HANDFULS OF AIR

HANDFULS OF AIR

Stories and Poems

Jim Gold

Full Court Press
Englewood Cliffs, New Jersey

Second Edition

Copyright © 2013 by Jim Gold

Published in the United States of America
by Full Court Press, 601 Palisade Avenue
Englewood Cliffs, NJ 07632

ISBN 978-1-938812-03-3
Library of Congress Control No. 2013938256

*Editing and Book Design by Barry Sheinkopf
for Bookshapers (www.bookshapers.com)*

Colophon by Liz Sedlack

To Bernice

My anchor as I reach for handfuls of air.

TABLE OF CONTENTS

Crusader Tours and Beyond

Crusader Tours

Beyond

Business

Language

Handfuls of Air

Poems

Songs for Open Ears

Crusader
Tours
and Beyond

CRUSADER TOURS

C H A P T E R ONE

Recipum Magnum

ON MARCH 22, 1105, PIERRE ROUGET de Toulouse le Bon-bon fell to his knees before the cross. *"Teins!"* he cried. "I am ready!" He touched the soft earth. "I'll leave this stiff, dull place!" he proclaimed. "No more stuffy cells, dank walls, and miserable company. And all for the love of God. Ha! How can I love God when my hand creates worm scribblings instead of calligraphy, when morning matins stink, and when Abbé Ron-sard's knowledge of God goes no deeper than a grass blade?

"I'm tired of translating Plato and Aristotle into Latin, tired of kneeling every day to the Virgin Mary. Man was not made for kneeling. . . but for walking. And I'm walking out of here! Adieu to the monk's life.

"Besides, I like to fornicate."

On the morning of March 23, Pierre rose from his genuflections, brushed his knees, lifted his head high, and strode through the St. Boeuf's Monastery gate. He roared with excitement to the expanse of heaven above him: *"Je suis un homme libre!"* Swinging his arms and singing his favorite troubadour song, "Cant Par Le Flor" by Bernart de Ventatour, he headed down the long dirt road towards Toulouse. Crisp, cool air brushed his face as the Provençal sun shone upon him. Up ahead lay infinity. Inhaling deeply oxygen of the future, his pointed leather shoes lifting puffs of dust behind him, he trod forward.

After an hour of walking, he passed a strange bush on his right. He paused to watch its leaves and branches tremble. Suddenly, it the bush burst into flame!

Pierre jumped back. *"Tiens!"* he cried. *"Ca bruille!"*

A mellifluous voice sounded through the funnel of smoke. *"Tais toi,* fool! I am speaking to you!"

The burning bush consumed itself, crumbled into a sulfur heap, and a blond maiden wearing a high-peaked hat rose from the ashes.

Pierre's mouth fell open as he stared in amazement. "Who art thou?" he asked.

"Beaux Beaux La Belle. Call me Bobo. I am your hidden lover."

"I didn't know I had a lover," Pierre answered, kneeling before her and kissing her feet.

"Wait," she commanded. "Do not kiss me. Not yet. First, you must earn my love."

Pierre's wide brown eyes gazed upon her. "What can I do for you, beauteous maiden? How can this humble servant earn your love? Command, and I shall obey."

Bobo arched her back, stretching to her full five feet. Her blond hair cascaded down her shoulder; a wild, far-away look filled her blue-blue eyes. "Oh, knight of the sword-pen," she said, "Find the *Recipum Magnum*. Then my love will be yours forever."

"The what?"

"*Recipum Magnum*," she repeated. "Ah, Pierre, you have studied the great books behind monastery walls, yet you know not of the *Recipum Magnum*, lying hidden in the Holy Land. Near Jerusalem, they say. Written at the beginning of time, the *Recipum* contains secrets of the universe. Know these secrets and you can run without stopping for a year, and fly across oceans as well. The owner of the *Recipum Magnum* can conquer the world and live forever!"

"If it is such a secret, my lady," Pierre asked, "how do you know of its existence?"

"*Bête stupide!*" Bobo cried. "You dare to question me? I know because I was born in a cloud." Her eyes narrowed. "Every knight would love to find the *Recipum*, as would every king, emperor, and the Pope. But no one knows the exact location of this treasure. Only that somewhere . . . in a land overrun by Saracens. . . beneath a rock, perhaps. . . . Find it, Pierre, and my hand shall be yours. And after my hand, who knows?"

"I shall find it, my lady!" Pierre declared. "My quest has begun. Fear not. Soon I shall lay its secrets at your feet."

Bobo pointed to the east. "Go, then. Your destiny has been written."

Pierre closed his eyes. He imagined Jerusalem and the Saracen conquerors of the Holy Land gouging out the eyes of Christians, smashing their brains. The hated Saracens lived so near the treasure.

He vowed to find the *Recipum* and deliver it to Bobo.

CHAPTER TWO

History

IN THE YEAR 1071, ten miles north of Toulouse, in the village of Crouton-en-Main, Virginie Marie le Bonbon bore a son. Moments after the birth of Pierre Rouget de Toulouse le Bonbon, three Persian fools burst through the east door of La Maison du Bonbon. The first entered dancing, the second singing, the third laughing. They circled Pierre in his cradle, shouted, *"Tellement laide!"* gave him a potato, a cup of earth, and a stick—and rushed out the door on their way to Persia.

All le Bonbons grew up within the medieval confines of the Henri Raymond castle, whose steeple towered over the Church of Crouton-en-Main. Spanned by a drawbridge and surrounded by a moat filled with stagnant water, frogs, and fish, the castle had been built as a refuge from raiding Norsemen two hundred years before. Its courtyard, housing cattle and movables of the peasantry, served as a stronghold location for festivals, marriages, feasts, and games. Mills, a forge, a cooperage, leather works, and surrounding arable land completed this medieval tapestry. The wise Abbot le Pruneau dispensed justice and levied fines.

Lord Raymond's vassals contributed to his wealth with

goods and services, and, of course, his court had an official chancellor, chamberlain, butler, and seneschal, Popeaux de Vaux, an able administrator who knew how to count.

The 12th-century theologian, Abbé Benefois described Pierre Rouget de Toulouse le Bonbon as an extremely ugly lad with blond hair, a flat, laughing face, and brown eyes that danced with the light of both God and the Devil. Benefois tells how a wild boar attacked Pierre on a rabbit hunt in October 1089. Before the lad could kill the beast with his sword, the boar broke Pierre's right leg and sliced a huge gash down his thigh. Bleeding and in terrible pain, Pierre dragged himself to the village barber, who questioned him: "Has this wound had been caused by stars, comets, or storms? Would you like a tooth pulled, an enema or leeching? No extra charge."

Pierre shook his head. Before operating, the barber mixed an anesthetizing drink of opium, lettuce, hemlock, ivy, and scraped-off pus before pressing the concoction into the gaping wound.

He handed Pierre a glass of brown liquid. "Drink this magic potion of frog fluid, sheep excrement, snails, snakes, and curative emeralds," he said. "Then sleep under relics for three weeks." One month later, Pierre, seeing no improvement in his right leg, decided to cure himself by breaking his left leg. Limping evenly on both legs for one month, he soon walked straight.

CHAPTER THREE

Pierre Becomes a Troubadour

PIERRE TRAINED AS A troubadour from April 1091 to December 1096 in the Castle of Ventatour. Here he learned his favorite troubadour song was "Cant Par La Flor" by Bernart de Ventatour.

> Lo tems vai e ven e vire
> Per journs, per mes e per ans. . . .

All his lessons took place in the castle dungeon, where his teacher, the famous Bernart foix-Voie de faux de Ventatour, taught singing and verse writing.

When Pierre arrived for his first lesson, he descended a long circular stairway of stone to the cells and underground rooms beneath the dungeon. Damp air filled his nostrils and chilled his bones. Candles and torches lit the way. Soon he heard screams and shouts; heart-breaking cries echoed through the corridors. He gasped as he imagined prisoners chained to the walls, their skin torn by red-hot pincers, their bodies stretched on the rack, their feet roasting over fires. Perhaps torturers were crucifying a rebellious serf or breaking him on the wheel.

What a surprise when he found, not a torture chamber, but a singing school! To his right, in a cell, he saw a young knight in full armor, grunting as he counted off push-ups on the damp earthen floor. In another cell, a duke, dressed in tunic and metal shoes, ran in place, heehawing like a mule. Beyond, in a former fruit-storage room, a viscount sat on a Roman curule chair, rowing an imaginary boat and shouting, "Haey, haey!" to an imaginary oarsman.

Pierre walked down a tunnel into a large cell with an arched ceiling. There he found his teacher, the proud, tall, muscular Bernart foix-Voie le faux de Ventatour, waiting for him.

Bernart approached his new student. "Sing! he commanded.

Pierre straightened, cleared his throat, and sang. "Let my face be your footstool"

> I laid my head upon the ground that my face
> Might be a footstool to my beloved;
> My beloved said, "Rejoice, for you may
> Set your lips upon mine!"

Bernart shook his head, his eyes filled with tears. "Young man, your songs are empty. They do not express the highest ideals of courtly love in Provence. Hopefully, I can coax your talent out of hiding—if I can find any."

Bernart's strict, disciplined teaching style drew strength from his religion. His oily face, seamed with battle scars, and calloused hands smelling of horses and dirt, befitted a former knight, trained to kill by flinging himself against the enemy and howling like a wild beast. Bernart never cut his long unkempt blond hair or shaved the matted, burr-laden beard that flowed

over his breastplate. Nor did he believe in bathing. A flute virtuoso and excellent harpist, he accentuated his teachings with
grunts, burps, and animal noises. He often wore armor to
Pierre's lessons.

Bernart taught Pierre voice production, pantomime, jug-
gling, acting, somersaults on stone floors, and how to lead a
dancing bear. He helped improve his *vielle* playing and taught
the lad to read and write music using the *neume* system, with its
series of accents above the words, and the four-line staff invented by Guido of Arezzo. Pierre learned to play harp, flute,
bell chimes, and *organistrum*.

Bernart trained his pupil in all troubadour arts. One Tuesday
morning, he said: "Pierre, you arrived five years ago. Now you
have learned everything I can teach you. Time to leave Ventatour. Go! Make your way through the Latin lands."

CHAPTER FOUR

Pierre Joins a Monastery

PIERRE BID BERNART ADIEU; he packed his tunic, walking stick, and pointed shoes, put vielle on his back, and, with powerful strides, crossed the Ventatour castle drawbridge. The following months found him journeying from castle to castle, braving brigand-infested roads, exploring the lands of Aquitaine, Toulouse, and the Kingdoms of Leon and Castile. Traveling by foot or mule, he sang troubadour songs in the courts of Poitou, Albi, and Carcassone. In July 1096, he joined a pilgrimage to Santiago de Compostela but soon decided to expand his worldly horizons by attaching himself to a band of brigands. In six weeks, he became their leader. However, four years later, a decline in robbery revenues, coupled with a longing for God, convinced him to abandon this position. Barefoot and repentant, he walked eighty miles to the Monastery of St. Boeuf, then stood naked for six freezing December days outside the monastery gate until Abbé Ronsard, finally convinced of Pierre's contrition, watched the troubadour faint into the courtyard.

Ronsard dragged Pierre's prostrate body into the monastery *dormitorium*, laid the lad on a wooden bed, and covered him with a woolen blanket. Upon awakening, Pierre said, "I am most grateful. The Lord sent me to fulfill His mission."

Ronsard offered him chicken broth and wine. A revived Pierre rose and, taking Ronsard by the arm, traversed the halls of St. Boeuf to meet the other monks. *"Bien matins, Dieu adieu."*

Pierre called out with merry smile. Spying a monk praying on his knees, he quickly fell to his knees and said, "Forgive me, fair friar, for I have sinned. *Canis videt cervum."*

Ronsard listened carefully. "Hear how the lad speaks," he said. "None from Provence to Normandy speak in this manner. Is it a madness, divinity, or both? The lad is blessed with able wit."

After Pierre had made a full confession, Ronsard and other friars decided to educate him in the ways of a monk. On December 17, 1096, he knelt before the abbot and listed his sins from robberies to countless fornications.

Next day, purified and cleansed of his past, he began his monk's education. Under Ronsard's the tutelage, Pierre learned to copy books in the calligraphy of the Carolingian hand. He developed his gift for writing, learning to relax and and let God dictate his words; he became God's instrument. The young monk dedicated himself to the Lord, consecrating his mind and soul to the Higher Power. He prayed to understand the nature of the universe. Soon however, Pierre concluded he could not know God through intellect.alone. Limited and frail, this faculty of the mind could not envision the infinite, or grasp the eternal. Only direct experience of God's grace could show the path; only faith and divine intervention could help him write.

"To work is to pray." Abbé Ronsard emphasized this rule of St. Benedict as Pierre studied grammar, rhetoric, dialectic, arithmetic, geometry, astronomy, and music. Through these

Seven Liberal Arts, Ronsard hoped to free his student from many defects, especially the desire to fornicate.

Every morning Pierre sat in the *scriptorium*, copying pagan and Christian manuscripts. He read the lives of the Latin fathers and developed a fondness for Tertullian, who claimed that "things are credible only if they are absurd." He studied St. Jerome's translation of the bible, and St. Augustine's *City of God* and *Confessions*.

However, aberrant behavior exhibited itself early in Pierre's monastic life. During matins, when monks sang *melismas* and *alleluias* of the Gregorian chants, Pierre often broke into falsetto. Late at night, he climbed the church walls and sat by the barrel vaulting beneath the steeple, yodeling "*Veni Creator Spiritus*," "*Improperia*" from the Gallican liturgy, and the Mozarabic chant "*Gaudete Populi*."

While working in the monastery fields, he sang love songs from Provence, using the trochaic rhythmic modes to punctuate his hoeing. Often his powerful voice upset the other monks, causing Père Poursuivre to rush from his scriptorium to insist on silence.

Once Pierre stole candles from the church altar even though he knew stealing was a sin. Stealing had been encouraged during his childhood in Crouton-en-Main when his father, Jean Le Bonbon, told him bedtime stories of the legendary folk hero and thief, Alvin le Pauvre, a laughing giant who stole from the rich and kept the proceeds, then robbed the poor and kept those proceeds as well. Pierre's penchant for stealing had been enlarged by an inferiority complex created by the three wise men from Persia who had called him *tellement laide!*

Pierre knew God would punish him for his sins. He had

joined the monastery because he needed help and hoped more religion would cure him of his vice. Abbé Ronsard tried confessional and counseling methods. When these didn't work, he used the fear of damnation. "Rob your fellow man and you will spend eternity in Hell," he warned. "The Inferno is no easy place, Pierre. You will be hung by your tongue and boiled in oil. Your arms will be sawn in pieces and your greedy fingers frozen in ice!"

Pierre broke into a cold sweat and swore he would never steal again. The sudden fear of Hell had a curative effect. But after a few days rest, he forgot his fears and drifted back to his habitual abominations. Habits are hard to change, and for Pierre, it seemed, only a miracle could change them.

CHAPTER FIVE

Toulouse

WHEN PIERRE OPENED HIS eyes, only a wisp of smoke and the smell of burnt wood filled the air where Bobo had been. "Ah, a visitation," he breathed deeply. "God has defined my road. I must travel to the Holy Land. But how can I get there? By sea? By land? Is there a map of Jerusalem? And, when I get there, how can I find the *Recipum?*" He fell to his knees and prayed. "God help me to succeed. *Aidum Deum ergo vanquinum.*"

On April 29, Pierre walked through the Toulousian gates and entered this most important city of Provence. Fixing his eyes on the steeple of St. Jacques le Pecheur, he walked up narrow Rue des Poissons until he came to the town square. Today was market day, and hundreds of artisans, merchants, and peasants were displaying their goods on tables and blankets.

Pierre saw all kinds of people in the square: Spaniards, Franks, Byzantines, Arabs, and Jews. He roamed through the oriental bazaar where knights in bright-colored fabrics, returning from their Crusade, paraded over the cobblestones. Everyone was talking about the Crusades; everyone wanted to go.

A form of madness, a Crusader fever, filled the air—quiet

ferment, subtle, but visible, too.

Now a secret fear rose in Pierre's breast; his heart fluttered and his veins ran cold.

At age three, his mother, Madame Le Bonbon, had abandoned him for three days on the Cliffs of Malveaux. Although ever drawn to wander, memories of that frightening incident, had created, in contrary fashion, a dark spot in Pierre's soul which soon developed into a fear of travel. Often, when he was alone, a fog of vague panic descended upon him. This secret fear now converged with the real, ever-present, external dangers of travel on local roads.

Suddenly, in a flash of inspiration, his fertile mind gave birth to an *idea:* Why not organize his own Crusade to the Holy Land? By force of numbers alone they could soften the perils on the road to Jerusalem.

Pierre felt a surge of excitement. "Why wait?" he cried. "*Carpe diem!* Seize the moment!" He surveyed the people milling about the marketplace. "My Crusaders stand before me. Speak to them now! Tomorrow they may be gone." He raced to the stone fountain in the middle of the square, mounted it, and preached to the people: "Ye villagers, Toulousians all! Join me in a Holy Crusade! Our scriptures and the cross of the Lord himself rest in the hands of the infidel Saracens. Heart-breaking. Join me, friends. Is not eternal life a worthy reward? Sell your possessions, sell your land, your farms, your vegetables, your horses, geese, chickens, and barley, even your children, or bring them along. Free yourselves, and join my Holy Crusade!"

Wiping the sweat from his brow, he climbed down from the fountain. Many in the marketplace crowded around him.

"Do you do laundry?" asked a fat woman.

"Can you sing?" asked a merchant in a pointed hat.

"We need grape pickers," said a passing count.

Pierre realized they had misunderstood his message. Getting a Crusade together might be harder than he thought.

The fat woman approached him again and leaned into his face. "Do you not perform the cleansing of clothes?" she asked.

Pierre pushed her away. "Beg pardon, fair madame," he said, "I am from the monastery."

"You slop-fed stinking pot of vermin!" shouted the woman. "May the curse of Jepetuthala blight your Crusade!"

"Why suffer a Crusade," asked the merchant with the pointed hat. "Better to remain under the blessed skies of Provence in Toulouse."

The count stepped forward. "Holy Land?" he sneered. "Pick grapes instead. My neighbor, Viscount Belfromage Journée de la Fondé, tells me the Holy Land is a stinking place filled with infidels who bathe."

"How will you travel, young man?" asked the merchant. "The Mediterranean is infested with pirates. Sea captains charge outrageous prices, which you cannot afford, and if you *can* afford them, your ship will be captured by pirates, your belongings pillaged, and you will be sold into slavery, if you are lucky."

"I would not travel by ship," Pierre said to the merchant, "but by land."

"Land!" the count laughed. "Land travel is too dangerous. The miserable roads—whenever they exist—go through rutted, mud-soaked swamps. Paths are choked by weeds and thickets; they crawl with snakes. Wild boars hide behind tree trunks. Sea pirates are beneficent creatures compared to the brigands and thieves roaming the forests. A traveler to the Holy Land could easily be robbed, beaten, even killed."

The fat woman pushed the count aside. "I'd fly to the Holy Land in a laundry basket," she explained. "Jepetuthala, the Witch of the Wind, flies every seven years to dump her foul body wastes upon the hills of Galilee. Every fourteen years she visits Jerusalem, too. Fly with her."

"Who will finance your trip, young man?" asked the merchant.

"Who will guard you?" asked the count.

"So many obstacles," sighed the fat woman. "Stay home. Devote yourself to laundry."

Pierre bowed. These are not *my* Crusaders, he thought, politely pushing them aside. He made his way to the Cathedral of St. Jacques le Pecheur. There he sat on its cold stone steps until a shiver went from his spine into his brain. But these shivers were mild compared to the big question that lay before him: How could he organize a Crusade?

He sat, head in hand, pondering the question. The bustle of the marketplace grew silent as dusk settled upon the town.

CHAPTER SIX
The First Crusader Plan

W HEN THE FIRST RAYS of dawn illuminated the church steeple, Pierre saw the shadow of a boot before him. Upward from the boot towered a burly man. He poked Pierre with his cane. "Looking for a vision?" he asked.

A full beard, flecked with gray, surrounded a wide, sensuous mouth dripping with spittle from yesterday's beer. Around his tattered cloak he wore a brown scarf for extra warmth. A fur hat held his long hair in place and his squinting eyes shone with light and clarity rare for a drunkard. As he touched Pierre's knee with his boot, the young crusade organizer got a closer look at the cane with its carved Egyptian scarabs and Greek mythological figures dancing up the knob.

Pierre gazed up at the weather-beaten face. "I am, sir," he answered.

"And might that be a vision of the Lord?"

"No. A vision of a following."

The man rocked forward before stroking his beard. "What following would that be?"

Pierre's flexed hand called the stranger towards him. "Sit down, my friend. Listen to me. I sit on these stone steps hoping

| 17 |

St. Jacques le Pecheur will inspire my vacant mind. My love of God and Jacques saintly love of fish have called me to lead a Crusade to the Holy Land.

The man sat down at Pierre's side. His breath smelled of a strange brew, not quite beer but not dew either. "Ah, the Holy Land," he muttered. "A wild and beautiful place."

"You have been there?"

"Aye, on the first Crusade."

Pierre's eyes widened; his heart trembled. "Then you have seen the Holy Land!"

The man nodded. "Allow me to introduce myself. I am Charles Cheval le Brun, former Captain of the First Crusade's Peasant Regiment. Count Raymond of Toulouse appointed me to mold peasant riffraff into a dependable and respectable fighting unit for our Lord. I taught them to fight with sticks and broken lances, and after two weeks of training, my unit learned not only discipline and organization, but received the word of God as well. Indeed, the first Peasant Regiment was first to scale the walls of Jerusalem."

"Do you know the way to the Holy Land?"

"My young friend," Charles replied. "I was on the front lines during the entire Crusade. I helped Count Raymond plot our route, not only through France and Italy, but through Asia Minor as well. Had it not been for my ability to find hidden mountain pathways, the massacres in Phrygia and Cappodocia might have become total annihilations."

"Wonderful, wonderful!" Pierre cried. "You are no doubt a leader of men. But how did you convince others to go on Crusade?"

"Easy," said the old warrior. "Leadership and followings come from God. Just ask him."

"I've been asking, but, so far, no answer."

"Perhaps you have been asking in the wrong language."

"Impossible. I always use Latin, the language of The Church."

"Have you tried French?"

"French? A language of peasants. God would never listen."

"Try it," Charles coaxed. "If you want a following, people must understand what you say. People understood Peter the Hermit. He spoke their language. What a following he had. If not for his preaching, there never would have been a first Crusade. Even his ass spoke French."

"I never thought about that."

"I know you haven't. That is why you are sitting *outside* the church."

Pierre liked Charles's tough demeanor. Perhaps the captains's earthbound energy, combined with his own training as a troubadour and monk, might create the perfect Crusade leadership. "If I got a following, could you guide us to the Holy Land?"

"*Cogito ergo peregrinarus,*" Charles told him. "It is my calling. Since the first Crusade I have led many groups to the Holy Land. I even have a travel plan." He reached under his cloak and withdrew a faded parchment.

"It is written in the Langue d'Oc," he explained. "Any native of this region can understand it. Unfortunately, most natives cannot read, so I often must read it aloud, but you, an educated man, will have no problem."

"How do you know I am educated?"

"Your smooth hand informs me." Charles unrolled the parchment. "I think you will like my travel plan."

Crusader Tour to the Holy Land
Led by Charles Cheval le Brun

Departure date: April 23, 1103

Travel Plan:

April 23: Depart from Toulouse on foot.

May 23: Depart from Constantinople on foot.

May 28: Depart from Nicea on foot.

May 30: Sightseeing in Dorylaeum. Accommodation
on the ground; search for buried Turkish treasure
and armor. Optional side trip: pillage a village
and/or local shrine.

May 31–August 5: Walk, walk, walk. Then trek across
Phrygia. Climb Taurus mountains.

August 5–September 23: Arrival in Antioch. Storm
city walls. Operate a battering ram and siege engines. Plunder tour of inner city. Search for
relics. Touch the Holy Lance. Meet an Armenian
(optional).

September 23: Depart for Jerusalem.

October 4: Arrival in Jerusalem.

December 2: End of Tour. Departure via mule
through Dung Gates.

General information: Average temperature: 10 to 106
degrees.

Fee: 15 bezants.

Pierre read and reread the travel plan. "I like it," he said, rising from his stone step. "Surely, you were sent by God to help

lead my Crusade. Now I will spread the word to others. Let us meet here again in one year along with my following. You shall receive ample payment in both material and celestial form."

Charles agreed. They shook hands.

The next day Pierre went to the monastery of St. Boeuf, gathered the monks together, and offered them free travel to the Holy Land if they would create four hundred copies of the Crusader Tour Travel Plan. They agreed and started writing immediately. In six weeks Pierre had four hundred copies in matchless calligraphy with illuminated capitals of gold, blue, red, and green, delicate filigree pen-work, colorful floral line finishings, and borders of arrows, swords, and lances. He even convinced three Benedictine abbots to preach to his Crusade during morning services.

He walked the countryside, posting copies in village squares, handing Plans to anyone he met who could read. He visited monasteries and castles throughout Languedoc and northern Italy, haranguing crowds in market places, preaching in peasant homes and stables, haunting Sunday church services, talking to pilgrims on lonely roads, and generally speaking to anyone who would listen.

But no one listened. Perhaps, Pierre thought, if I were a bishop, a count, or a king, I might inspire more confidence. But a simple troubadour and monk at the beginning of a career change. . . . Alas, his beautiful Crusader Tour Travel Plan remained unread.

How could he convince people if he had never led a crusade before? How could he lead a crusade when there were no crusaders?

How could he win the fair hand of Bobo?

CHAPTER SEVEN
Pierre Finds a Following

WHY DO THEY REJECT me? Pierre groaned. "I am a failure. Has the Witch of Crouton cast her evil spell, haunting me with unlucky spirits? Or has the Laurentian Dragon, that claw-toed, fire-belching monster in Le Cave Putreuse, four miles north of Crouton-en-Main, decided to avenge my theft of her Montagne Malfactueuse golden treasure?" Pierre fell to his knees. He could not forget the sting of rejection, and callous faces of the ignorant townspeople. "I have failed," he cried. "Oh God, what is wrong with me?"

Weeks passed as he vacillated between Satanic rage and hapless confusion. In frustration, he pounded the stone walls of shuttered houses, or cried on doorsteps, begging for forgiveness. After drinking a gallon of wine he staggered down the muddy streets of Toulouse, shouting at the evil spirits and swatting the demons of bad luck with the loose sleeve of his tunic.

Pere Genoux, a friendly priest, pulled him inside, laid him in a pew, and slapped his face a few times. When Pierre sobered up, the priest counseled that drinking was no way to worship God. "Man clings to what he has," he said. "It takes a superhuman act of self conquest to surrender the ego. No one who hesitates between God and Mammon will reach perfection. Young man, give up the desires of this world, and eternal life will be your prize."

Abandon desire? It sounded right. The next day he walked to a cave in the hills outside Toulouse. There he dwelt for three months, determined to free himself from his mad desire to run a Crusade. Fresh purpose entered his mind. Through self mortification, he planned to root out his desire He wanted to destroy his foul flesh with its disgusting needs, to rise above his body and reach a closer union with God.

He posted a daily mortification schedule on his cave wall. Every morning, in strict adherence to his rules, he rose before dawn and whipped himself. Then, after a breakfast of water, he hung upside down from the bough of an apple tree for an hour. This was followed by forty-five minutes chanting holy St. Boeufs and twenty minutes kneeling on crushed glass to pray. After a lunch of water, he bowed to angels in his cave and with each bow, made sure to strike his head against the stone wall. Most days he bowed six hundred and fifty-five times, but sometimes he managed eight hundred. Once, on a chilly November afternoon, he broke his record with one thousand twenty-seven. Pierre concluded each day by supping on a leaf.

Mortification helped him forget his body and his desires. But, in spite of his trials, visions of a Crusade kept reappearing.

Three weeks later, another hermit took up residence in a cave nearby. He said Pierre's example of abstinence, piety, and self-denial had inspired him to follow the spiritual path.

Two days later, four more hermits moved in. By the following week, sixteen more had arrived.

The neighborhood was changing. Caves were at a premium.

Real estate values went up as crowds of anchorites descended upon Pierre. Noisy and young, these ascetics chanted and flagellated themselves with more vigor than he. Their wails and screams filled the daytime hours; at night he heard their sighs and snores. Worst of all, he found himself competing! These young upstart hermits were punishing themselves better than Pierre! Some came from wealthy families and could afford to purchase sturdier whips; others lived with servants who helped hang them higher in the trees. They even had better trees: oaks and maples with branches in the sunshine! How could Pierre hang himself so high or hold his own against these rich aristocratic anchorites?

One tall, thin lad, a count from Perpignan, cut off his fingers to show his disdain for counting. Another stood on one leg for six weeks. Although Pierre increased his mortifications, he kept slipping behind. "Sure I'm competitive," he rationalized. "So was Moses, the prophets, and Jesus. You must perfect yourself and be the best. Otherwise God will not care about you."

Creating new penances, he walled himself up inside his cave for forty days with only a loaf of bread and a cup of water. He survived the ordeal but found himself no closer to God. Visions of Crusade kept haunting him. Perhaps his cave was too luxurious. He moved to a barren rock on top of a mountain but, after three months, felt no closer to God. He craved followers, followers, followers. His foul desires were winning the day.

All his ascetic practices appeared useless. The more he practiced, the more he wanted to go on Crusade.

One night Pierre returned to his cave in deep discouragement. He sat on the damp earthen floor for two weeks, rocking to and fro and wringing his hands; he felt like giving up.

But while he sat lost in morbid thought, many of the common people of Toulouse were hearing about his ascetic practices. In their eyes, his virtue did not remain hidden. Evidently, the more he mortified himself, the more rapidly his fame increased.

On Monday morning, September 14, 1105, a cripple visited Pierre's cave. The man crawled towards him begging to be cured. "Help me walk," he pleaded.

Pierre snorted with disgust. "I am not a miracle worker," he sneered, "but a poor penitent hoping for a cure. Make you walk? What a laugh." Pierre was so nauseated by the sight of the man's hideously deformed legs, so annoyed that this creeping disambulator had dared interrupt his solitary prayers, that he kicked the cripple in the backside. "Succubus of Satan! Get out of here!" The poor man's eyes opened wide in shock and disbelief. He trembled as if struck by the hand of God himself. Then, to Pierre's amazement, he jumped to his feet and ran down the hill!

Word of the miracle spread among the townspeople. The next day, hundreds of supplicants appeared before Pierre's cave: A train of maimed, sick, plague-ridden unfortunates, some bearing boil- covered children, others carrying leprous, emaciated old women on their backs or leading one-legged soldiers on crutches. Stalwart dukes and merchants arrived demanding health and fertility for their wives. a scrofulous fellow with lice in his hair came only to touch Pierre's body. A thin man, wearing a bearskin and holding a horse's hoof, seized a piece of Pierre's trousers and tore it off to use as a lucky charm.

That evening Pierre felt a surge of indescribable joy. These unfortunates needed him, and he needed them. He understood their potential. Here was his following! Here were his Crusaders!

Weeks went by. As hundreds more came to see him, he realized that soon success would be within his grasp.

On October 17 he abandoned his cave. Followed by the thousands in his retinue, walked down the mountain and returned to Toulouse.

On the steps of the Cathedral of St. Jacques le Pecheur, he found Charles waiting for him.

CHAPTER EIGHT
The First Crusader Tour

THE ARMY OF CRUSADERS, all believers in Pierre's leadership and the miracle of redemption. They consisted of peasant, serfs, the blind, lame, and deaf, knights, feudal lords, the mute and illiterates gathered in the field of Vauntauge. Facing the stream of Pearls, Popus Urbanus Requiem Supremamus—specifically asked for by Pierre to bless the Crusade —mounted high on a platform of broken branches.

Popus spoke to the crowd of wretches before him. "Oh, ye staggering chosen, how lucky you are to engage in a battle for the Holy Cross. Go ye now. Follow Pierre to the Holy Land. Wrest the sacred Cross from the Saracens! God will be your guide. Pierre works with him. Yes, my Crusaders, as you travel, know that travel means travail and to torture yourself on the Roman *tripallus*, the three stakes of misery, movement, and constipation. But such travail brings you closer to God and the Holy Land. Go, my children. I bless you. With the Lord's help and Pierre's leadership, you cannot fail."

Popus Urbanquet II blessed the Crusaders.

Three days later, on March 15, 1108, twenty thousand souls gathered behind Pierre. Cheering knights raised their swords, shouting peasants held hoes high, and horses brayed. The first Crusader Tour began.

Marching peacefully through the country side, they reached the great trading town of Cologne on the Rhine. Pierre stopped to preach Crusade to the locals. Soon German knights, such as Count Hugh of Schwatzberg, Otto of Tubingen, Friedrich the Penniless, and Walter Zimmern, impressed by Pierre's cause, joined the Crusaders. Continuing along the banks of the Rhine and Danube, they reached the Hungarian border where Pierre asked King Coloman for provisions and guidance. The Hungarian king, happy to rid his kingdom of these nuisances, offered it gladly. Pierre's Crusaders passed without incident through the villages of Kecskemet and Mohacs.

Two days' march from Belgrade, Pierre and Charles Cheval le Brun consulted on travel directions. Pierre preferred the more traditional route, hoping to walk the Via Egnatia from Dyrrhachium to Ochrid. However, Charles insisted the northern route across the Balkan peninsula was best. After lengthy discussions, the leader acquiesced to Charles' more experienced judgment. The Crusaders now crossed the frontier at Belgrade, and headed southeast through Nish, Sofia, Philippolis, and Adrianople.

One week later, the horde of travelers stood before the walls of Constantinople. To their happy surprise, the Byzantine Emperor Alexius came out to greet them. He offered fruit, vegetables, grain, and seven horses. However, in Nicea, the Crusaders ran out of food. A group of hungry knights pillaged a village. This created a local uprising. During the ensuing fight, Crusaders and townspeople were wounded. Departing quickly, and heading towards Dorylaeum, they were attacked by brigands.

When they reached the treacherous Taurus Mountains of Asia Minor, continuous harassment and attacks by wild local tribesmen killed hundreds of Crusaders. Others deserted, or were captured and sold into slavery.

On July 17, 1109, when Pierre's Crusade reached the Holy Land, he had lost most of his following. Starting out with twenty thousand crusaders, he arrived in Jerusalem with fourteen.

Once safely in the Holy City, these survivors dispersed along the Via Dolorosa to meet with their respective destinies.

Now totally alone, Pierre continued his search.

He visited the Church of the Holy Sepulcher, then moved to the burned-out site where the Holy Temple had once stood. Here he knelt and prayed before the Western Wall.

After many days under the burning July sun, God appeared in a vision.

"Welcome to Jerusalem, Pierre," said the Lord. "Why are you here?"

"I came to meet you!"

"Why did you come *here?*"

Pierre looked puzzled. "The Holy Land is where you live."

"That is true. But I have other residences as well—Spain, Germany, streets of Kiev, alleys in Vienna. I live in Alpine caves, Antioch fishing boats, walls of Constantinople, peasant homes, and forests near Toulouse. I live everywhere. Pierre, you may enjoy exploring new places, but if you want to visit Me, you could just as easily have stayed at home."

"Did I make a mistake?" Pierre asked. "Should I have remained in the monastery?"

"Your search has brought you wisdom."

"But have I wasted my time traveling to see you?"

"Know this: I live in your home. I *am* your home. Revere your vision. Look within. You'll see me sitting behind your eyelids."

"What about Bobo? "

"All is One."

"I must find the *Recipum Magnum* for her."

"You have already found it."

"I have?"

"The *Recipum Magnum* is *you*."

"Me?"

"Yes. You have a piece of Eternity inside your heart."

"But how can I show it to Bobo? How will she know?"

"She will know when *you* will know."

"Can't you give me *something*? A sign?"

God gave Pierre a pebble.

"What will a pebble prove?"

"It will prove as much as a mountain, or the sun. It will prove as much as a drop of water, an elephant, or an ant. It will prove as much as you need it to prove."

"Maybe I don't need proof."

"Aha!" God smiled.

All at once, a bush appeared to Pierre's right. Its leaves and branches trembled, then burst into flame!

Pierre jumped back. *"Tiens!"* he cried. *"Ca bruille!"*

A familiar voice sounded through the smoke. *"Tais toi,* fool! I am speaking to you!"

As the burning bush consumed itself, a blond maiden wearing a high-peaked hat rose from the ashes.

Pierre's mouth fell open in amazement. "Bobo!" he exclaimed.

"Fair Pierre, at last you have found me. And because you have found me, I have found you." Bobo then placed her fair lips against the fair lips of Pierre. . . . And both fared very well.

Next morning, Pierre packed his all belongings in his satchel and threw it over his shoulder. A bright sun rose in the east.

He took Bobo by the hand and placed her close to his heart. Then they began their long journey back to Toulouse.

BEYOND

King Diamond

ADAM HAUSNER SOLD DIAMONDS on Forty-eighth Street in New York City. His store, Sweet Diamonds, Inc., stood between the Diamond Emporium and the Olympia restaurant. Merchants, potential customers, cyclists, pedestrians, police, tourists, and shoppers paraded up and down the street.

Adam arrived at work early, before the rush of the city descended upon his narrow preserve. He'd sit behind his desk in back of the store away from the display cases of diamonds, necklaces, rings, and green carpeting. Here, along with the tranquility only a good night's sleep can bring, he enjoyed a morning walk down Philosophy Street in the city of his mind. He'd ask himself questions about meaning, purpose, and the nature of the world: Was life really a waking dream? Who created customers? Who created diamonds? Who created the first man? Was his name really Adam?

He never came up with answers. Often, when he got close to understanding the relationship between body, mind, and spirit, he'd be interrupted by a telephone call, or some practical early morning business matter.

One morning his reveries were broken by a heavyset man with dark glasses and a black overcoat. He barged through the door, pointed at the display case, and asked, "What're ya gettin' for dis stone?"

Adam got up, walked to the case, and looked at the diamond set in a gold ring. "Eighteen hundred dollars," he answered.

The customer glared at Adam, grunted, and without another word, walked out.

Adam returned to his thoughts. What was he really selling in his store? What is the true nature of a diamond?

Suddenly, it struck him! *Diamonds had no intrinsic value.* Rather, they were reflections of inner worth, symbols of the "real diamonds" people searched for in themselves.

Adam was selling *reflections*.

This realization startled the merchant. Could his business be, in a sense, superfluous? Was he a fraud? Maybe he should have listened to his father and become a teacher. Then he could have given people something useful, guided them, and helped them find their lost parts. His father knew value; he could tell the difference between a lasting truth and a bauble with an ephemeral shine.

Then a positive thought rose: All people owned "real diamonds." But they weren't aware of them. And the few who *were* aware often didn't know how or where to find them. By selling precious stones, Adam was performing a social service: He was supplying his customers with reminders.

Now his brain was cooking! He thought up new copy for his next ad: When you're feeling down and out, remember your diamond within.

He unlocked the display case, picked out his most valuable DeBeers gem, and slipped it into the vest pocket just above his heart.

He drove home in a good mood that evening. Hitting a traffic jam and slowing to a stop on the Long Island Expressway, he turned on the radio and listened to Bach while exhaust fumes and waiting cars piled up around him.

After a fifteen-minute wait, traffic began to move again. He cruised through Queens.

When he passed the Great Neck sign, he patted his vest pocket. *Nothing there!* Where was it? He felt again. Still nothing. Hadn't he put the diamond in his vest pocket? Or had he? He couldn't remember.

Trembling, he searched his other pockets but found nothing. His mind flew back to the store. Mentally, he combed the display cases, desk drawers, safe, and rows of catalogs lying open on his desk. Blank.

He pulled over to the side of the road, stopped to search the front seat, the glove compartment, and the floor. Still nothing. He panicked. Where could it be? How could he have misplaced—or worse, lost—such a valuable jewel?

He finished the drive a physical wreck. When he arrived home he slumped into his living room armchair, unable to touch the martini his wife brought him.

He gazed into space. Try to remember. . .try to remember. His finger inadvertently slid over his breast pocket. Try. . . . *There* it is! He touched it. His diamond had been with him all along, safe and secure. How could he have forgotten where it was?

He held his hand over his heart. He pressed gently against the precious stone and resolved never to forget it again. Then he fell fast asleep.

"*Dinner's ready!*" Laura had prepared a huge spaghetti repast. All three kids charged down the stairs, plopped onto their chairs, and began grabbing food. "Wait a minute!" Laura snapped. "Don't be pigs! Wait until everyone is seated."

Adam yawned, stretched, and took slow, leisurely strides towards the dinner table. The kids eyed him eagerly. As soon as he sat down, they dove for the food. "Where are your manners?" Laura shouted. The kids started yelling at each other. Adam's peace of mind vanished. "Shut up around here!" he said, slamming his fist on the table. "I want quiet when I eat!"

"Listen to your father," Laura echoed.

The dinner continued in silence until Liam, the eldest son, dumped his plate of spaghetti on the floor and ran upstairs.

Adam's appetite disappeared along with the spaghetti, which he forced Liam to clean up and flush down the toilet.

He took a walk around the block to help digest what little food he had eaten. As he passed the candy store, the old panic returned. Where was his diamond? He wanted to touch it, see it, feel it. He wanted to remember how valuable he was. But he kept forgetting. And when he did, a terrible panic ensued, a heavy cloud darkened his world. He felt like a fool, weak, even stupid. Why must a grown man need to touch a diamond for hope, security, sustenance, self-knowledge, and wisdom? Did everyone need a diamond as he did?

He bought four halvah bars in the candy store and raced

down the dark side street, tearing off wrappers and shoving the bars into his mouth one after another. He hardly chewed them.

He walked through the park and sat down on a park bench. The night air was cool and clear. A sweet breeze blew. No cars passed. Adam listened to the silence. His heart stopped pounding. He sighed, slouched forwards, relaxed his shoulders. The stone moved above his heart. Found. His eyes lit up. Why had he been afraid? Why the panic? It had always been there.

Nevertheless, he kept forgetting.

Why was it so hard to remember?

His treasure lay, always and forever, deep within him. But evidently, he needed a diamond to remind him.

He headed home along the darkened streets thinking about reminders.

Mama Clock

MAMA CLOCK LED HER son Ben down the road. She tied his wrists to a watch and strapped his brain to a schedule. Although Ben lived in a lovely village surrounded by trees, fresh air, and flowers, he couldn't see its beauty. Handcuffed by Mama Clock, he dwelt in Time Prison.

Every day was exactly the same. Mama Clock tolerated no deviations in her schedule. If Ben tried avoiding it, Mama Clock shook her rusty head, twisted her tin face, and scowled as she shouted: "Moron, get back on schedule! I'm not ticking here to *amuse* you. Drag yourself out of your Stupidity Swamp. Follow my *schedule!* It will tell you what to do, and your watch will tell you exactly when to do it. Listen to me, my son: Until you can run your own life, *I'll run it for you!*"

Mama Clock called Ben stupid so often he believed it. As a docile and willing prisoner, the thought of freedom frightened him.

One day he met a lively girl with dancing blue eyes. Her name was Frieda. She laughed easily, seemed unafraid, and had a good time wherever she went. Her smile and ease made Ben feel sad.

"Why can't I have fun, too?" he asked Mama Clock.

"You're too dumb for fun," she answered.

But Frieda thought Ben was just as smart as anyone else.

"Mama Clock wants to keep you prisoner," she said. "She does it by convincing you you're stupid. She keeps you hand-cuffed to your wristwatch, so you'll never find out how smart you are."

Ben had many talks with Frieda. After lunch, they walked in the park, or sat by the ocean watching the waves roll in. Slowly he began to understand he wasn't stupid after all. Belief in himself grew. As it did, he started to argue and fight with Mama Clock.

Fearing he might break out of Time Prison, she hurled one accusation after another at him: "You blithering, blundering idiot! Your brain is softer than an egg yolk. How can a moronic, loathsome creature like you expect to succeed in the world?"

Ben defended himself and fought off each accusation with his newfound belief. The more he fought, the more he emerged from Time Prison. Soon he unlocked his wrists, dropped his wristwatch in the gutter, and tore up his schedule.

Then he said goodbye to Mama Clock.

Mama Clock screamed when she lost her son.

When that didn't work, she shook her fists.

When that didn't work, she calmed down.

She took an easy breath, and muttered "At last!"

Then she smiled.

Ben held Frieda's hand as they danced down the road together.

Mama Clock waved goodbye to her son.

"Good luck, Ben," she called. "And have a good Time!"

The Elephant Who Wanted to Become a Rabbit

ONCE UPON A TIME there was an elephant who wanted to become a rabbit. All the other elephants laughed at her. "Elly," they asked, "why do you want to become a rabbit? You can't hop like a rabbit. Rabbits don't have a trunk, tough skin, or big floppy ears. You're too big to be a rabbit. Besides, you're an elephant. It's best to accept what you are.

"That's ridiculous," Elly answered. "I can be whatever I want to be. I hate elephants. I want to hop around, have fur and a short nose. I want to be a rabbit and you can bet I'll try to change."

Then Elly tried to hop. She rose about a foot in the air, then crashed to the ground. The elephants laughed at her and walked away. A few nodded sadly and said, "It's tough when you don't like yourself."

While Elly was lying on the ground a rabbit hopped by. "Can you show me how to become like you?" she asked the rabbit. The rabbit didn't understand. As it hopped away, Elly realized she'd have to learn Rabbittilli.

She began studying right away. After two years she spoke the rabbit language fairly well.

One hot July day she tried hopping again. Again she crashed to the ground. But this time, when a rabbit came by, she was able to say in Rabbittilli, "Can you teach me to become a rabbit like you?"

"Illi fortrattimucutti calducky plook," muttered the rabbit. "I must be nuts. How can an elephant be talking to me?"

"How can I become a rabbit?" Elly repeated.

The rabbit blinked his eyes a few times, then said, "I cannot teach these things. Most rabbits are happy just being rabbits. However, on rare occasions when another animal seeks to join our ranks, we generally send them to the Russian Rabbit Dr. Hopquick Stepsky. He is an excellent teacher although many think him unethical. He will teach anyone to be a rabbit if they can pay his fee of four hundred carrot pounds."

"Please take me to him," Elly pleaded.

"If you insist," said the rabbit. "Follow me."

The rabbit hopped across a field, brook, and hill, and finally came to a wooded grove. There, sitting on top of a rock, was the famous Dr. Hopquick Stepsky. The rabbit introduced Elly to Dr. Hopquick.

"This elephant wants to become a rabbit."

"Very well," said Dr. Hopquick as he studied Elly. "I can teach you to become a rabbit. In my ten week course you shall learn the complete Rabbit Method including hopping, nibbling at green vegetables, ear wiggling, fur combing, and relating to other rabbits as equals. I shall not teach you to become an inferior rabbit or a superior rabbit, but only an ordinary rabbit. Although most rabbits are content in the knowledge that they are what they are, I shall teach you to be happy in the knowledge that you are what you are not. My fee is four hundred carrot pounds. Our lessons begin tomorrow morning at nine o'clock."

"Thank you, thank you!" Elly left beaming happily.

She studied her lessons every day and after ten weeks completed the entire Rabbit Course, receiving her certificate in Rabbitology from Dr. Hopquick.

"Now it is time for you to make your own way in the world," said Dr. Hopquick knowingly. "What I have taught you is only how the rabbits in the past have handled the problems of Rabbithood. However, the future is ever changing. Your problems will be different from those of other rabbits. Use the core of my teachings to help you hop over the hills of life and may you land safely in the carrot patch of your choice."

Then Dr. Hopquick said goodbye and hopped across the field. As Elly saw him disappear behind a tree, she thought, "At last I have accomplished what I wanted. I feel so proud!"

Elly worked with Dr. Hopquick's methods, but she still had trouble. She hated carrots and lost weight eating them. When she hopped, she still came crashing to the ground. She still couldn't nibble at green vegetables or wiggle her ears. Now the elephants in the neighborhood had nothing to do with her, while the rabbits paid no attention to her either. Finally one day she tried hopping across a stream and fell on her head. As she lay semi-conscious in the mud only the flies settling on her hide seemed to notice her.

Three of her old elephant friends saw what happened. They came over, dragged her out of the mud, and laid her down in the grass. As one elephant stroked her head with his trunk, the other blew cool water across her body and the third whispered in her ear.

His whispers made her dream a strange dream. She was on a hill overlooking a field of rabbits. All the rabbits were sitting absolutely still and looking at her. Slowly the rabbits began changing into elephants. Then the elephants changed into an enormous elephant as big as a mountain. The enormous elephant looked down on little Elly with a kindly expression on his face. He stroked her, saying in a soothing voice, "Elly, you are beautiful. No matter how you act or what you do you will always be beautiful to me. If you are a rabbit, to be a rabbit is beautiful. If you are an elephant, to be an elephant is beautiful. And if you are Elly, to be Elly is beautiful. Go and enjoy yourself. No one can take your beauty away."

Elly woke slowly from her dream. Her eyes blinked. She lifted her head. Gently her friends helped her up. She seemed different now. Her burdens had been lifted. A strange peace came over her. Her trunk swung from side to side as she walked down the road with a new freedom. She felt there could be nothing better in the world than being an elephant.

Brain Arthritis

JACK'S BRAIN WAS GETTING stiff. When he spoke, words stiffened in his mouth and fell out like sticks. He decided to see Dr. Hartmind, who did an immediate brain scan. "Jack," he said, "you are suffering from brain arthritis. It is a curable disease, but the treatment is very painful."

"So is the pain, Doctor. I'll do anything to get rid of it."

"Good." The doctor nodded. "A positive attitude is important in this treatment. Traditionally, we give our patients only aspirin. However, a laboratory in New Jersey has developed a special drug for treatment of brain arthritis. It is now available in pill form. At your stage, the disease is so advanced only concentrated doses can help."

The doctor reached into his drawer and pulled out a small bottle. "Take these pills. They'll make change easier and lessen the pain. Take them every day for one year. After that, you won't need them anymore. You'll be able to change all by yourself."

"Thank you so much," said Jack. "I feel better already."

"That's one of the miracles of these pills," the doctor explained. "You feel better even before you take them."

Jack went home. After lunch he took his first pill, a round white one with a sweet fragrance. Then he left his house for his afternoon stroll. Every day for twenty-three years he'd walked the same street, and always turned left at Baker Avenue. Today, however, he decided to turn right!

The pills were working.

He passed the dull, red-brick houses. Suddenly, he noticed sparkling window panes, polished handrails, and black-shingled roofs. Maple trees stood proud and straight, their sturdy branches, vibrating and dynamic, like powerful hands reaching towards the sky.

He glanced at the street. Even the asphalt shone!

Everything looked so different, so new. The fire hydrant seemed to survey the neighborhood like a conquering general.

Then Jack began to feel uneasy. This was enough adventure for one day.

He returned home, sat down in his familiar living room

armchair, and opened *A History of the Black Sea Trade; Cumulative Effects on Eleventh Century Expansion During the Byzantine Empire* by Heinrich von Schledenhofer. The book's 543 pages had been translated from German into English; many sentences went on for two pages and more. Jack began reading even though the von Schledenhofer tome was a marvel of dullness. He read every word, comma, period, page number, and footnote up to page 34. By page 35, he was almost asleep. Suddenly, new daring had pumped adrenalin into his stomach. He slammed the book shut and threw it across the room. It smacked against the wall, then fell into the garbage can where it belonged. Jack smiled triumphantly. He rose, stepped to his book shelf, and picked out *Martin Eden* by Jack London. Licking his lips, he sat down to read.

Slowly Jack began changing many attitudes. He learned to formulate a thought, act on it, and, if it didn't work, try a new thought. As he changed and became more flexible, he took fewer pills. Eventually, he didn't even need them anymore. Although, like all suffers of brain arthritis, he had occasional relapses, he nevertheless struggled to bring a new vision to each day. Brain arthritis loosened its grip on him. He had a better grip on life.

Morgan the Gorgon

MORGAN THE GORGON HAD difficulty making friends because snakes grew out of his head; they hissed whenever anyone came near him.

Morgan was very upset. The number of snakes was increasing each year. Finally, in desperation, he went to a snake doctor who understood his problem immediately.

"There is a snake coming out of your head for every evil deed you have committed," the doctor explained. "The only way to get rid of them is to reverse the effects of evil deeds. This is a very difficult task."

"I'll do anything to get rid of the snakes," said Morgan.

"Then follow me to the Room of Mistakes."

The doctor led Morgan downstairs to a large underground chamber. As soon as they crossed the threshold, all the snakes began hissing furiously.

"Shut up!" shouted Morgan. But the snakes kept hissing. He had no control over them.

"Look through this window," said the doctor. "See the Field of Evil Deeds?"

"What evil deeds have I done?" asked Morgan.

The doctor laughed. "There are so many. I don't have time to tell you all of them. However, judging from your most prominent snakes, you have robbed mailboxes, cheated your friends, lied to your parents, stolen from your classmates, and bullied little children. I see countless others, too."

The doctor put his hand on Morgan's shoulder. "You must go to the Field of Evil Deeds," he said. "Uproot every plant you find."

"Will it get rid of the snakes?"

"Absolutely."

As Morgan explored the Field of Evil Deeds, he found it extended much further than the doctor's basement. It spread over many city blocks. Morgan couldn't see the end of it. Some plants were taller than he was. One looked like a small tree, with iron blades growing out of its trunk and razor blades coming from its leaves. There were cacti, rose bushes, and nettles. It might take weeks to uproot one plant alone. He got down on his hands and knees and started weeding. The first plant he pulled up cut his thumb. He worked for hours on a huge cactus; his fingers blistered and bled. After nine hours of weeding, he had uprooted only four plants.

He fell on the ground, exhausted. It seemed hopeless.

But when he awoke, he saw that two of his snakes had fallen out. They lay dead on the ground beside him.

Encouraged, he spent the next three days weeding furiously. He worked in the field, ate in the field, slept in the field. When his hands got bloody, he bandaged them and continued weeding.

He weeded for months. Every few days another dead snake fell off. After a year had passed, the field was completely cleared.

Morgan felt much better.

He visited the doctor again.

"Look at yourself in the mirror," the doctor said.

Morgan did. The snakes were all gone. He looked wonderful without them."

"*Fantastic!*" he exclaimed.

He was ready to face the world again, no longer as Morgan the Gorgon, but as Morgan the Fair.

Flight of Imagination

FREDERICK WANTED TO FEEL flight. So he joined the race up the Empire State Building. Two hundred runners elbowed and shoved their way up the stairs towards the finish line on the roof. Frederick's untrained legs were no match for the well-muscled runners. But coming in last didn't bother him. After all, he hadn't come to run, but to fly.

By the time he arrived on the roof, all the runners had gone.

Frederick climbed the protective wall and spread his arms. The clouds of pollution were thick that day. When he jumped, his descent was slow and gentle.

He flapped his arms.

As he floated down, a history book passed by. Taking hold of it, he paused to read: *The Icelandic Sagas of Erik the Red*. These adventures by Snorri Snurlson held him until the second floor, when, realizing his flight was over, he tossed the sagas away.

He landed on the sidewalk by a new stand. Headlines read: "Nuclear War Postponed."

He lunched in a deli.

Then he took the subway home.

Phrygian Knots Drive Phrygian Fred Knuts

WHO IS PHRYGIAN FRED? Did his mother walk across Armenia? Was his greatest of grandfathers a Hittite? These questions haunted Fred as he trod the Phrygian plateau on his way to Gordium. There he hoped to cut the Gordian knot.

But when Fred got to Gordium, the town elders told him Alexander the Great had already cut the knot and left the remnants for chicken feed.

Fred was twenty-three hundred years late! Tough times on the Phrygian plateau.

He sat down on a Hittite ruin and looked up at the stars. Then he put on his Phrygian cap, checked for marauding Cimmerians, and headed towards Central Asia to check out his Indo-European roots.

Fred Watches TV

ON MONDAY, JUNE 22, Fred carried the TV to the fireplace, doused it with gasoline, and tossed on a lit match. In a blaze of glory, the set began to burn.

Fred sat in his armchair, beer in hand and watched the fire. He saw the eleven o'clock new burst into flames, followed by a movie. Channel after channel went up in smoke. "This is the best TV I've ever seen!" he said.

Then he went downstairs and began a new life.

Fred Speaks Bulgarian

FRED WENT TO HIS first Bulgarian lesson with Natasha. She sat opposite him in her furnished Palisades Park apartment and fed him tasty morsels of large and small Bulgarian words.

Ah, it felt good. Fresh Bulgarian verbs, nouns, adjectives, and pronouns funneled into his brain, helping to generate a lively debate among his brain cells. His heart beat faster. Even his knee joints felt the hard-sounding phrases. By the end of the lesson, Fred's head swam with images of St. Cyril and Methodius and their Cyrillic alphabet.

After his lesson, Fred drove back home. Just outside his house, his wife, Clara, was sitting in a tree. "Why are you late?" she asked.

Fred dropped his books on the doorstep. "I am not late," he replied. "I am early for tomorrow's meeting with you. Clara, for years you said we couldn't communicate. That is why I am learning Bulgarian. I know we can communicate if we speak Bulgarian." He asked in Bulgarian, "Clara, do you want to move down from your tree trunk into the house with me?"

"I don't speak Bulgarian," Clara answered.

"Then write it down in the Cyrillic alphabet."

"This won't work, Fred." Clara shook her head. "I think we should make an appointment with a marriage counselor."

"A Bulgarian teacher is better."

They compromised by going to a marriage counselor who spoke Bulgarian. After one session, Clara said, "I'll try anything, even Bulgarian."

"Good," Fred said.

They looked at each other and shook their heads in the Bulgarian "yes" manner.

"Da."

"Da."

Shining Jewel

FRED GAZED INTO THE lake. He saw his father's face rolling across the water towards him. "Pa, why are you here?"

"I came to visit you, son. I came to give you support."

Fred watched his father's body coalesce, step out of the water, and come closer. He could smell the familiar cigar and old white shirt.

"How do you know I need support, Pa?"

"Easy. When you were little, you used to sit by the lake, cross your left leg over your right, and gaze into the water. That's what you're doing now, so I guess you must be in a bad way."

"You're right, Pa. I am sitting by the lake. But it is my *right leg* that is crossed over my *left*. You may remember, my right leg is my victory leg; my left leg is the leg of defeat. True, I used to sit here with my left leg crossed, but things have changed. Since you left, I've been on my own. I've discovered a shining jewel in my brain. When I visualize it, I feel confident. You mentioned something about a jewel before you died, but back then I didn't know what you were talking about."

Fred's father nodded. "Ah, yes, the jewel. I remember telling you about it when I was in the hospital. It's a legacy that can help you through tough times. You have to experience such a jewel to know it. I just didn't know how to tell you then. But when I saw death approaching, I decided to tell you anyway, even though you might not understand."

"You're right," Fred said. "I didn't. I thought what you said was just babbling, the ravings of a dying old man."

Fred's father looked down at Fred's leg. "I should have noticed your right leg crossed over your left, but I didn't. Guess I've been under water too long."

"I miss you, Pa. But don't worry about me. I've seen the jewel. You can return to the lake and rest in peace."

His father smiled. "You're right, son. No need to stay any longer." Fred's father embraced his son. Then he walked into the lake and disappeared.

Fred and the Turks

WHY ARE YOU WRITING a great 19th-century novel?" Fred's mother asked. "Wouldn't a mediocre 20th-century one be better?"

"Ma, everyone is trying to write a great 20th century novel. If I want to stand out, it would be better to write a 19th-century one."

"Freddie, when will your writing phase end? Why don't you get out of the house, go to parties, meet a girl, and get married? It's unhealthy for a young man to sit around the house writing a 19th century novel. Writing is a disease only marriage can cure."

"Will marriage make me write a better 19th-century novel?"

"No, Freddie, I didn't say that. I said marriage will stop your writing completely. You'll raise a family, get a job, and forget about this business. Writing is for children. Grown-ups work for a living."

"But, Ma, if I work for a living, how can I go to Turkey?"

"Turkey? Why go there? I'm surprised at you. Look what the Turks did to the Phrygians."

"That wasn't the Turks."

"Well, whoever it was. Don't go to Turkey. You won't be safe there."

"Turks are very hospitable."

"Hospital is right. That's where you'll end up, with hepatitis and diarrhea. Turkey is dangerous. I'm afraid of Turks."

"Ma, you said you were afraid of the French, English, Germans, Austrians, Portuguese, Finns, Kurds, Armenians, and Hungarians, too."

"I'm afraid of them all."

"They're not so bad. Hundred of books have been written about the people you're afraid of. Many were written in the 19th century."

"The 19th century? Aren't you writing a 19th century novel?"

"Yes."

"That's wonderful, Freddie. I'm proud of you. Imagine, a 19th-century novel. I'm telling all my friends about it. Do Turks know how to read?"

Fred's Personality Change

FRED SUFFERED FROM BOILS-on-the-brain, a disease inherited from his mother. How could he get well? How could he become more selfless, caring, sensitive, and open? How could he break out of his self-created prison with its delicious meals and kind waiters?

The Personality Changing Mental Meat Grinding Machine, then being sold in Pathmark for $29.95, was his only hope. He jumped in his car and drove off to buy one.

He put the machine on his kitchen table, opened the steel

door, put his head inside, and turned on the switch. Warm currents began heating his brain. When he heard a ping, he was done. He opened the door, and out came a new personality, a kind Fred—caring, sensitive, and open. Only his head was burnt to a crisp, and, instead of ears, he had ashes.

He told his friends about the machine, and many jumped in their cars, too.

Jasper Gratz, Modern Composer

JASPER GRATZ HAS BEEN employed during the past three years as composer in residence at the Ford Motor Plant in Detroit. His work here has been hailed by many as an outstanding contribution to America. He has learned to compose with one hand, and put on bumpers on cars with the other. His contribution to the mass production of both music and cars has thus been considerable. He is also one of the few working composers in America today.

We interviewed Mr. Gratz on the assembly line. The time was Monday morning at 11:26 a.m. His words are as follows. (Dots indicate a new bumper being attached.)

"I...am a com...poser in res...idence at the...Ford Mo... tor...Plant... My work...here...has...been—"

We had to conclude our interview at this time for a lunch break. However, over a three day period, we managed to learn of Mr. Gratz's personal view of his life and work.

Jasper Gratz feels that factory work has put him closer not only to the workers, but more important, to the machines themselves. In order to feel at home in modern industrial society Mr. Gratz believes that man must befriend his machines. "Take a machine out to lunch," he says.

Although Mr. Gratz is not married, he does live with the machines he loves. These include three radios, two TV sets, a staple gun, and four hundred and two "little gadgets." He says, "As long as...I am with...the...machine, I...am...never lonely."

Mr. Gratz's work in the factory has enabled him to live and work intimately with machines and thus capture their true essence in his musical work. "Factories and Trucking Number 1" was written in 1972 and first performed for the annual meeting of the Local Brotherhood of Machines, of which Mr. Gratz is president.

Ludwig Learns to Staple

LUDWIG WAS SITTING IN the subway on his way uptown, reading his *Bavarian Times*, when a mugger grabbed him by the collar, yanked him out of his seat, and said, "Gimme you wallet!"

"*Bitte?*" Ludwig replied.

The mugger, a lean sixteen-year-old fresh out of ninth grade, glared at Ludwig with eyes so filled with rage that the German art student was sure he saw knives coming out of them. He wasn't too far wrong. A very visible knife gleamed from just beneath the mugger's coat.

"You wallet!" the mugger repeated. Ludwig knew he meant business.

"*Bitte,*" he nodded and reached into his back pocket. He had just come from Parsons School of Design, where all month long he had been taking a course in the stapling arts.

"Faster! Move faster!"

This was too much. Ludwig replied by pulling his staplegun out of his back pocket and releasing a well-aimed barrage of 5/8-inch pointed copper-clads, which stapled the young hood firmly to the subway wall.

Then he returned to his *Bavarian Times*.

Identity

I LOOK IN THE MIRROR. What dark romantic eyes. I identify with my eyes.

What a fine nose. I identify with my nose.

What a strong jaw, sensuous mouth, and firm teeth. What a face! I identify with my face.

Whoops, I feel a pain in my neck. I stop. I think. *I become* the pain. Now I have a new identity: I am a pain in the neck. Don't laugh. At least I know who I am. Do you know who you are?

Look at that gorgeous brunette walking by. I've already forgotten my pain in the neck. That gorgeous brunette—she's my identity now. I open the newspaper to the financial section. My oil stock has gone down again. I identify with my stock as it sinks. Its value is being depressed and so am I.

Luckily the phone rings.

"Hello. Who is it?" I ask, completely identifying with the voice on the other end.

"This is your identity."

I hang up. You think it's easy? I have so many identities. They change from moment to moment. Sometimes it makes me feel insecure, but when it does, I identify with my insecurity, and this removes my insecurity by giving me a new identity.

Yesterday I saw a sign outside a church: *Spirit Wanted? Inquire Within.* I walked inside. I looked at the rows of empty pews, the stone pillars, and the high vaulted ceiling. It was very quiet. Slowly I began to identify with the silence and emptiness around me. I felt better; all my former identities were forgotten.

A strange peace filled my mind. It was a new identity. I sat in silence for a long time.

Then, cleansed and refreshed, I rose and returned to the world.

Clothing

GOD SAT ON HIS throne. He spoke to Man: "Man, I want to take a look at you. Take off your clothing."

Man took off his shirt. "That's not enough," God said. Man took off his shoes and socks. "Still not enough. More!"

Man took off his pants. He stood in his underwear before God. "More!" God roared. "Reveal yourself. Remove it all!" Man removed his underwear. He stood naked before God. "Don't play with me!" God thundered. "Remove it all!" Man trembled. He fell to his knees before his Maker.

"Lord," he cried, "I stand naked before you. What more can I do?"

A deafening command rolled through the universe. "Use

your imagination! Remove it all!"

What did the Lord mean? Fueled by fear, man's imagination began to work. Suddenly an idea seized his mind. Quickly he stepped out of his skin, drained his blood, and removed his bones.

He stood before God only in spirit.

God looked at man. He said: "Man, you look like me." Man looked at himself. "You're right, God. I feel like you too."

Then they embraced.

Music
for
Real Fans

A Real Fan

JOHN WAS BLACK, TALL, and strong. His rough face, sharp features, and full lips made him appear menacing to Martha. She was so pale and frail that she seemed almost helpless.

When he met her at the Brahms concert, sitting alone in the corner, nervously clasping her hands, he strutted over. His hand fell roughly on her delicate shoulder. "You pathetic creature," he said. "Why are you trembling in the corner like a frightened mouse? Sit with me! I groove on defenseless chicks. They don't call me Fowl Man for nothing."

Martha swooned when John spoke so forcefully. She stole a furtive glance at him and cooed in a high-pitched voice, "I'm so glad I can be near you. I love your powerful arms holding my thin body. Strong trees must support weak branches."

They sat together in the mezzanine. The conductor emerged on the stage, bowed, waited for the audience applause to diminish, then lifted his baton. The orchestra began playing Brahms' *Third Symphony*. Martha's face relaxed. But John's contorted with rage.

"I thought this was a Bach concert!" he roared.

The people in the seats nearby glared at him. One young man told him flatly to shut up. John paid no attention. "I want

Bach!" he repeated.

The musicians kept playing. John saw an usher racing down the aisle towards him. His eyes swelled with fury. As the music rose to a crescendo, he picked up his chair and threw it down at the musicians on stage. Martha was mortified, but all she could do was coo admiringly, "Oh, you're so *strong*."

The chair bounced off a tuba and knocked over the French horn player's music stand. The orchestra stopped playing. The conductor turned and shouted at the audience, shaking his fist, "Who threw that chair? What do you think this is, a wrestling match?"

John ripped a chunk of rug from the floor and tore it into tiny pieces with his teeth.

"I want *Bach!*" He spat out the rug. "If I don't get Bach, I'll sing him my self!" He turned to Martha, picked her up by the scruff of the neck, threw her over his shoulder, and marched out of the hall singing the *St. Matthew's Passion.* Martha tried to harmonize as she hung upside-down, her face bumping into John's buttocks.

He slammed the hall door behind them, pulled off the doorknob, and threw it at the delicatessen window across the street. As the glass splintered, you could hear hams singing counterpoint in their sandwiches.

"I *love* your manliness," Martha hummed as John pulled a stop sign out of the sidewalk and used it like a battering ram to smash cars and spear buses as they crossed Seventh Avenue.

Police sirens started to wail in the distance. John stopped. He listened. "Is that Bach I hear?"

A squad of police cars surrounded him. "Put down that girl!"

one of the officers commanded.

"Only if I hear a good fugue."

The officers huddled for a plan of action. Then they broke out of their huddle and began singing the *Parking Violations Fugue in E minor*. John was enraptured by the superb counterpoint. He relaxed, put Martha down, and smiled happily. As an officer handcuffed him, he said with a touch of awe in his voice, "You guys are really good. How do you get so much feeling in your music?"

"By handing out parking tickets," answered the squat officer with the big mouth.

"Can you sing the *Speeding Laws*, too?"

"Naw, you gotta go to the state troopers for that one."

The officers pushed John into the paddy wagon. As they drove off, the radio was playing "Courthouse Gavotte."

Meekly, Martha waved goodbye. She walked across the street, flagged down a cab, and went home.

The next day, she saw John's picture in the paper. He had been sentenced to six months of Brahms. She held the picture in her small hands, saying, "We'll go to more concerts when he gets out. He's a real fan."

Knorbert and the Kneecaps

THE KNEECAPS GAVE OUTSTANDING concerts in every city. Eastern European countries swelled with pride when they appeared in Budapest, Prague, and even Vienna. State treasuries burgeoned as well. The American concert tour was a smash hit. In short, the Kneecaps had it made.

How had this happened? How had these small body parts built themselves up? How had knees reached beyond mind and heart?

It all started when Knorbert Kneecap left his house early one morning to go to his job as an obscure clam stripper in a local fish market. The job didn't pay much, but it was a living, and, as his wife declared, "A job is a job."

"Yes, a job is a job."

"A job is a job is a job," he added inventively.

Such communication went on for years in that clam-dominated household.

Then one day everything changed.

Over the years, Knorbert's knees had begun to hurt. Arthritis, perhaps, or even osteoporosis of the tibia. The stiffness and pain increased until, one morning, Knorbert couldn't get out of bed. This was too much for his wife. "Knorbert," she said, "your pains are becoming my pains. It's time you went to a doctor. I know a bone specialist, a graduate of Knie University in the Knetherlands, and whose radical work in knee surgery has won him honors in the medical insurance race. He'll cure your knees."

Knorbert consulted the doctor. "I'm putting you on a music diet," the doctor said, handing Knorbert some tapes. "Play these four times a day. Take them with plenty of fluid. Music cures everything. You'll be fine in three days."

"Thank you," Knorbert said as he hobbled out of the office.

Sure enough, after three days of playing the tapes, Knorbert's knees got better. So did his mental state. He began to sing and dance every morning, and his clam shelling improved. I'll bet other people would benefit from this cure, he thought. That's when he formed a singing group from among his coworkers at the fish market. At first they called themselves "The Torn Cartilage"; then they changed their name to "The Kneecaps." The Kneecaps' unique style and sound captured the nation and shot their songs to the top on all music charts. They created the Knee market and made the selling of Knees the megamillion-dollar business it is today.

The Kneecaps first hit tune, "Kneecaps For My Honey," made $20 million. It was followed by "Knees for Jesus," "Oh Darling, I Knees You," "Megaknees Dioxide on my Mind," and the blockbuster monster "High Knees."

Last year the Kneecaps finally disbanded after a long and successful career. Knorbert returned to the fish market, but as the owner. He has since purchased several hundred fish markets throughout the United States and is now reputed to be one of the richest men in America.

Recently, he spoke before the world body of the United Kneetions and proposed the creation of World Knees for Peace.

After that speech, he went home for a good night's sleep. But in two hours he awoke.

His elbows hurt.

A Death in the Finger Family

ONCE UPON A TIME there were five Fingers. They lived together at Edge-of-Hand in northern New Jersey. Each finger worked six days a week, pressing strings for a guitarist.

Every month family members would set aside a few musical notes in a Retirement Plan especially designed for older Fingers. The Fingers knew that although today they were strong and flexible, eventually time would weaken them. Each one wanted an early retirement in Florida where they would collect Social Security, lie in the sun, and live off their notes.

One day, Index Finger pulled a muscle and collapsed. The burden of leading the other fingers on the guitar neck, plus barring chords without any help, had been too much. The pain in his segments was terrible, and after a few days, he died. The other fingers were horrified. "How can we get along without Index?" they cried, as Index hung limply at Edge-of-Hand. "Who will point the way?"

After recovering from the shock, they decided a proper burial was necessary. Thumb called the undertaker, who wrapped Index in a white bandage, ordered guitar funeral music, and called the family together for a memorial service. Prayers were offered, and a moving eulogy by Thumb told of how the two friends had worked together, spending so much of their lives grasping things, or touching each other on walks through the park.

After the service Thumb said solemnly, "Index Finger had hundreds of notes put away for retirement. We must make sure they are equally divided among us."

"That's not fair!" Middle Finger cried, rising to her full height in indignation. She rocked on her knuckle base as her joints turned purple with rage. "I stood next to Index all his life! I supported him; I gave him strength. I should get the most notes. Index would have wanted it that way."

"Don't make me laugh," yelled Pinky, who always leaned on the other fingers, and was so dependent that even during the Vivaldi Guitar Concerto—a concerto in which she had almost nothing to do—she nudged Ring Finger when her trill came up, and pleaded, "Please help me. I can't trill all alone." (After the concert she was fined twenty notes by the Musician's Finger Union for her unprofessional attitude.) "I'm the smallest and the weakest," she continued. "I need the most support. Inheritance should be based on need, not greed."

Ring Finger fumed silently as the other members of the family argued about the money. Finally Thumb, who was in charge of things, spoke with authority: "We must all live together. An uneven distribution of the notes would only cause conflict among us. A few notes one way or the other are not as important as family unity. The notes must be divided evenly."

"Amen," said Ring Finger.

Middle Finger was about to protest, but Thumb silenced her by stepping on her cuticle.

The next day was Sunday. All the Fingers rose at 7:00 a.m. They gathered round the meeting place of Palm. Thumb was about to divide the inheritance when, suddenly, Index Finger began to move! The Fingers jumped. They rushed over to Index, stripped off his bandages, and saw him squirming about. Evidently the pulled muscle had only put him in temporary remission. He rose slowly, gazing at the Fingers standing around him.

"I'm glad you're well," said Thumb, beaming happily. "This must be the Sunday Resurrection."

"Yeah," squealed Pinky. "It's great having you back!"

Index looked healthier now. "I'm glad to be back," he said hoarsely. "It makes me glad to see my family sticking together, even through my death."

On Monday all the Fingers went back to work. Once again Index pointed the way as they closed in a chord around the guitar neck.

Paul's Piano Lesson

"CAN'T WE HURRY THIS Beethoven sonata?" Mrs. Pathby asked at her son's lesson.

The lad was quite goal oriented.

"Absolutely not," answered his teacher. "Paul must play it *even more* slowly,"

"What?" Paul complained. "You must be mad. I need goals. Just like the termites eating this house, my music must have goals. When I play the Beethoven *Pathetique*, my goal is to finish! That's why my fingers fly so fast. I play to win! It's a contest. First pianist to finish wins."

Mrs. Moreon blew her nose. "Pretty bad," she sneered. "Luckily your mother pays me a pretty penny to tolerate your boorish, perfectionist attitude. Otherwise, I'd take your piano and stuff it—"

Mother Pathby piped up from her seat by the window, "Steady now, Mrs. Moreon. There's no reason to berate my son. His goal-oriented attitude has brought benefits. Last week, after his waltz lesson, he danced to the store to buy groceries."

Mrs. Moreon sizzled. "How crass!" she snorted. "I've never heard such a hedonistic attitude. Luckily you're feeding my coffers. Otherwise, my high standards could not be compromised."

"That's easy for you to say, Mr. Moreon," Paul piped, glancing up from the watermelon he had squeezed between the piano keys. "Not everyone can attend the Jewelyard School of Music as you did and graduate Summa Cum Kumquat from the fruit department."

Paul's piano lessons continued for three years until the termites ate Mrs Moreon's house.

Voice

THAT LOUSY ROTTEN VOICE! Who does he think he is? Left me. Just like that! You call that gratitude? And after all I've done for him.

I gave him the best place in my body—and he leaves.

I'm not the kind of girl to let just anybody in. I've got my standards. I'm very particular. But this Voice was real nice. You know the type—smooth and soft-sell, yet strong and macho, supermasculine yet somewhat laid back. And oh, so attractive! All the other girls in the office wanted him.

At first I didn't mind sharing. But after awhile I wanted him all to myself. I've got so little time. After working all day typing papers, serving coffee, bringing buns into executive meetings where all those dark-suit creeps clean their hands on my public and private parts—oh, they are disgusting! I hate them!

But I had to do it. I had to. After all, what could I say? I had no Voice.

Then I found my Voice!

Ah, sweet Voice. He's protecting me, speaking up for me. Why should I have to share him with the other girls? Let them find their own voice.

Dental Musician

TOM WAS A DENTIST. He wanted to move beyond his cavity of ignorance by expanding his aural knowledge.

An oboe and bassoon soloist for the San Diego Orthodontial Symphony, an orchestra specializing in serial music extractions, he needed to know the art of music from all ends. Teeth were his business by day but at night he dreamed of intestines.

Saturday morning, when he entered the aviary section of the San Diego Zoo, he asked the guard: "Please let me hear the sound of canary intestines."

The guard promptly handcuffed him to a restroom post, dialed the Aviary Intestinal Research Institute in La Jolla on his cellular phone, and asked for Dr. Jonas Fawk, director of the Fowl Intestine Department, who immediately sent an ambulance filled with canaries.

Now the guard handcuffed Tom to a backseat monorail—protecting the canaries from unauthorized dental work—and sent the hawk-faced ambulance driver back to the lab. Bobbing and through the freeway rush hour, Tom suddenly heard the belching, intestinal traffic sounds he was looking for.

Arriving at the Institute, he emerged from the van, thanked Dr. Jonas, smiled, and, with a wild scream, ran down La Jolla Mountain.

Romance in E flat

JOHN STENCH, NEWEST MAN on the rodeo squad, adjusted his blue ascot. "What in blazes is going on here?" he asked. Betsy, his pervert nag, stood silently to the right.

"I bought this dang thing to please Lisa, but all I get is a whirlwind of blade-dodging danger."

Larry Phillips, boilerman from Petusa, ambled over. Wiping swibble from his lips, leveling his chin four inches above Stench, he barked, "You'll never get that gal. She took off with Dog-Face Rhino two days ago. Now all you can hope for is Stallion."

John shook his ponytail. Tightening his saddle, he said, "No use complaining, Larry. That girl won't listen. Every time I bring my turnip soup to her shrivel on the prairie, she stoops on her sit and howls. No dog will go near her."

"Takes after her mother. A linguist, you know." Larry leaned on his empty foot, then added, "When the gravedigger threw dirt on her coffin, she pushed open the lid, shook her finger, and shouted, 'Don't you dare!' You don't see corpses like that around here anymore."

John pulled out a squirter and shot protoliquid on his metatarsals and bunion cushions. "I won't try that again, Larry. This is the last time you catch me with Heinrich Blieberhaft's *Weltanschaung Plus*. Lisa couldn't understand a word in that book, though she's an Aramaic scholar."

Larry polished his glasses. "I wouldn't push book reading

too far. Besides, scholars are for frying."

Both lads rose, tightened their diapers, grabbed teething rings, and fell asleep in the playpen.

Three Tales
of Jimenez

JIMENEZ!

JIMENEZ DEL ORO, DRESSED in black with guitar in hand, strode across the stage. "*Ole*, Jimenez! Jimenez!" Cries of adoration from his fans resounded through the hall.

Alphonso carried the master's footstool from backstage. He set it before the gold embroidered concert chair and scurried away.

Now the spotlight narrowed. Cheering of the overflow audience diminished until, mesmerized by expectation, only the shuffle of ushers feet remained. Soon even that was gone.

Total silence.

The master guitarist smiled, revealing two gold teeth scattered among the white.

He bowed in all directions.

Jimenez sat down on his gold-embroidered cushion. Cradling his Ramirez guitar on his lap, he stroked the ebony neck and inhaled the rosewood aroma emanating from the sound hole.

Focusing his mind, reining in all stray thoughts, a look of other-worldliness crossed his face as he strummed a C chord. The rich sonority flowed through the hall. He smiled again.

Leaning into the guitar, the fingers of Jimenez slid rapidly up and down the neck on a C scale. Lingering on a succulent low C, he held the root until its vibrations vanished into a shadow of silence.

Jimenez stopped, stood up, leaned his guitar against his concert chair, raised his right hand, and spoke:

"Thank you, my beloved audience. The scale you heard is from my village. I heard my first when I was five years old. It has haunted me ever since.

"Ah, my village, home of my beloved parents, Madre Gansa and Juan Plastico. Our ancestral tree dates back to ancient Phoenician traders who docked at Jerez around 1000 B.C. At that time my grandfather Bannibal was on a trading mission selling alphabets to Celtic and Iberian tribes. Sailing with sacks of alphabet blocks, he carried his vision of universal literacy throughout the Mediterranean world. During that time, interest in the alphabet was steadily growing. Prices for letters soared. Fleets of Bannibal's boats sailed, not only to Etruria, but to Mycenia, Troy, Marsala, and Egypt, where they cut into hieroglyphic sales and even dented the demotic market.

"Then Bannibal succumbed to greed, a common failing in our family. Instead of restraining production, he increased it. Competitors stepped in. Soon inferior letters were produced selling at lower prices. The price of alphabets plummeted as thousands of inferior letters were dumped, first on the open market, then into the Mediterranean. Bannibal's business was ruined. His boats laden with letters drifted aimlessly from port to port.

"Bannibal died a poor man. His son, Kartobal, tried resurrecting the business by specializing in vowels. In the chronicles of our family you can read descriptions of Kartobal traveling through the Iberian countryside, hawking his vowels. When an Iberian tribesman expressed interest, Kartobal would grab his arm and pull him into the Alphabet Sales Cave, serve him Sidon wine in a V-shaped goblet, and bombard him with the importance of owning, not only a complete set of consonants, but all the vowels as well. When a deal was concluded, Kartobal presented the vowels to the Iberian in an oakwood box."

Jimenez paused to reflect. His black eyes darted to three women sitting in the mezzanine. He listened to the silence, then went on:

"Bannibal and Kartobal loved sound and the magic of speech. They didn't invent the alphabet, they only promoted it. As the first sound salesmen in history, they risked insecurity and financial ruin, speculating in a market of illiterates, taking chances, doing whatever possible to spread the joys of letters throughout the world. Both were visionaries; letters their form of music. And they suffered for their apocalyptic visions."

The guitarist scanned his audience once again.

"What have the visions of Bannibal and Kartobal to do with you or me? How does their suffering relate to us? Well, I don't know about you, but I've suffered a great deal."

Jimenez wiped a tear from his eye.

"A musician's life is not easy. Guitarists suffer from low funds, malnutrition, joint diseases, arthritic fingers, lower back pain, poor housing, inadequate clothing, and lack of calcium. Often our twisted bodies are deformed, one shoulder higher than the other from hours crouched over the guitar. Notice this hump on my back, a scoliosis of the trapezius malformation caused from playing too much Bach."

Jimenez extended his arms towards the audience.

"Look at my left arm: It is longer than my right because every day I stretch it on the rack of Tarrega, Sor, and transcriptions of Beethoven, Mendelssohn, and Bach. My right-hand fingernails dwarf those of the Transylvanian demon; these digital spears enable me to play fiery scales *piccado* style and roll my fingers over the strings in thunderous *rasgueado* flamencan rolls. How many times have I broken fingernails, bones, and even guitars pounding on the face of my guitar as I *golpe* my way through a passionate Farruca?

"Long hours of left leg elevation on the foot stool have made one leg shorter than the other. Like many guitarists, I suffer from a limp. Add to these woes, a fear of falling off the stage, danger from sitting on wobbly chairs, unglued piano benches, stools, broken backstage toilet seats, and so on.

"Yet I would not trade my career for anything. Such pains bring me pleasure. I love to suffer. It makes me creative."

Jimenez opened his arms to embrace the audience.

"My beloved audience, let me tell you about my life, and the many lives I have led.

"My suffering did not begin today, last week, last year, or as the Freudians would have you believe, in my childhood. No, no, no! Truth is, I have been suffering for *ages!* Not only at birth but *before* birth. I suffered in previous l i v e s....

"I remember life as a brick in Babylonia in 2000 B.C. My memory of those days is hazy. What can you expect from a brick? During that period, I lived in the wall of a ziggurat until it was torn down by invading Hittite tribesmen. Then I traveled as a flu germ inside the lungs of a Chinese peasant; I was also a frog on the Euphrates, a vulture in Africa, and a horse in Central Asia where I first heard spoken Mongolian!

"I even remember my incarnation as a Phoenician. During that time, my parents believed in education. I learned to read, write, and study the stars. Papa loved music and encouraged me to play a stringed instrument.

"Of course, guitar as we know it today did not exist then. Phoenicians called their guitars 'harhars'. When I was seven, Papa hollowed my first harhar out of a cedar tree and stretched a sheepskin across it.

"My harhar had only one string made from the guts of my favorite sheep. Whenever I plucked it, I imagined bleats echoing from the valley behind our home.

"Indeed, the "music" I produced distanced me from other living creatures. Birds, insects, animals, my father, mother, and brother all scattered whenever I plucked that string. What power it gave me! Whenever I wanted to be alone, I'd simply play my harhar.

"Ah, but I was a clever lad in those days. Creative. Driven. I loved playing my harhar. Even though I could only play one note, I played it over and over again. It became my favorite note. I called it My *Note*, or simply *Note*. I played My Note beneath date trees; I played My Note as I climbed Mount Har-el-Jibar; I played My Note strolling the beaches by the Mediterranean; and I heard My Note echo through the Wadiel-Moof-Qoof as I sat on the stones of the dried up river bed, strumming while buzzards flew in circles above my head.

"But the artist in me kept growing. Soon I got bored playing the same note over and over again. I began experimenting by pressing my fingers on the higher and lower parts of the string.

The muted tones I produced showed the limitations of my instrument. I yearned to reach beyond my limits, to expand, to grow!

"I needed more strings.

"So I started searching for sheep. I killed my first at night by the Nahr River. Using a knife from my father's cloth shop, I cut open its belly and pulled out a long piece of intestine. I could hardly restrain my excitement.

I ran home humming a Canaanite hunting song, sat down on the floor in my room, and attached the intestine to my harhar next to the first string. When I ran my thumb over two strings a miracle happened: Two sounds at once!

"During the next few weeks, the intestine dried and the tone on my harhar improved! I was ecstatic.

"I loved the feel of the strings under my fingers. I practiced every day. Neither food nor sleep could tear me away from Phoenician sailor songs, Canaanite hymns, and Hebrew psalms.

However, after a month, the old boredom returned. Once again I yearned to break the bonds of limitation and expand.

"I returned to Mount Har-el-Jibar where shepherds grazed their flocks. I looked with longing at the mountainside dotted with strings or grazing sheep.

"Over the next three months I killed a sheep a week, and added twelve strings. From a simple harhar, I went to a two-har, three- har, then four- and five-, to a six-har. I made it up to twelve-har, and might have gone on to a hundred, but a shepherd caught me prowling among his flock one night. He brought me to my father, whose rage, when he found the strings and knife I'd stolen, knew no bounds.

"I was led through the streets of Byblus by a leash. How humiliating! Friends, neighbors, and townspeople looked on and threw me clumps of grass to eat. Then he sent me to live with a flock of sheep for three months. The very shepherd who caught me was now my shepherd.

"But my father was a wise man. He knew living among sheep would teach me many lessons. We shared food, drank from the Nahr River together, and searched for tasty grasses on the slopes of Mount Har-el-Jibar.

"I began to see things from a sheep's point of view. In three months, I developed a loyalty to these kind animals. These days we still get together on weekends down by the river. I joke about their cousins who became strings on my harhar, and, although they don't laugh, at least they remain politely silent. I've learned to respect sheep.

"My father understood I needed a positive role model in order to grow as an artist. He gave me lessons with the famous Byblus music seer and teacher, Ibrahim-al-Moosiq'bal.

"Ibrahim had blinded himself at age five, believing it would improve his hearing. No one knew his real age, but as headmaster of the local Chaldean Music School, he was the best listener in Byblus, and taught me singing, astrology, and to improvise on the harhar in local modes."

Jimenez sat down on his chair, placed his left foot on the footstool and played the *Pavane in C* by Luis Milan. The audience cheered as the final C chord faded away.

Jimenez rose and picked up his footstool. "An unseen power resides within this magic, four-legged wonder," he said. "Every morning, with body cleansed and mind purified by three cups of coffee, I retire to the chapel in my garage and fall on my knees to pray before my footstool." Jimenez held it aloft for the audience to see. "Gazing upon this marvel brings me a deep inner peace.

"But I wasn't always peaceful. I used to suffer daily from anxiety and depression. I needed therapy. Madre Gansa told me about a Dr. Sigmund of Vienna who treated broken-down performers.

"So I went to Austria.

"The sun was shining when I arrived at the Vienna city gates. A breeze from the Hapsburg palace brushed my cheeks. I heard horse-drawn carriages rolling over cobblestones, and smelled the fresh Viennese manure. My guitar case slung over my back, I traversed the inner city, inspected shops on Fleischmark and Rotenturm Strasse, and compared the Gothic arches of St. Stephen's with those in my garage. For lunch I ate a sausage, washed it down with beer, and proceeded north to the Ringstrasse. Circling it for the next two hours, I searched for Dr. Sigmund's house. Finally, at 19 Bergstrasse, guitar in hand, I climbed the three flights of stairs to his apartment.

"Stroking his beard, Dr. Sigmund greeted me at the door. Or rather, he greeted the door as I passed through it. During my first therapy session he went downstairs for a walk while I sat in his office. By the time he came back, my session had ended.

"That didn't stop me from returning, week after week. Finally, after two months, Dr. Sigmund said something. But it was in German, so I couldn't understand. Then he ripped the guitar from my hands and threw it out the window!

"'*Aufwiedersehen*,' he said.

"I knew what that meant, because he left.

"Dr. Sigmund had said the magic words! Now I understood. Even though a week later he said in Spanish, '*Las papas estan cocinado,' Aufwiedersehen* stuck in my mind.

"*Aufweidersehen* changed my life. By throwing my guitar out the window, Dr, Sigmund made me realize I didn't need a guitar to express myself. Even without my guitar, my essence would remain. It could be expressed, depressed, post-pressed, or simply pressed, but no matter what happened, nothing could destroy it!"

Jimenez smiled remembering his revelation.

"One day the doctor arrived looking very tired. He sank into his armchair opposite me and placed his foot on the embroidered footstool by his chair. Suddenly, the muscles of his face relaxed, his lips parted in a smile, and he fell asleep. While he slept, I had thought about the nature of existence, the relationship of divine to mundane, free will versus predestination, impermanence of life, the transitory nature of history, transmigration of souls, and the role of the intestines in psychotherapy.

"When Dr. Sigmund awoke, I thanked him for these powerful insights. He uttered a meditative 'hmmm,' and took his foot off the stool. Suddenly, his expression froze! Anxiety lined his face. He straightened his jacket, rose from his chair and left.

"I realized what had happened: Dr. Sigmund had taken his foot off the footstool!

"I put together the meaning of these events:

1. *Foot on footstool: Doctor relaxes, smiles, is happy.*

2. *Foot off footstool: Doctor tense and worried.*

3. *Conclusion: Foot on footstool brings happiness!*

"I grabbed Dr. Sigmund's footstool and ran out the door. I never returned. Fleeting memories of stealing sheep in a former life crossed my mind as I raced down the stairs to freedom."

Jimenez raised his right fist in a militant salute and intoned:

"Footstool, footstool! When God created Heaven and Earth, he placed a footstool in the Garden of Eden. It became a symbol of man's higher calling."

The guitarist sat down again.

"I remember the tomb of Pedro the Magnificent outside my village. As a youth, I used to hear Pedro playing guitar beneath his tombstone. Born in 1525, he had a magnificent court career as a *vihuela* player, performing for kings and princes throughout Europe as well as Spain. What scales the man played! Pedro was buried with his footstool. I plan to be buried the same way."

Jimenez played *Recuerdos de la Alhambra,* composed by the 19th-century Spanish guitarist Francisco Tarrega. Entranced by the hypnotic repetitions of this tremolo masterpiece, the audience swooned.

Arpeggiating the final A chord on the second fret, Jimenez let the bell-tone sonorities illuminate the darkened hall. A desert of silence as minutes passed. Moonscape of inner peace, eerie and haunting.

The master now played a Bach gavotte. He moved easily from A minor to C, pounding out rhythms of the Gap natives in southern France where he'd seen his first gavotte danced in 1725.

Ah, 1725: That was a good year. He remembered meeting Bach, Telemann, and Haydn.

Jimenez lashed into the gavotte, tearing out rhythms and ripping bass notes to shreds. Too many bass notes in Bach. He destested the surplus. Imagine Bach trying to show his macho by writing so many bass notes! He had argued with the composer, coaxing him with encouraging words about his masculinity: "Johann, what a man you sre! Women love you. No one writes *gavottes* like you. No need to *prove* yourself." But Bach responded by crawling under the organ, sitting beneath the pipes in the full Leipzig lotus position and weeping. That night, to prove himself, he went home, and for spite, added even more bass notes to his *gavotte!*

Well, Jimenez wouldn't stand for it. No no! He dropped bass tones right and left. The notes lay paralyzed in corners, under windows, beneath drapery, and in aisles. He plucked a big one from the lower E string, crushed it in his fist, and hurled the remnants at the critics sitting in the front row. "*Perros!*" he growled, "Here are pieces of Bach for tomorrow's reviews."

Suddenly, a witch flew out of the sound hole. It circled an usher's head, then headed for the exit. Then another flew out, and another and another. Round the ceiling clothed in black bass notes they flew, waving pointed hats, flapping their dresses and screeching in unison *Ich bin Made von das Leben.* Jimenez leaned forward while the train of unearthly elements grew in size, hissing as they stumbled one after another out of the sound hole. A broomstick got stuck. The witch squealed and squawked until Jimenez strummed a religious cadence of C, F and C. Suddenly, like the whirlwind funnel of a tornado, *Chuuuuuup!* the witch was sucked immediately back into the guitar. This harmonious sound caused all her flying colleagues to fly past the rosette and into the sound hole again, settling in the dark interior of the guitar.

Jimenez coughed. Sweat rolled down his cheeks. He rose, paced the stage, stretched his legs and cleared his throat.

"Bach and I were competitors," he admitted. "Both of us started at a young age. My first composition was written in the basement while my parents, Mutter Gans and Hans Plastisch fought upstairs. I found their fighting restful. I began my first *pavane* at age seven, completing the one-page manuscript by age thirteen. For the next ten years, I wrote music for obituaries. I liked writing for the dead. They never talked back; they never criticized. Many of my earlier works became morgue standards. For example, I wrote a piece for the Egyptian Pharaoh Akhenaten, hoping it would be buried in his pyramid. He never thanked me. Although writing for the dead has advantages, they *never* send thank-you notes.

"That's the reason why after graduation from the Academia Del Escuela de la Musica Pura y Classica, I decided to spread my music among the living.

"My main problem was notes I composed kept sliding off the page. I'd write hundreds of them, but when I put the manuscripts in my briefcase, they'd end up blank. At first I thought my pen was faulty. Then I double-checked the paper. Both were fine. Yet my notes kept slipping off the page. As soon as I held the paper vertically, *poof!* Publishers didn't even believe I wrote music. At first they looked at me strangely. After awhile they didn't look at me at all. A few wouldn't let me in their offices. What could I do? I was the only composer with this problem. All the others wrote notes that stuck.

"This situation depressed me for years and cut into my income. However, my earnings were zero anyway, so at least financially I wasn't going backwards.

"Then one day I had a revelation: My notes were not *meant* to be written down. God kept removing them from the pages for a reason. Written on air, carried by the wind, my notes were not bound in galleys but were forever free!

"How can you sell free notes? How do you promote the invisible?

"Well, you can *feel* them fly from the concert stage, sing in your body, dance in your heart. I would compose free notes and bring my freedom-loving musical compositions to the world.

"Suddenly my life had purpose."

Jimenez sat down. His left hand closed around the guitar neck. His right hand spread over the sound hole as he played the opening notes of the *Jota de Aragon*. Serpentine fingers danced, creating magnificent arpeggios climbing three octaves towards the high E.

The fans sighed.

Jimenez moved into the A major theme, embellishing it with harmonics and legatos. His fiery finale made the audience gasp.

Jimenez drew a tuning fork from his pocket, tapped it on his chair and touched its base to the face of his guitar. Vibrations from the note A chimed through the hall.

"When I tune up, I am really tuning myself," he explained. "There are times when I desperately need tuning. I concentrate on the mystical sparks, those pieces of God scattered around the world. It helps me keep my sanity.

"If I remember God, he'll remember me. We work to-gether—pooling our resources, so to speak.

"But even when I work with God, concerts sometimes get cancelled. I take it personally. I believe God is sending down re-jections to punish me for my greed that put me into the Amsterdam tulip market in 1634. At the time, I worked for Rembrandt, grinding paints. He paid me a miserable salary, though I was the best paint grinder in Rotterdam. Franz Hals loved me; so did Jake von Ruisdael and Vermeer. As a young man I wanted to become an artist, but, after working for the likes of Rembrandt, I realized it was no life for me. Slowly my goals shifted from a desire to become an artist to a desire to be rich. That's when I bought my first tulip bulb for ten guilders. Next day I sold it for twenty guilders, bought two more, then sold both for a big profit.

"I bought and sold for months. I made one hundred, one thousand, then five thousand guilders. I was getting rich. I had one setback when that ignoramus Rembrandt saw one of my bulbs lying on the kitchen table next to a loaf of bread. He sliced it up, made a sandwich, and ate six thousand guilders worth! On that day, I left his employ. I went into speculation full time. In two years, I had close to half a million guilders! I was rich beyond my wildest dreams! I bought a house with my own windmill and even considered buying into the Dutch East India Company.

"Suddenly, in 1637, the market crashed. Bulbs I'd bought for several thousand guilders in expectation of a quick profit plummeted to near zero! I panicked. So did everyone else. Hundreds, including myself, were ruined. I went crawling back to Rembrandt and asked for my old job back. During those frenetic up-market years, Rembrandt hadn't bought one tulip. All he'd done was paint, paint, paint. He still didn't know the difference between a tulip bulb and an onion.

"Reduced to the poverty from whence I'd come, at least I was wiser. I saw the connection between money and hope. As I watched my funds dwindle, fear destroyed my hope. Well, that's reality for you.

"Why am I still optimistic? Because I live in another reality. As I review my many lives I've lived through thousands of years of history, I see cycles: Business cycles, psychic cycles, emotional cycles. Everything moves in cycles. Succees soon leads to failure; failure soon brings success. After traveling in cycles so often, I don't believe in their transience anymore.

"I'm optimistic because I think long-term, beyond the cycles and their changing forms. Cycles are merely illusions moving in a circle. Why believe an illusion? Why believe that a short-run movie is the essence of life?

"Indeed, given this truth, why bother doing anything?

"I've been asking that question for years. Finally I came up with an answer: Fun!

"I play guitar for fun. Fun is my bottom line.

"What a startling revelation. Millions of pages of esoteric philosophy about the nature and purpose of the universe; thousands of books written about man's suffering, redemption, sweat, self-torture, death, agonies of creation and morality fill religious institutions and libraries.

"But none of these mention the concept of fun.

"I don't see the word mentioned in the Kabbalah or the Bible. Neither Hebrew prophets or Christ preached its benefits. Plato in his *Republic* never talks about it, nor does Aristotle in his *Ethics*. Buddha, Zoroaster, Mohammed, Moses, even the "moderns" like Kant, Hegel, Marx, and Swami Vivekananda, do not speak of fun as an important force in the universe.

"If none of these world leaders and philosophic giants mention it, how can I, a guitarist with only a master's degree and footstool, offer fun as a fundamental?

"Well, who cares what they think? I *know* it's important, and that's enough. As my father, Juan Plastico, said in a lucid moments: 'Me gusta la vida ingenuo.' Enjoy the process. You never know how the product will turn out."

Jimenez stroked his chin. His eyes shone with pleasure.

"It's my happy nest egg, my day at the beach. Some believe that fun is, as a word, so disgusting. They say there is something nauseating about an adult whose goal in life is fun. Fun is for children. Adults should only 'enjoy.'

"Well, I admit it's difficult for an adult to feel the fun high. Sometimes it's hard even for me. There are times when life stinks—like when I started my career. No agent's calls, no mail, no concert tours, nothing. Things got so bad that one day, I decided to end my life. I tied a low E string around my neck, stood on my footstool, and was about to hang myself from a beam, when I thought: Will suicide work? Will it solve my problems? Fingering the wound steel around my neck, the obvious answer came immediately: Suicide doesn't work. Why? Because no matter how many times I die, I keep coming back. I keep reincarnating. If I don't get guitar bookings in this life, I'll get them in the next one. And on and on. . . and on....

"So I decided that instead of killing myself, I'd practice. I untied the E string from the beam, put it back on my guitar, and played *Testamento de Amelia* by Miguel Llobet.

"I'll play it for you now."

Jimenez cradled his Ramirez. His fingers curled round the neck, simulating the technique he had perfected strangling chickens on his uncle Jose's poultry farm. He tuned his "hanging E string" down to D before focusing on his right hand, which dangled loosely above the sound hole. He studied the corpuscular traffic flowing through his right arm veins into his drooping dexters.

"When the wrist hung limp and relaxed like a moist sardine,

he began to play the *Testamento*. Delicious, cream-colored notes exited, floating like silk above the heads of his audience. Once more, the mind of Jimenez left this world and traveled upward to paradise.

The *Testamento* ended with a cluster of harmonics on the 12th fret. Notes drifted into the distance, leaving a wake of silence behind them. Fans sat stone still, frozen in a beauty moment of vibrational epiphany.

Jimenez stood up. "Thank you, *Testamento*, " he said. "You brought me luck. Ever since I played you on that dark day twenty one years ago, my destiny changed. Agents began calling. They offered me a concert tour, radio and TV appearances, a record contract. It felt so strange. I had been ready to face total failure but what did I get? Success!"

Jimenez heard a chuckle. "Why are you laughing?" he asked the fat, bearded man sitting cross-legged in the second row. "Sir," Jimenez added. "You remind me of Sigmund Freud."

The man, wearing a maroon vest and tweed jacket, uncrossed his legs, and muttered. "Never met him."

"Good answer, sir," Jimenez replied. "Come up here on stage. The audience will hear you better. You will also be closer to me. I thrive on intimacy." Jimenez turned towards the stage door. "Alphonso," he cried, "bring out the second chair."

The man made his way up the aisle. He mounted the stage, shook Jimenez's hand, nodded to Alphonso, and sat down beside the master guitarist.

Jimenez looked him over. "Say, aren't you Lawrence Smert, the archaeologist?"

"Indeed I am. How did you recognize me?"

"From the Hittite buttons on your vest. Those are worth a

pretty penny. Tell me, Mr. Smert, isn't that considered stealing? I mean, to pick up buttons at an archaeological site and appropriate them for personal use—"

Smert raised his hand in protest. "I am not a performer like you, but a shy retiring professional humbly trying to unearth artifacts and explain their meaning to an ignorant public. The Hittite buttons I wear are simply part of the education process. As you've no doubt noticed, I'm also wearing an Eighteenth-Dynasty brooch I excavated from the Valley of the Kings during last year's season at Luxor."

Jimenez examined the brooch more closely. "It looks familiar, Mr. Smert. I'm sure I saw the exact one last year in the Egyptian Museum in Cairo. Are you sure you didn't 'discover' them there?"

"Never! The ones in the museum are fakes."

"Well, if you say so. You're the expert. I was sure I saw them in the case just behind Nefertiti's chair. In any case, Mr. Smert, how were your travels this summer?"

"It was a terrible summer, Mr. Jimenez." Smert settled back in his chair. "I never want to repeat it again. I emerged a human wreck."

"Sorry to hear that."

"I'd love some peace and quiet in my future travels—at least for myself."

"You can get that, Mr. Smert. Just learn to play guitar."

"You may have a point," Smert agreed. "Could I try now?"

Jimenez shook his head. "Call me after the concert," he answered. "We'll arrange lessons. Meanwhile, I suggest you keep suffering. Mental anguish makes one strong."

Jimenez led Smert off the stage. "Thank you for sharing

your thoughts with us."

As Lawrence Smert headed up the aisle, Jimenez turned to the audience. "Perhaps Smert is right. There are times when failures or successes shatter my equilibrium. Cycles of the music business can drive you crazy. In fact, the music business forced me to go into therapy with Dr. Sigmund again. But this time the sessions only lasted three years. Thank God that's over. Thousands of *pesetas* to put my head on straight. Result: It's still backwards. I know other guitarists with heads like mine who haven't spent a dime. Where's the justice of it all? It's an unfair world, except, of course, for Freud. He cleaned up on me. The doctor sat for years answering every question I had with a blank stare. Once every three months, he blinked. Then I knew I'd said something significant. Periodically, when he wanted to exercise his voice, he'd answer my question with a question. And only 400 *pesetas* an hour. Well, it's hard to fault him: I couldn't sit for an hour without blinking. Anyone who can do that must be worth 400 *pesetas*. How that cures you, I'll never know. One thing that Dr. Sigmund didn't offer, though, was joy. I can dance *a Farruca*, read *Historia de la Civilizacion Espagnola* by Lopez, play *Recuerdos de la Alhambra* on my guitar, walk down Calle de las Vacas, even breathe the fresh air of my village. Simple movements, simple ideas, simple people, simple, simple. All of them, at one time or another, have brought me a brief meeting with a higher force. However, Sigmund did not give me one epiphany. I could have saved a lot of time and money going for a walk."

Jimenez strummed an F bar chord with his thumb.

"Strangely," he went on, "my best therapeutic experience took place in prison. It happened when I gave an all-Bach program for the Bach Society of Long Island. I made so many mistakes the chairman called the police. As the muscular sergeant and his Bach-loving rookie buddy handcuffed me and pushed me into the paddy wagon, the program chairman growled, 'You don't mess up Bach on Long Island and get away with it!' The judge, an obvious lover of the Baroque, sentenced me to five years of solitary confinement in State Prison for the Musically Insane. My punishment was to write the *Music History of the World*.

"At the time I had been concertizing steadily for seven years without a break. I was tired and on the verge of burn-out. I needed to get away from the prying eyes of the public. I thanked that judge.

"My prison sat on a swamp behind a nuclear waste dump. To reach my cell, we marched along a long narrow corridor with pictures of musicians, performers, and composers along the walls. Heading south, we finally reached a windowless iron door. My guards opened it and pushed me in. 'Here's a minor prelude for you,' they grunted. I heard the door click shut behind me. Home at last.

"I looked around my cell. Whitewashed walls. Not one book. No book-shelves either. A toilet stood in the corner, opposite a steel bed frame covered with a foam rubber mattress; to the right sat a wooden desk and straight-backed chair. A 100 watt bulb dangled from a wire above my head. A shoe box filled with pens and pencils sat on the corner of the desk; on the floor to the left, a Pathmark carton was filled with writing paper. Here was solitary confinement with refinements, plus plenty of equipment to write the *Music History of the World*.

"'They won't let me out until it's finished,' I mumbled to

myself. 'No reference books either. I'll have to write it from memory.'

"I looked at the wall above my desk. Although it had been whitewashed, evidently it hadn't been whitewashed enough. I saw traces of writing. Upon closer examination it turned out the wall was covered with the history of the State Prison, scratched onto the wall in Dutch with a fingernail. I remembered my speculation sheets on the tulip market, so I could easily read the language. Periods, commas, and exclamation points had been made with teeth marks. Many paragraphs were separated by cracks in the wall formed by banging some kind of head. It might have been a human head; I noticed strands of hair stuck in the plaster.

"When I finally sat down at my desk to write, my hand cramped. I couldn't move the damn thing. I sat for days, pen and paper in hand, but nothing happened. How frustrating. Yet I didn't give up hope. I knew somewhere within these personal sufferings, God was trying to teach me a lesson. Someday the inner light would shine, but until that moment came, I could only sit at my desk and wait. While I waited, I read the Dutch notes scratched on the walls of my cell.

"During my time in solitary I often spoke with the imaginary inhabitants of my cell. I lay on my back and transmigrated through my many lives. As I lay there traveling through time, visiting paleolithic relatives in their caves, talking to Rembrandt, cuddling with my community of trilobites in their homes beneath the Precambrian mud, speaking Hebrew to the prophets, or playing my harhar by the Nahar River, I realized my calling was not to write about the past, but to tour through it. *Travel through History:* How I liked the ring of that phrase!

Suddenly, I understood what Lawrence Smert must have known long before: Tourism was a good business. What better way to travel than by organizing tours?

"Tours. Ha! Imagine that. Me, a humble guitarist running a tour. Why, it was laughable. Impossible. Crazy.

"Thus, why not give it a try?

"Naturally, I saw problems. My biggest was how to combine tourism and transmigration. Capital expenses would obviously be low. How much does it really cost to sit in one place and recall your past? But how could I teach people to remember past lives?

"Suddenly, I heard a stentorian voice: 'Stand up! Be a man! No more shall you take abuse from agents and audiences. No more shall you depend upon music to earn a living. Jimenez, I am the Voice of Business.'

"From that day on I had many meetings with the Voice of Business. It turned out his name was Stan. Born in Germany near a Volkswagen factory, he had moved to Great Neck, Long Island, propelled by his passion for watching traffic on the Long Island Expressway. He was tall, wore blue jeans with a red blazer and had a white handkerchief in the vest pocket. I never knew how he got into my cell, but he always appeared whenever I needed to talk to him.

"Before I met Stan, the idea of commerce disgusted me. After all, I was an artist. My job was to create art, not handle filthy lucre. But God and the music business work in mysterious ways. No doubt He had put me in jail for a reason. I thought about Moses on Mount Sinai, Jesus meditating in the desert and Buddha sitting under the Banyan Tree forty days. If great religious leaders had to retreat in self-imposed exile before returning to the world with revelations of newly acquired wisdom, perhaps I had to do the same thing. Five years in solitary might bring me the wisdom I needed. The tourist business might be a part of my return. Plus, I was no longer alone in my cell. Although Stan remained silent, sometimes for weeks, I always felt his presence.

"Once Stan was gone for months. Then suddenly, without warning, he appeared. 'Wake up,' he said.

"I rubbed my eyes, moaned a melody from a Palestrina motet, and sat up.

"'You haven't been around for months,' I said.

"'I've been giving you time off.'

"I rose from my bed and took a cup of imaginary coffee from the imaginary kitchen table in the imaginary kitchen of my cell. Holding it in my hand, I paced across the floor.

"'Time for you to give up music,' Stan said. 'Trade it in for business. Businessmen don't look for chords. They look for markets.'

"I lay down on my bed and pulled the blankets over my head. How could I even consider such a blasphemous idea? Trade in my old way of life on the *chance* that markets were more powerful than music? It didn't sound right. Yet I was in prison. Why? Mistakes at the Bach concert.

"I had reflected upon those mistakes. After three years, I knew why I made them: Because I *wanted to*. Deep down I had a need to self-destruct. But it took two years to realize it. Not only did I want to destroy Bach: I wanted to destroy *my old self* as well. A life change was coming.

"I reviewed my performing career. At the beginning, my playing spoke for something greater than myself. But over the years I'd lost touch with my original beatific vision. As I traveled from one concert to another, performing had gradually become a 'job,' a tawdry attempt to please the public instead of an art form. I should have recognized the first signs of this spiritual malady when audiences began falling asleep at my concerts. But I had denied it. Things had gotten worse. Soon I was falling asleep, too. Even when playing Tarrega, Sor, Albeniz, and the fiery Flamencan Farruca, my mind wandered. I thought about my mother's cooking, beautiful women, picturesque beaches, mountain villages. I thought about many things, but rarely about what I was playing.

"In time my audiences began falling asleep *outside* the concert halls. They couldn't even work up enough enthusiasm to enter. This meant they *didn't pay*. Gate receipts fell rapidly. I performed in half-empty halls, even empty ones. Once, in Toledo, instead of giving my concert from the stage, I had gone outside the hall, set up my chair and footstool, and performed for the lines of sleeping Jimenez fans surrounding the place. A sad day. They never awoke, not once, even though I played with all my heart. But my heart was empty, and so was my mind. Then came the Bach Society Concert in Long Island....

"I was ready to listen.

"'Stan,' I said, as I lay in bed, looking at his face on the ceiling. 'Where should I go? What should I do? My goal in life has crumbled.'

"Stan looked down at me, said nothing, and disappeared for a month.

"I knew he wanted me to figure out answers by myself. But I refused. I kicked, screamed, beat on the walls, fell to my knees, and begged Stan to return. Finally, I had to answer my own teleological questions. For the first time in my life I wanted a TV set to watch any vapid program, commercial, or anything to escape the torment of self-analysis. But I had no choice. Once I came to the border of the questions I was doomed to cross over and answer them.

"Who am I?

"Where am I?

"Which way shall I go?

"What is the difference between a vacuum and emptiness?

"Suddenly, I heard Stan's voice speaking to me from behind the toilet. 'Jimenez,' he said, 'you are at a crossroad. Like a crucifixion, a crossroad is a form of torture. Self-torture. But growth, too. You can't leave prison without being crucified first.'

"'OK? That's easy for you to say, Stan,' I said. 'I don't see *you* carrying a cross.'

"'Do you doubt me?' Stan looked hurt. 'Long ago I bore my own cross. But I matured and transcended it. Today I no longer need it. I have moved from the corporeal to the in-corporeal. But you have not. So, back to basics: What is bothering you, my friend?'

"I stayed silent for a month, mulling over the question. Finally I asked, 'What about art?'

"'What does art have to do with any of this?' Stan asked.

"'I am an artist,' I answered. 'Can business be an art? If not, I will live forever in conflict.'

"'You will live forever in conflict anyway, Jimenez,' Stan answered. 'Conflict is life.'

"'Conflict is *your* life, Stan. But I don't want it to be mine. I'm looking for peace.'

"'You can find it in business.'

"'That's a laugh. How?'

"Stan sat down on the imaginary chair opposite my bed. 'Jimenez,' he said, 'I have started many companies. Most recently, I founded International Detrimental Detergent—IDD, a multinational company that produces and dispenses detergents throughout the world. I started IDD by myself. During the early years, it existed only in my mind. Then it moved from my mind into the basement of our house. Soon I built a second office in my garage. I hired an employee. He was such a miscreant I rented office space in another town to avoid him. Nevertheless, he was a detergent genius, so I appointed him head of our second branch. Delighted with my management decision, he started a third branch. Although I didn't see him again for three years, profits from those branches flowed into my pockets. When that happened, I knew I was on the right track. IDD grew into an international company. As president, I traveled all over the world, meeting business and government leaders, negotiating detergent deals, and cleaning up the environment with our superior detergent products.'

"'What does all that have to do with me?' I asked.

"'A great deal. The next phase of your existence will be the business phase. When you leave this cell, you will leave on business. Your business will become an art, and your art will become a business. You'll create a work of a r t — b u t in business! Combining the mysteries of creation with the practical aspects of accounting is a big challenge, Jimenez. Business and art must blend.'

"'But I have no experience,' I pleaded.

"'Sorry, but I cannot help you,' Stan replied. 'I am merely

you. But to assuage your fears, remember that lack of experience means nothing. Those streaks of fear bolting through your gut are signs from Above that you're on the right track. They're directional signals from Him-Who-Knows. So listen to them and plan accordingly.'

"I sank deep into thought. Silence pervaded my cell. Finally, after three months, I looked up at Stan. 'How about the tourist business?'

"Stan didn't answer. But there was a tangible grey quality to his silence which drifted back and forth across my cell. I developed back sores as I lay for weeks contemplating the vacuum of my lost career. My guitar playing and concert career would stop. 'I am lost!' I moaned. 'Where shall I go? *Madre, Madre!*' I cried, falling to my knees.

"Finally, one day after weeks of questioning, I stood up straight and boldly faced the wall. 'I'm through with you, Wall!' I said. I'm going into the tourist business and I'm taking Stan with me!'

"Sure enough, as I stared at those whitewashed walls, they started to recede. The next day I received a phone call on my imaginary phone. It was the warden telling me my time was up."

Jimenez stood before his audience. "Listen to my 'Song of Silence.'"

He held up his right fist. Slowly, he released first his index finger, then middle, ring, and pinky. The audience listened. Total silence filled the hall.

Jimenez placed his gold embroidered cushion on the floor, lay down beside it, pushed it under his head, and fell asleep.

Ten minutes later, Jimenez awoke. He slowly rose to his

feet. He rubbed his eyes, stared blankly at the audience, then wandered about the stage.

"I remember. . ." he hesitated, stumbled . . . "I remember when . . . yes, I was sitting on the porch of my Villa in Tuscany, or was it my latifundia outside Pompeii before Nero visited? . . . No, I was walking with Marcus Aurelius, carrying straw for the baby . . . wait, I think . . . no, Heraclitus, that's it. I pushed Heraclitus into the stream near Miletus so he wouldn't step in the same stream twice."

Jimenez wiped his brow. A sweat came over him.

"No," he grunted, struggling with himself. "It wasn't Heraclitus; it was the Emperor Justinian trying to calm me down. I was a cook in his kitchen in Constantinople. I put a table leg instead of a cowhead into his burnt-offerings. It was an accident, I swear. . . . Or was that Theodosius? Or Ramses?"

The cold sweat came again.

Jimenez sat beneath the spotlight, staring into space. "Who am I?" he asked again. "I can't remember."

"You're Jimenez del Oro," his manager whispered through a crack in the stage door. "You're Jimenez del Oro, you fool! Start playing the damn guitar before you lose your audience!"

"You're Jimenez the Magnificent," Alphonso offered. "Do you need an aspirin?"

"Come on, Jimenez, play!" called a woman from the upstairs balcony. "We're not paying to see you blink."

"Yeah, give us a song!" shouted a man from the front row.

Programs rustled, people shifted in their seats, rhythmic claps of frustration started in back of the hall. But Jimenez kept staring straight ahead.

"Who was I?" he repeated. "Who will I be? I can't remember." A tear rolled down his cheek.

A thin woman wearing a fur hat stood up in the third row. "Jimenez," she called, "I'll help you. I've been your fan for years."

"Help?" Jimenez scoffed. "You must be joking. Why, even Madre Gansa couldn't help me. When I forgot the 'Concerto de Aranjuez' in the middle of a concert, she ran on stage, slapped my face, and whispered the notes in my ear."

"Did it help?" asked the fur hatted woman.

"I don't remember."

The woman stood up. Her wraith-like body swayed as she declared in a high-pitched voice, "Jimenez, you never trusted women. I remember when you brought home that boar's leg after hunting in the forest near Lake Baikal. You never let women hunt with you, especially when you hunted mammoth. You said a woman's place is in her cave. But times have changed. You can no longer judge women by your past lives."

"I don't remember any of that," Jimenez answered.

"I do!" The woman approached the stage. "You used to point to our cave walls and demand to paint pictures on them, 'I want to become an artist,' you'd shout. Pictures, pictures, that's all you thought about. You wanted to visit France, cultural capital of the Ice Age, study with the master cave painters and visit their studios in Altamira and Lascaux. When you got frustrated because you couldn't paint mammoths on our walls, you beat our children."

"I don't remember beating children," Jimenez protested. "Maybe that was Gurki. He was jealous of me."

"Ah, you remember your brother?"

"Vaguely."

"Let me remind you," the woman said. "One night, after we stacked our axes and spears in the corner, you decided we should migrate to France. Three days later we started our trek westward across Siberia, with a brief stop in Verteszollos, Hungary, where, a few years ago, Laslo Vertes discovered part of Gurki's skull—the occiput, I think it was—and three of his teeth. Ah, Gurki. What a piece of Pithecanthropus he was. Girls loved him. He had a way with buffalo and wild boar, too."

Jimenez reddened. "Gurki? That worm!"

"Every girl wanted him," the woman taunted. "He was not unattainable like you, Jimenez. You loved only ax handles and paints. He loved girls. Your attitude improved when we reached the Dordogne Valley and moved to Vezere, our final home, but you got snobbish again when you won the Neanderthal Painting Competition.

"Then you elected yourself shaman of our family. Chief hunter, too. Nobody opposed you, because nobody could paint."

Jimenez shook his head. "I don't remember."

"Jimenez," the woman said. "Don't you recognize me? I was your sister back then!"

"My sister?"

The woman nodded.

"Did mother love me?"

"Sometimes."

"Did I want fame and recognition?"

"Yes. You got it, too. Today, your cave paintings are world famous. That's what happens when you believe in your art. Today you're a big success even though it took thirty thousand years. That's not too long when you compare it with two billion years of geological time."

The woman blew a kiss to Jimenez and sat down.

A man in row seventeen stood up. He wore black pants and a jacket with patches sewn over the elbows. "Hey, Jimenez," he called out. "Remember the good old days? We played together on the ocean floor in the Cambrian mud. Just you and me and all the other trilobites. We had the whole floor to ourselves in those days."

Jimenez blinked.

"Those were good times," the man went on. "Nobody fought. Nobody talked. We got along real well."

"What about the brachiopods?" Jimenez asked. "Didn't they swim near us?"

"Naw, you're off, Jimenez. That was forty million years later. I'm talking beginnings. Before the continents drifted apart, before the Atlantic Ocean was created. We were one happy arthropod family. Trilobites ain't snobby; it's not the trilobite way. We accepted everyone. We lived in peace with worms, graptolites, brachiopods, scorpions. . . . Trilobites were active, too—especially in housing, trying to get a fair deal for our friends, and for protozoa as well."

"Hmmm. Was I handsome?"

"Oh, you were a beauty, Jimenez. A perfect body. You worked out every morning under the sand, while the others slept. Your thorax segments were beautifully jointed, and your chiton reflected a pale yellow light whenever the sun was out. Your tail stood in a class by itself—such majesty and power! That's why females wanted to lay eggs with you. You had a certain undulation, a watery wiggle that sent shivers of excitement through the egg-laying community."

Jimenez looked at the man in the seventeenth row. "How

do you know all this?"

The man cleared his throat. "I am Professor Jan Sweezhof from Ham University in Mouth-of-Delaware, New Jersey. I head our research department. We study river bottoms and ocean floors."

The professor raised his finger. "But who I am is not as important as who *you were*. After all, you are the one who cannot remember. At the university lab, we have been studying Jimenez del Oro genealogy and Orobite eating habits for years. We know, for example, how you used your legs to dig worms from the ocean floor and shove them into your mouth. We know that every spring, you haunted the egg-laying pits of female trilobites, hoping to catch them unawares. Through our research into prehistoric psychoanalysis, we study ancient feelings. Our researchers examined your antennae, many legs, and hundreds of eyes, all of which made you sensitive to criticism. This sensitivity led to your downfall. To protect yourself, you let your chitinous shell grow harder and harder until, towards the end of your Cambrian days, you were stiff and inflexible."

Jimenez looked puzzled. "Are you sure it wasn't my sister, Bumastus?"

The professor pointed his finger. "It was you, Jimenez. We've researched it. We've got all the facts. Just because you don't remember doesn't mean it didn't happen."

"You're absolutely right!" shouted a short man from the fourth row. He wore a Road Runners Club sweat shirt, sweat pants, and running shoes. "Jimenez has always been a rare breed, whether he remembers it or not. During the Triassic, he was the swiftest of dinosaurs, the thin-legged *Jimenez del Orosaurus*. He was in superb condition when he entered the

Saurus Marathon. Hundreds of racers showed up: brontosaurus, stegasaurus, triceratops, even hadrosaurs and plateosaurs, and, of course, Jimenez del Orosaurus. At the start of the race our competitors lined up at the continental divide. When they heard the crash of a fir tree, they ran like crazy. The Saurus Marathon went through swamp, dry land, and over one hill. Some contestants took a year to finish, but Jimenez won in under a week! That record still stands today. No dinosaur has ever beaten it."

Jimenez shook his head. "I don't remember any race."

"Visit the Museum of Natural History," the runner told him. "They have the fossil remains to prove it."

Jimenez stroked his chin pensively. He stood up.

"Ah, yes, it's coming back!" He straightened, leaped across his footstool, and charged to the apron of the stage.

"How could I have forgotten? My friends, I must explain that my identity appears whenever I forget myself." He brushed his shoulder. "I have never walked the one-way track, never ridden the monorail of existence. My path has always been crooked. Doing many things has kept me sane in an insane world. Living beneath appearances is no easy task. How do you wear a mask and simultaneously remember that the mask you wear is not you? Well, never mind. Why should I ask these questions of you, my audience? After all, it's my show. I should be telling you.

"And I will.

"I stand before you today as a guitarist, but also as a stamp collector, linguist, insect specialist, and tour guide. Plus I read books, practice yoga, stand on my head, and walk on shallow water. Doing a variety of activities gives me perspective.

"I have lived many lives. For example, four hundred million

years ago, during the Silurian period, I enjoyed life as a snail on a coral reef. Much later, in Mesopotamia, not only did I live as a brick embedded in a Babylonian ziggurat, but also as a fish in the Euphrates, and as a cleansing agent in the Babylonian Temple of Marduk. During the Paleolithic Age, I joined the Homo Erectile group of counter-Neanderthals as we rebelled against the traditional cave life of our Neanderthal contemporaries. During the 12th century, I organized tours to the Holy Land, and made pots for the pope."

Jimenez paced across the stage. "Ah, my beautiful audience," he exclaimed. "You are my ladder to heaven. I look into your faces and see infinite aspects, miracles of variety!

"And now, my friends, I shall communicate with infinity through Bach's *Prelude and Fugue in E minor*.

"You shall hear the ultimate performance! Fulfilling. Magnificent! After this, you will never want to hear another performance again. Hear this!"

Jimenez began the Bach *Lute Suite in E minor*. He advanced through prelude, fugue, allemande, courante, and lively bourree. Scales rose and fell. But when he completed the fiery contrapuntal gigue, instead of ending the piece, he returned to the beginning and played the entire suite again! First slowly and elegantly, then in rapid tempo. In the process, he deleted some passages, improvised others, added jazz chords, and turned presto phrases into largo laments.

Jimenez drifted into a fantasy, traveling the road of his dream. The notes flowed as he forgot past lives and merged with the Moment.

Hour after hour, Jimenez kept playing, He would not stop. Time disappeared. . . . Space disappeared.

And gradually, so did his audience.

Knowing that deadlines had to be met, critics in the balcony got up and left. After several more hours of non-stop playing even his fans, realizing supper was at hand, rose quietly and tiptoed out of the concert. By 2 a.m. the hall was completely empty.

But Jimenez didn't notice. He played on, mesmerized by Bach's magnificent Lute Suite.

By 9 a.m. the next day, new fans trickled in. By early afternoon Jimenez was playing to an entirely different full house audience. Still oblivious to their presence, he continued exploring new passages of Bach's musical stratosphere.

Days passed. Audiences came; audiences left.

Jimenez lost track of time.

Was it today? Was it yesterday? Was it tomorrow?

Which concert was he playing? Last week's? Last year's? Last century's? Or next year's?

Where was he? New York? Spain? Sweden? Somewhere else?

Was it the 18th century or 22nd? Ancient Roman times or the Middle Ages? Had the Renaissance passed yet?

Which life was he in? Was he dead? Alive? Or in transition?

He no longer thought about such questions. Now there was no differentiation, separation, polarities, or dualism, no conflict or pain. Only oneness with Bach. Only union with the musical forms he projected to the transient world around him.

Jimenez took no food or water. He did not sleep. Music fueled his body, sustaining him on the cross of guitar, creating an everlasting bridge between heaven and earth. Time vanished as he traveled through birth, life, death, and into eternity.

One morning, a beatific smile appeared on his face and he collapsed.

Doctors came to examine his body. Heart attack? Exhaustion? Starvation? None could determine the cause of death.

And why was he smiling?

The doctors didn't know. Newspapers carried the story but they couldn't figure it out either.

As his body lay on stage, blissfully his soul departed.

Jimenez traveled through the universe, visiting souls of all ages and realizing how limitless was the Limitless.

One day he felt a push.

It hurt.

Then came another push. Harder and harder.

He tried avoiding it but to no avail.

Suddenly, a strange face appeared before him. He saw blood and surgical instruments. A man wearing a white jacket picked him up and smacked him on the back. Jimenez gasped, then started to cry.

He heard the doctor shout: "It's a girl!"

The audience cheered as the artist rose, bowed in all directions, and left the stage.

CATSKILL MOSES

IT STARTED ABOUT TEN years ago. I couldn't find my center. My bones and bladder ached; head, lungs, and chest, too. Backstage, before concerts, I belched, coughed, and spat. None of the notes I played sounded right. I couldn't relate to any composer, even myself. Added to that, all my friends deserted me: Madre Gansa went to visit her relatives in Santiago de Compostela; Juan Plastico flew to Paris on business; Pedro, Juanita, Raphael, and the Loco Brothers went on vacation in the Canary Islands. Even my musical mentors—Tarrega, Sor, Mozart—stopped inspiring me. I felt lost. I was tired of individuality and separateness, tired of being an artist. I just wanted to be like everyone else. Only trouble was, I didn't know what everyone else was like. Who exactly is everyone else? Is everyone else just as much of a mystery as I am?

Love had deserted me, and so had my dog, Hector. I went on eating binges, hoping food would fill my spiritual emptiness. I consumed vast amounts of asparagus, broccoli, cauliflower, green beans, bananas, pears, oranges, and grapes. When sated on fruits and vegetables, I devoured roast beefs, lambs, hams, sardines, spiked mackerel, sea trout, and tuna.

I added lobsters, shrimps, and crabs, and flavored them all with generous helpings of seaweed. Finally, weary and bloated, I rose on my hind legs and, in my new, rotund, mammalian form, went to the first Malaga bakery, filled my duffel bag with pastries, and fled to a nearby grove of trees. There I sat in the shade, stuffing myself still further with cookies, cakes, *pates au glace*, almond horns, chocolate chip cookies, whole banana cream pies, platters of vanilla cream puffs, and foot-long seven-layer cakes.

I overate for almost a year. I became the size of three Jimenezes. I got so fat I could hardly walk. Every day I trudged to the bakery for more sugar creations to feed my stomach. But of course, I couldn't fill it. I was looking for the wrong food in the wrong place.

After eating enough sugar to sink Spain, I realized I couldn't find unconditional love in a Malaga bakery. Where could I find it? Who would give it to me? No woman I knew. Not even Madre Gansa could do that. I needed some ideal form. Who? What?

Life is so strange. I remember so much about my past, and yet I can't understand why I have so much trouble with the present. Do I transmigrate too much?"

During my Fat Period I gave some concerts in New York City. One night, after a hundred-dollar supper in a cheap Greek restaurant, I decided to take the subway back to my hotel. At that time I could hardly fit into a cab, but I could still squeeze through the turnstiles. I like riding subways, especially when I'm depressed. Going underground is soothing to me. I like hundreds of people crushing me during rush hour; it gives me a feeling of security.

I boarded at 57th Street and headed downtown. Riders kept getting off. By the time we hit 14th Street, much of the crowd had departed. Then I noticed a bearded man, dressed in a yellow saffron robe and sandals, sitting beneath a subway map.

He sat quietly, staring straight in front of him with a serene smile on his face. Was he an idiot? An undercover cop? Had he been released from a mental institution? Hard to say. There was an empty seat next to him and, tired of standing, I took it. When I did, I caught the faint aroma of incense. Then, as the train sped along the track, I felt a wonderful vibration passing through me. It filled me with a delicious peace and a put a serene smile on my face—the same smile as the bearded man's next to me. Where was this vibration coming from? Could it be from the subway train itself? We were between 14th and Chambers Street, always a pleasant part of underground travel in the past, but it had never felt like this. No one else in the car was smiling. They all sat stone-faced or abstracted, some lost in thought, others reading the newspapers. No one on that subway car was smiling except the bearded man and me. Why was this?

Then I realized the vibrations were coming from the bearded man. They passed to me directly through the subway seat. This guy was making me feel wonderful! Even though most riders avoided him because he looked unkempt, he had a power. I tapped him on the shoulder. "How do you do it?" I asked. He kept smiling, looking straight ahead. "Pleasee," I repeated, "I am looking for some happiness in life. I haven't felt so good in months. Your vibrations are like a heavenly massage. How do you do it?" The man kept staring straight ahead and smiling. Finally he reached into his robe, pulled out a card, and handed it to me. It read:

Yogi Schwartz

Itinerant Transcendent

14 Orchard Street, New York, NY (212) 947-0978

or Bodhi Tree Ashram Rishikesh

Uttar Pradesh, India   Himalaya-2-0400

Yogi Schwartz is available for silent lectures, weddings, parties, bar mitzvahs, and club and social events. Vibrations at a low fee. Prices available on request. Yogi Schwartz's vow of silence, has made him a desirable resident in quiet neighborhoods. He will answer your questions with a special style of silence based on the wisdom of the sages and yogis of ancient India.

I learned about Yogi Schwartz through his vibrations. As a young man, he had gone to India seeking the Truth. He wanted to meet a *rishi*, one of those wise men who lived about 3,000 years ago. He met one of their descendants, a maharishi who led him to Swami Vishnu Deva. Schwartz studied with the swami for three years. They communicated mostly by vibrating. For a year Schwartz kept asking the swami questions: What is life? How old is the universe? What is the meaning of existence? The swami became annoyed with these questions and never answered. In fact, during those three years, he only said two words to Yogi Schwartz: *Shut up!* The words had a profound effect on Schwartz. He contemplated each syllable. Was there a secret meaning in the swami's message? What did the *Sh* stand for? And what about the up? No direct answers were forthcoming from the swami. Schwartz even asked the Swami's disciples, who answered with a silence of their own. Finally, Schwartz figured it out. The swami wanted him to take a vow of silence. Silence would reveal the truth to him.

He came back to New York a changed man, opened an ashram on 72nd Street, and started recruiting followers. In four years his ashram had hundreds of members taking lessons in hatha yoga, pranayama breathing exercises, and meditation. The amazing thing was, he built his entire following without saying a word.

I learned many things sitting on the subway next to Schwartz. It was my personal Upanishad. He taught me the ways of the seers, how to sit still, listen to the silence, block out the sight of other subway riders, and through deep breathing, find inner peace. Subtly, he taught me about the seven chakras and related them to the seven stages of guitar playing and the seven stages of my guitar career. He showed me how to move up the chakra ladder, and that a crucial change in my life was coming and would be reflected in my guitar playing and the direction of my performing career. He didn't elaborate beyond that point—after all, how much can you say without talking? However, he did intimate that, some day, I would reach a point where I would no longer have to talk to my audiences, to anyone, not even to myself. I would reach a higher stage of evolution beyond the spoken word where I would dwell within the vibrations of the words themselves. When that happened, words would seem like shadows—formless, empty, and meaningless. I would smile and live beyond all the opposites, in a universe of beauty and splendor and unitary consciousness. Yes, I had quite a future. That future was here and now, but I was still too ignorant to recognize it.

Schwartz convinced me to go to India, the land of the sages. There I would find my personal guru, one who would lead me to salvation. If it happened to Schwartz, why shouldn't it happen to me? This made sense. Also, nothing else was working at the time. I was ready to move on, ready for an adventure. India sounded right.

So I packed my traveling bag, strapped my guitar to my back, put on my best walking shoes, and, bright and early Monday morning, crossed the George Washington Bridge, set my feet on Route 4 in New Jersey, and headed towards India.

When I hit Ohio, I realized India was the other way. My feet were giving out too, so I returned to New York and took a plane, first to London, then straight to Delhi. When I got there, I slept two days in the back room of the broken-down Maha Savasana Hotel on Sundar Nager Street. Next morning, following the directions of Yogi Schwartz, I headed northeast through Hardwar straight to Rishikesh. I couldn't find my guru in the dusty streets of Rishikesh, so ı traveled further north towards the Himalayas. As I walked up a steep mountain path, I met a man in saffron robes with a white beard, long hair, sandals, and a beatific smile. He looked like an older version of Yogi Schwartz. I said hello to him, but he walked right past me without saying a word, smiling all the time. He had a distant gaze, as if he were watching a plane disappear on the horizon of his inner landscape. I ran after him, tapped him on the shoulder, and asked, "Excuse me, sir, but are the Himalayas this way?"

To my surprise, he stopped smiling, looked me straight in the eye, and asked, "Are you a guru hunter?"

"Indeed I am," I answered.

He pointed ahead of me where the mountain path bifurcated. "Guru hunters take the path to the right.'

"Thank you," I said. Was the man speaking Hindi or English? If he spoke English, something about it just didn't sound right. Was it Spanish with a Hindi accent? Was it Sanskrit? Very strange. I wasn't sure of the language, yet I understood him.

"What language are you speaking, sir?" I asked.

"I speak in the universal tongue," came his reply. His smile returned, but the curl in his lips showed a more worldly air. "What kind of guru are you looking for?" he asked.

"Just an ordinary guru," I replied.

"An ordinary guru?' he asked. "Are you sure? Don't you want an *extra*ordinary guru, one who can lead you easily to enlightenment?"

"Well, yes, I suppose that would be good."

The man's smile became more worldly with each sentence. Finally, he said, "Young man, do you think it was an accident that you met me on this path?" The word *accident* made me think of my D string breaking. Are accidents accidents, or are they subtle celestial messages pointing out new paths of learning? Maybe there is no such thing as an accident, and only my narrow perspective made me perceive one as such. The man saw my hesitation. "It was no accident. I have foreseen this day for three months. Young man, I am your guru. I know all about your subway rides, and your meetings with Yogi Schwartz. Allow me to introduce myself. I am Swami Pajami. Many in the West know my name. I am also known as the Pistol of Brahman because of my rapid teaching methods. Over the years I have developed a sure-fire program of enlightenment that really lasts. None of the two-month or six-month or four-year enlightenment guarantees those fake swamis from Rishikesh give. Their miserable degrees and guarantees are meaningless. My enlightenments last a lifetime. And they are fast! Really fast. You never forget them. I use tapes and videos, too. Very modern. I'm the only one to put movements of your astral body on video, and your personal mantra on a cassette."

So this was what Yogi Schwartz was "talking" about, I thought. This was the swami. How clear his message was. When you communicate through silence, the message comes through so much better.

Our mountain path was surrounded by rhododendrons, pine trees, and oaks. Majestic and peaceful. Far below, in a ravine to our right, a stream flowed. Dramatic boulder formations of metamorphic and sedimentary rocks, carved by thousands of years of erosion, ran below.

I looked directly at the Swami standing in front of me. Was he the real thing?

"I'm lost." I said. "Can you show me the way?"

"I know you're lost, son. Showing you the way is my business."

I took off my knapsack and laid it on the ground. "You're right," I agreed. "I'm not sure which way I'm going."

The Swami stroked his beard. "Lots of folks coming here say that." He shook his staff. "First admit you're lost. Then learn to live with it."

"That's not comforting.'

"You'll get used to it. Order is an illusion. Lost is the way to go. Lost is the way we are. Once you know that, it's not too bad. I've been lost for years. By now it feels comfortable."

He pointed to a boulder. We walked over to it.

"Behind this rock," the Swami said. "Built myself a nice home."

I was intrigued. I liked this old guy.

"I'm Jimenez," I said, offering my hand. He shook it. A tough, calloused, strong hand. It surprised me. Where does an old guy get a grip like that? I looked into his eyes, trying to read them. "Glad to meet you, Swami. Funny, your accent is so familiar. It's not Hindi, is it? Sounds like New York to me."

The swami sighed. "You have a good ear, son. That's why you play guitar so well and can hear the vocal nuances when I speak of the ancient wisdom. For years I hunted down the roots of words. Etymologies. I am able to speak many foreign languages and imitate many foreign accents. I chose to speak to you in English with my New York accent because I thought you would be more comfortable with it."

"That is very kind of you, Swami. You did make me feel comfortable. Still, your accent is so good. Did you ever live in the United States? In the New York area?"

The swami hesitated. "Young man, you seem like a sincere seeker of truth, unlike many of the Neanderthals who pass this way, hypocrites who inundate these wonderful mountains, miscreants from the West, looking to escape Western decadence. Yes, more and more are pouring in each day. They are disgusting. Driving Lincoln Continentals, Jaguars, and Mercedeses up these narrow mountain roads, polluting the air, pissing in our streams, and defecating under our sacred trees. They are destroying our conifers, to say nothing of our oaks and rhododendrons. We need pure souls here, sincere searchers. Young man, you seem to be a pure soul. Therefore, I shall reveal the truth to you: I have lived in New York City. I was born in the State of New

York—Westchester, to be exact. Lived there much of my life, too. My real name is Moses. Friends call me Catskill. That's because I worked as a waiter in Catskill Mountain hotels for many years."

"Catskill. Catskill Moses, eh? It's got a nice ring to it."

"I like it, too. But I call myself Swami Pajami on the trails here. It gets me customers. Fills my begging bowl."

"I'm glad we met, Catskill. Maybe it was fated."

"We met because you're lost," Catskill declared. "If you weren't lost, you would have walked right by me."

"I would have heard your voice—"

"Nope. You wouldn't have heard a thing. Only lost people hear me." He pushed his eyebrow back with his fingertip until his hand rested on his cheek. "Now listen, son," he said, "I've been around a long time. You wouldn't know from looking at me that I used to be a vice-president of Pepsi-Cola. That was a straight life—every day planned. I could see my future for the next twenty years. Real security. Then sales started dropping. One day they fired me! What a blow. Had to sell my house in Westchester, sell my Mercedes, take my kids out of private school. My wife went to work." He leaned his staff against the rock. "Still, bad as I felt, it was a valuable lesson: I learned that nothing lasts, not even a job at Pepsi-Cola."

I considered his story. "That's not too comforting either," I said.

Catskill shook his head and chuckled to himself. "You want comfort?" He stood up. "I'll give you comfort. Ever since I got bounced at Pepsi-Cola, I've been working off balance. It takes some getting used to, but at least you know you're living the real thing." He pointed to an old oak tree towering above his head. "That old tree could fall on me," Moses said. "It could happen any day. Am I worried?" He scratched his robe. "Yes I am." He must have seen my jaw drop. "You're surprised, eh? You didn't think old Catskill would be afraid of getting hurt." He chortled eerily. "Well, let me tell you something, sonny. My position isn't easy. It's better than working for Pepsi-Cola, but still. . . ." He looked me straight in the eye. His commanding gaze forced me to pay close attention. "People hang on to my every word, listen to every syllable, wait for me to give them some truth to make their lives better. It's no joke being a sage. And all my followers say, 'Gimme, gimme, gimme. Gimme some wisdom, old man, get me through the day.' I'm tired of giving. I wish they'd give me something for a change.

"But that's my fate. Everyone's got a job, and mine is sag-ing."

Moses sat down. He leaned forward on his staff and looked through the forest surrounding us. Far in the distance I heard the Ganges flowing—or was it the Yamuna?

Who was this guy? Where had he come from? You don't find many like him in Andalusia.

Why had he chosen to come to India?"

We traveled the road from Yamnotri to Gangroti, sharing the path with walking sadhus—old men on their path to Nir-vana. We passed through tiny villages like Barkot, encircled by pine forests with incredible snow-clad peaks forming a pictur-esque background. I liked Yamnotri, huddled against the west-ern bank of the snow-covered Banderpunch Mountain. We reached the Ganotri, then passed the Ganotri Temple commem-orating the source of the Ganges. Working our way through hundreds of pilgrims, we finally managed to reach the river, where Catskill kneeled down, cupped his hands, and guzzled mouthfuls of water. "Jimenez, this stuff is the purest water you'll ever find. Comes from the glaciers of Gangroti. Great minerals here. It'll cure your skin diseases. I keep a bottle in my hut. So does everyone else around here."

I got on my knees next to Catskill. We both guzzled long and hard. Refreshing, delicious, you betcha. I was ready for some real walking after that, and we left Gangroti heading in the direction of Lake Manasarovar at the foot of Mount Kailasa high in the Himalayas. Canyons, cascades, and rushing rivulets surrounded us as we walked on the right bank of the river. After hiking about four hours, we reached Catskill's hut. We sat down to rest among lilacs, orchids, and a few mountain cacti. Blue-and-white rhododendrons also. A large oak tree shaded us. Catskill pulled a few roots and vegetables out from near the oak tree, and we consumed a vegetarian dinner.

After eating, Catskill sat quietly for an hour. Then I heard a moan. At first I thought it was the wind rustling the leaves of the branches above my head, but I soon realized it was Catskill meditating. He swayed slowly from side to side, backward and forward, trying to put himself in touch with his fount. I could see he was doing interior research, and, before he could put his thoughts into words, he had to take them through various stages of verbal evolution. The moan sounded decidedly paleolithic.

While I waited for him to speak again, I looked up at the criss-cross of branches above me. A leaf fluttered through the air and landed at my feet. I picked it up, turned it in my hand, then glanced above me as the thousands of oak leaves rustled in the wind.

Catskill sat absolutely still on his rock, his eyes fixed on some distant point, or was it somewhere within him? I couldn't tell.

I also noticed he had stopped breathing.

There was an eerie sense of stillness about him.

My eye traveled up the oak. The tree had a certain grandeur about it. No wonder the Druids worshiped oaks as symbols of creation. I suddenly knew why Catskill Moses had chosen that spot to build his hut on.

He came back to life. "A tree surgeon," he muttered, wetting his lips. "That's what I need. Someone to prune this old tree. I'd like some security around here." He chuckled, then shook his head. "But I'll never find it. Security is a myth."

Moses looked at me. "You remind me of my son, Jerry," he said. "That kid wanted everything. And I used to give it to him. The more I gave, the more he wanted. When I wasn't around, he'd go running to his mother, or to his teachers, or, if they couldn't help him, to his friends. Sometimes, when the house was empty, he'd speak to his dog, Roland. That boy was impossible." Moses glanced at the tree. "Luckily, we had an oak like this in our back yard. After school Jerry started consulting with that oak. And I'll tell you, I was impressed with that tree. Some days, Jerry would come home from school mad as hell, or sullen, or crying; he'd go straight to his tree, sit down, and stare at it. Soon he'd calm down; after a half hour or so, he'd be perfectly still—just like the tree trunk. Then he'd return to the house with a such a peaceful expression on his face that it even relaxed me. I was amazed.

"After Jerry discovered that tree, he hardly talked to me anymore. I began to miss our conversations. After all, what's a father for if he can't help his son? Things got so bad, I had a private consultation with the tree myself. I asked what it had told Jerry that I couldn't tell him, and did it have any secrets about life that might help me. But the tree didn't say a thing. Maybe it only spoke to teenagers."

"The tree gave him security," I ventured.

Moses thought about that one. "Could be," he replied. "Course, you never really know what people are looking for-you have to kind of guess it. Besides, you've got to suspect anything an oak tree says."

"The Druids worshiped oak trees."

"Aw, what do Druids know," Moses barked. "Maybe Jerry was a Druid—or a reincarnation of one. Anything is possible in this crazy world." He paused, then started to draw odd figures on the ground with his staff. "I'm glad I'm out of it."

"Out of what?" I asked.

Catskill's staff stopped moving. He took a deep breath, stood up, and beckoned to me with his hand. "It's easier for me to talk about that indoors. Four walls remind me of those claustrophobic years in Westchester."

We walked along a dirt path, then up winding steps cut into the shale. A flat rock served as a porch to an old log cabin. I looked around its one room. Cellophane covered the only window. I noticed an Indian blanket and straw mat under it.

"Have a seat,"Moses said, pointing to the mat. "Make yourself at home." He sank into a half-lotus on the blanket.

I heard the straw crackling beneath me as it adjusted to my weight.

"Built this cabin myself," Catskill added proudly, "mostly out of logs. Used roofing tiles, too. I couldn't leave Westchester without a place to go." He ran his hand over one of the floor boards. "Yes," he reminisced, "I'd just about given up then. Thirty years ago. I was forty-four. I'd lost my job with Pepsi-Cola two years before, the kids were failing out of school, my wife was sick of working and warned me I'd better get a job or leave. That day I went to check out the Bowery as a possible place to stay. I packed a toothbrush, comb, underwear, and pants into a paper bag, and took up residence in the Men's Shelter."

"That's awful," I declared.

"It sure was. I probably would have ended up like the other bums if I hadn't met Swami Savhasana from Rishikesh. He's the one who saved me. Quite a guy. As soon as he walked into the Men's Shelter, I knew this swami was different. Even though he wore rags—ripped pants, torn shirt, faded gray overcoat—his eyes drew me to him. Today that swami is a big success. Through it all he's kept his vow of silence. But he still goes to the Men's Shelter once a week to keep in practice. Sometimes, when you're successful, you forget your roots; you get so caught up in it, you think that's all there is. But success can cut off as many options as failure. Swami Savhasana knew that, and he wanted to keep his options open. I follow Swami's footsteps."

"Wait a minute," I said. "If he kept his vow of silence, how did he teach you?"

"He sat next to me and vibrated."

"And that worked?"

"Sure did. After a few weeks with Swamiji, I left the Men's Shelter with a feeling of inner peace I'd never had before. He showed me *asanas* and breathing exercises. But the most important thing was that silence: It taught me how to meditate. Soon I made a decision to take a vow of silence for one year."

"That's tough," I said.

"It was easy with my wife; we hadn't spoken for two years anyway. Otherwise, it was tough, especially when I had to answer the phone."

"But didn't you feel isolated?" I asked.

"Isolated? Not at all. Some people got angry with me when I refused to speak with them. My cousin slapped my face. I turned the other cheek. He slapped that one, too. By then I had had enough, so I kicked him in the leg. He got so quiet after that, I thought he had taken a vow of silence, too."

Moses pulled his robe around him, protecting himself from the breeze blowing through the cracks of his cabin. I noticed the sudden chill in the air and glanced outside. It was getting dark. I had been talking with him for over six hours!

"*Silence!*" he cried. The word shook the cabin. "Silence," he repeated in a normal voice. "Silence, silence." Softer and more gently. "Silence . . . silence . . . silence. . . ." Soon he was whispering the word into his beard. At first I had been startled by his loud cry. But as he repeated the word over and over again, in almost imperceptibly softer gradations, I noticed its soporific effect. It was like a mantra charming me. The questions I had asked dissolved and were forgotten. By the time Moses was whispering the word into his beard, my heartbeat had slowed, my muscles had relaxed, and my mind, throwing off its defenses, was blank, open, and ready.

Catskill sat very still. Only his breath moved in long sweeping waves. Silence. I love it. Silence teaches you what words can't teach. Words only reflect the truth, but in silence you can *experience* it.'

I listened. I waited. I didn't want to disturb his thoughts.

"When you shut off the noise of the world," he went on, when you stop analyzing, judging, classifying, when you lay intellect aside and put yourself in touch with your deepest faculty—intuition—then you can feel the unity of all things. What most people call 'life' is a waking dream. Sit in silence, and you can wake up from that dream. The nightmare of this world fades away. You become enlightened."

Catskill closed his eyes and took these thoughts deep within himself. I was enchanted. Even if I'd wanted to speak or move, I don't know if I could have. Some greater power stilled my tongue and quieted my mind.

CATSKILL IN THE U.S.A.

AFTER A YEAR OF silence in India, Catskill decided to return to America. He moved to Delhi in upstate New York, named after Delhi in India.

"I rented an acre of land deep in the woods," Catskill said. 'I built me a cabin—actually a lean-to—and lived like a hermit for seven years. Didn't speak to hardly anyone. Only the sky. Sometimes the clouds. Jerry was beginning to worry about me. He came to the Catskills, searched for me in the woods for a couple of weeks, but he couldn't find the place. Finally, he gave up. As soon as he did, I started getting his message. I'm a vibrational kind of guy. So, one day, I just decided to leave my mountain and re-enter the workaday world of the living, real estate, advertising, business, heavy traffic, and dualism. Why

I did this, I don't quite know. Maybe I wanted to help Jerry, or bring my message to the world. Or maybe I was just bored with my Delhi mountain existence. In any case, on April Fool's Day, I packed my toothbrush and headed for the city."

Catskill cleared his throat. 'I kicked over some rocks, pushed aside a rotting tree, and headed down the mountain path towards the roadside. Think big, I said to myself. Make the big effort, push the big dream. Man is a fleck floating by, a fleeting thought racing through the cosmos. Make the most of your time: cough, spit, scratch, giggle, fight, show you're alive. My mud-layered boots clunked along the asphalt road. I stretched out my thumb to hitch a ride.

"'A Mercedes slowed. A well-groomed man in suit and tie looked me over, stepped on the gas and whizzed by. Other cars braked to observe me;, theyn sped on, too. I walked about two hours heading towards Monticello.

"'An old Chevy ground to a halt. Rattles. Squeaks. Brake linings ground paper-thin. Yet the Chevy did stop. Whether it would start again was another question. The front door opened. Thin white fingers curled round the door handle. I focused on the dirty fingernails-might be dangerous accepting this ride. But what the hell, I'd been waiting two hours. Grey sky, threatening rain, storm coming, maybe a hurricane, you never know....

"'Thanks,' I said, sliding into the front seat. I laid my knapsack next to my left, separating myself from the driver— just in case.

"A baseball cap was clamped on the driver's head. Curly brown hair covered the forehead of his weasel-thin face-this plus a four-day-old beard.

"'Mention it, mention it!" The Weasel squealed in a high-pitched voice; he floored the gas pedal and tore down the mountain road even before I closed the door.

"'Thanks!' Weasel shouted as we just missed hitting the wire fence protecting the reservoir. 'Mention *thanks!*'

"'Not feeling appreciated, eh?' I asked as the last of the brake linings ground away in a screeching halt behind a milk truck. Weasel passed him on two wheels.

"'You work?' I asked.

"'Course I work, old man. You think I'm a bum?' Weasel hitched his thumb over his shoulder, pointing behind him. 'I work in that mountain cutting trees. I'm a logger.'

"'Didn't know there was logging in these parts.'

"'I'm the only one.'

"'Is there much call for logs these days?' I asked.

"'Naw, but I cut 'em down anyway; I store the trunks in the river. Got about two hundred of 'em. Some day people are gonna want logs. They'll thank me then. Ha. They'll come crawling to me. Just like in the band.' Weasel strummed an imaginary guitar as the Chevy wandered off the road.

"I grabbed the wheel. 'Get your hands off, man!' Weasel screamed, and laughed like a maniac. 'Hey, buddy, you scared?'

"'Well—'

"'Nothing to be scared about, man,' Weasel giggled. 'I have a way of driving. I drive my Chevy like I drive my logs. Hey, yeah. I leave 'em both in God's hands. He's the big driver.' Weasel glanced at the sky. 'I just ride along with the flow... just like in the band...dum de doo, de dump, pum, pum,' and he strummed away, his eyes rotating, vanishing, then reappearing as he got into the music.

"'Tell me about this band,' I urged, gently guiding the wheel again.

"'A rock band, man. Did rock for years. Yeah, for years, 'til my strings went bad. Oh, I did clubs, toured, the whole bit, dum, dedoo, dum.'

"'You must have been pretty good.'

"Weasel stopped strumming. He eyed me. 'How do you know?' he asked suspiciously.

"'I can tell by the way you play.'

"'Oh.... Dum dee doo dee....'

"'Tell me more about your band.' Talking about the band calmed Weasel.

"'Don't worry, old man.' He started to speak with quiet control. 'I'll take the wheel now. I'm in charge of my Chevy. It's just I drive funny, you know, different from the others.'

"'What about this band?'

"'Band, band. Can't you think about anything else? Hey, there's more to life than a band.' Weasel wiped his overalls. He tugged on his suspenders. 'I hate belts.' He was clear on that one. 'Wore a belt once, but I pulled it off and started whipping myself. No more, though. Now I'm around trees all day. You see, uh, what's your name, old man?'

"'Catskill.'

"'You see, Catskill, I got a real mean streak in me. Real mean. I'm a killer at heart. I love killing things. I love taking them apart, too. I do bugs, especially ants. When I catch an ant I go to my workbench, pull off its legs, open its abdomen, and crush its head with my thumb. Oh, I love doing it. Makes me feel great.'

"'Weasel drove on. The more he talked about killing, the

calmer he got. I figured, if I could keep Weasel talking about killing, he'd stay on the road long enough to hit Route 17.

"'Yeah,' he added, his eyes narrowing as he remembered, 'ever since I was a kid, I wanted to be a killer. My mother was against it. 'That's no job for my son,' she'd say. My father tried persuading me to change my mind by holding my hands over a fire. But they couldn't keep me down. Oh, no. A dream's a dream. I read Nietzsche, Hegel, Plato, all the great killers. They all said the most important thing is to fulfill yourself, realize your dreams. So I said, 'Screw you, Ma and Pa, I got a goal whether you like it or not.' And you know something, Catskill? I'm still working at my goals. I'm making progress, too. Sure, some days I still think I'm just a lousy beginner. Working with bugs, what else could you be? Still, I'm hoping to graduate to cattle and livestock. Two weeks ago I filled out an application to work in a Chicago slaughter house. I sent 'em my resume and everything. Think I'll get the job?'

"He turned to me, a hopeful look in his eye.

"'You never know,' I answered. 'But I think you're on the right track. just keep sending out those resumes.'

"'Yeah, I guess you're right.' Weasel lapsed into silence. He was driving on the right side of the road now, and the car had slowed to a comfortable forty-five miles an hour. We cruised past farmhouses, deserted valleys, and a pine forest.

"'That's why I left the band,' Weasel continued. 'When you give those concerts, folks say, "Knock 'em dead!" Hey, that's my kind of language. But I never knocked 'em dead. Closest to death anybody in my audience came was falling asleep. My music put 'em to sleep. I knew it was time to quit. So I packed my guitar and headed for the country. I still got my guitar in my shed, but

I never play it. Naw, I just use it to stomp on toads.'

"I could see the lights of Roscoe up ahead. 'Where you driving now, son?' I asked.

"'Oh, I don't know, just driving. Looking for animals to hit. I'm practicing. I hit a deer once, and a couple of woodchucks, and a rabbit. They're tough, rabbits, real fast. I usually miss 'em, but I managed to get two this year. My aim's getting better. I'm improving.'

"'Maybe you are.'

"'Think so?'

"'Sure. Two is better than one.'

"Weasel thought it over. 'Hey, you're right. Two is better than one. I like that. Hey, Catskill, want to work with me?'

"'Doing what?'

"'Killing. Just you and me, you know, buddies. What do you say? We could start with rabbits, work our way up to cows, maybe even people some day. What do you say?'

"'I say you need a shrink.'

"'Naw, I've been through that. They're a waste of time.'

"'I can't work with you.'

"'How come?'

"'Killing's not my way. But how about the band? That would interest me.'

"'The *band? You* still into that?' Weasel slowed the car down, then floored the gas pedal. Bushes whizzed by. 'Band's out! I'll never play again.'

"'Were you good?'

"'You kiddin'? I irritated folks for miles around. When I played, real estate values fell. Neighbors moved because of me. Still I was real creative. I had licks you'd never believe. I could play guitar with strings or without, made no difference.'

"'A shame to quit playing-a creative guy like you.'

"'Yeah, they all said that. But I'm still creative. I do some pretty neat things with logs.'

"'You can't compare logs to a guitar,' I said. 'I love music. It's been my salvation in the mountains. Sometimes I'd hum for days. Real mellow. Peaceful, too.'

"'You like guitar, Catskill?'

"'I love guitar. My son played guitar before he started talking to trees. You and he would get along real well.'

"'I don't know,' Weasel mused. 'I think my playing days are done.'

"'Say *temporary* remission,' I said. 'It's closer to the truth.'

"'Aw, what do you know about the truth, old man?'

"'A lot. I'm on a mission to build the Truth right here in these Catskills Mountains. I'm looking to buy Truth Properties right now.'

"'You crazy or something?'

"'Want to join my band?'

"'Band? What band?'

"'Son, I've spent seven years living on the mountain. Now I'm ready to move out. I'm going to buy a hotel and make something special out of it. Want to be part of the staff? I'll need a guitarist. What about you?'

"'Me? Naw. I can't work in a hotel."

"'Look, son, think about it. I don't have the property yet, but when I get it, I'll give you a call. What do you say? Give me your address.'

"The Chevy pulled into Roscoe and stopped at the light.

"'Post Office Box 65, Downsville, New York,' Weasel said.

'Just address it to "Logs."'

"'I wrote it down on a piece of paper. 'Good,' I said. 'I've got to get off here. It's just a block to Route 17. Think about what I said, son. You'll like it at my hotel.'

"Weasel shook his head. 'Crazy, crazy,' he muttered. 'Why do I always pick up the nuts?' He turned towards me. 'Why you keep calling me son? You got a son?'

"I grabbed my knapsack from the back seat and slipped out of the Chevy. 'Maybe I do,' I said. Then I headed for Route 17 as Weasel zoomed off towards the town of Andes."

CATSKILL FINDS
THE PARADISE HOTEL

AFTER I LEFT WEASEL, I went for a sandwich at the Roscoe diner. 'I'm looking for property,' I said to the waitress. "Any ideas?"

"'Check the *Roscoe Reporter*,' she replied, handing me the diner copy. I flipped through the pages to the real estate section, ran my finger down the columns, passing ads for cows, horses, fertilizer, hundred-acre lots, barnless farms, farmless barns, quaint colonials with river frontage, until I spied a tiny three-line ad in four-point type. Clearly, here was an owner who wanted to save money. It took a magnifying glass to read it. I drew the ad to my face until the newspaper touched my nose and most of the letters were visible:

Hotel for Sale. Cheap. 250 Acres. Cabins, good
summer plumbing, indoor pool, lake, rowboats, spa-

cious dining room, chairs, microphones, many extras.
Call Owen Owings, (914) 424-4944.

"I thought it over. Sounded good. No price, though. That usually meant incredibly expensive or subject to intensive bargaining.

"I got up, went to the phone booth, and dialed the number. 'I'd like to speak to Mr. Owings.'

"'Go ahead,' answered a voice between a gargle and a cough.

"'Mr. Owings, my name is Moses. I'm interested in your hotel.'

"'Oh. . .'

"'Yes, I'd like to see it.'

"There was a pause.

"'What's the asking price?'

"'Under forty million.'

"'What?'

"'Well under.' Another pause. 'Come on over. I'll show you around. We're outside of Accord, along Route 209. Ask anyone if you get lost. They all know us.'

"'Sounds good, Mr. Owings.'

"I hung up. On the wall map, Accord looked pretty close to Roscoe, almost walking distance. I could visit it before nightfall. They'd probably put me up for the night, too.

"Between a hitch on a farm truck and a walk, I managed to arrive at a long dirt road leading to the hotel. A sign reading *Walnut Acres* stood by the road. Black paint had been splashed over most of it, and above, in red crayon, was the word *Devastation*. The sign was rotting. You could see its frame had fallen off years before. Well under a million, I thought as I headed up the dirt road.

"I arrived at the broken-down remains of a gatekeeper's hut. No Cerberus here; no one here. Empty and desolate. I looked ahead. A wide Victorian structure with shingles, some in place, others sliding down the roof, forming rusty rainbow patterns above the roof gutters.

"I walked further and came to the main hotel building. Clusters of bungalows huddled together as if to protect themselves from the guests. One of the roofs had already caved in. To the right, a wasps' nests hung under roof eaves beneath a window sill. A milk snake slithered under the bungalow to my right. *Well* under a million. The birds and reptiles had taken over.

"I mounted the stairs of the main building, crossed a porch, jumped the missing slats on the floor, and followed red arrows past rolled up rugs and an empty fireplace.

"I heard a flushing sound. 'Damn pipes!' someone cried. A tall man swinging a plunger stamped towards me. 'Who are you?' he growled, glaring at me. Long arms hung like wet long-johns from his T-shirt.

"'I'm looking for Mr. Owings.'

"The man stuck his thumbs through his clothesline belt and let the plunger dangle against his pants. 'I'm Owen Owings,' he drawled.

"I extended my hand. 'Catskill Moses. Glad to know you.'

"Owings looked me over, checking out my white beard, denim jacket, baggy dungarees, and worn, mud-encrusted shoes. 'So you are,' he replied.

"He motioned to a seat. 'You looking to own this place?'

"I put on my bored look, the one I had used as a buyer for Pepsi Cola. 'Maybe,' I answered flatly.

"'How come an old guy like you wants to buy a hotel?'

"'I'm old, Mr. Owings, but I'm not through. I'm just starting out. Got lots of ideas, too; spent years thinking about them, honing them down just right: what kind of life to lead and where to lead it.'

"'What kind of ideas?'

"'Okay, Owings. I'll give it to you straight. I'm looking to make a paradise here on earth, in the here-and-now. Your hotel's the place to do it. That's why I want to buy you out.'

"'Owings shook his head. 'You want to make a paradise out of this shit-hole? You must be nuts. Either that, or you've got lots of dough.'

"'I'm low on capital.'

"'How's your credit?'

"'Not good. Considering my age and financial situation anyone, including you, might think I'm a poor risk.'

"'Damn right,'

"'Mr. Owings, nothing could be farther from the truth. Not only am I not a poor risk, I'm a sure bet.' I leaned towards Owings and whispered, 'You see, I've got a secret.'

"'Oh?'

"'Yes. You'll get to know it. Meanwhile, let's just say I'll have no problem reclaiming your hotel.'

"'How're you gonna do it, Moses, without capital or credit?'

"'I've got a way,' I replied, 'a secret way. Learned it from studying the Upanishads. Ever read them?'

"'Can't say I have.'

"I opened my knapsack, took out two apples, offered one to Owings, and began munching on the other. 'Nice hotel you have, Owings. Why do you want to sell it?'

"'Shows what you know about the hotel business,' Owings snorted. 'Up here, every hotel owner has a dream: to sell his hotel. Course it doesn't happen all at once. No, in the beginning your dreams are different.' He leaned back in his chair. 'I came here as a guest fifteen years ago,' he reminisced. 'Liked my vacation so much, I figured, why not do it all year round? So I bought this dump. It wasn't a dump when I bought it. People packed this place then. But things change. Soon as I got my hands on it, business started going downhill. Guests went to Europe rather than Walnut Acres. The mountains died; hotels closed left and right. It's amazing I survived so long. Probably the only thing kept me going was my stamp collection. Reminded me of the fish store I used to own. That was a miserable business, but compared to this, it was heaven. Yup, I had hopes back then, but no more.' He cast his hand over the stained rug, broken chairs, and tilted stage platform in the corner. 'See what happened to those dreams? Dreams aren't worth shit if you can't pay for them.'

"'A lame excuse,' I observed. 'Money, accounting, finance, assets, liabilities, low-risk, it'll cost too much, no funds. . .I've heard it all before. To me the dream comes first. Keep your eye on the dream; then figure out a way to finance it.'

"Owings sighed and took the first bite of his apple. 'Sounds like horse-shit to me. . .but who knows. Ever since Chicken-Fat Butinsky put out a fire by pouring oil on it, I've started to think anything is possible—anything, that is, except making this hotel pay off. Maybe it'll be better if I give it to you instead of the bank.'

"'How much does the bank own?'

"'Most of it. I got four mortgages on the place.'

"'Well, no matter. I still want it.'

"'Take it, Moses. Maybe with a name like yours you can work a few miracles around here. A miracle's the only thing that'll turn this place around.'

"'Maybe we can work together, Owings. I'll push the dream, you take care of the plumbing.'

"'I don't know. I'm burnt out. I'll think it over.'

"Owings thought it over: Paradise on earth, bah, impossible. No one dreams that way. Besides, dreams are for kids. Plans, well, yes, but they lie within the realm of the achievable. They're usually short term and realistic. Dreams? First of all, you have to be asleep to have them. Then, when you wake up, they're not around anymore. Nah, I can't bank on dreams. But I can't bank on the banks either. They'll take over this place pretty soon. Might as well lend it to Catskill. Hotel on loan. A liability. Well, we'll see. In any case, it's something you can sink your teeth into. He wants to own sixty percent. That's a lot. It'll give him controlling interest. But it's not as bad as it sounds. I don't *have* much interest left in the place to begin with. If I could walk out tomorrow with a small profit, you can bet I'd do it. Small profit, ha. If I can walk out without too much of a loss I'd do it. Maybe I can make a deal with Catskill: sell him the whole place, but I'll stay on as plumber, or whatever. I know the ropes here. I just don't want the responsibility. Done. Sold. He's got it. Where are the papers to sign? Or should we just use the old handshake technique? No, not on a hotel. Papers, we'll need them. Well, whatever, my mind's made up. Done. Sold.

"Owings came out of his reflections; he rose from his seat. 'Sold, Catskill, you've got it. I bequeath this shit- hole to you.

Pay what you can. If you can pay anything, that'll be fine. If you can't, that's okay, too. Just assume my debts, take on my burdens. I've been weighed down by this joint too long. Anyway, being free of Walnut Acres is worth a hundred visits to a psychiatrist. The decision alone has made me feel light, even happy. I never thought I'd feel that way again. Take it, Catskill, it's yours. Just sign this little paper.'

"Owings scrawled a deed, last will and testament, lien, mortgage assumption agreement, title search, sub-soil rights, insurance, and air-rights clauses on the back of an envelope. Then he tossed it to me. 'Sign this, and I'm a free man.'

"I took the envelope, read the scrawl, put a line through the air-rights clause, then signed the bottom line.

"'Welcome to slavery,' laughed Owings.

"'A free man has the freedom to *choose* his form of slavery," I remarked wisely.

"Owings was laughing. 'Suit yourself,' he bellowed as he stamped around the room in fits.

"'This was a fine move, Owings,' I said. 'Someday you'll thank me for it.'

"Owings sank into a chair. 'I'm thanking you already.'

"'Well done,' I muttered to myself. 'Now I've got to get started on our building program.'

"'By the way, Catskill, I plan to stay with you here. I'm taking you up on your plumbing deal. You push the dream; I'll take care of the pipes. You see, I've got no other place to go. My family is mostly dead, and the ones that are alive don't want anything to do with me. Even my kids won't speak to me, probably because my ex-wife tells them I'm a nothing. Once they sent me a bagel on my birthday. But that was five years ago. I haven't heard from them since.'

"'That's fine, Owings. Leave your family behind and follow me.'

"'I didn't leave them. They left me,' Owings explained.

"'Doesn't matter. Once they see what we're doing here, they'll want to come back.'

"'No, no!'

"'Okay, don't worry, Owings, we'll leave them out of it for now. We've got plenty of other things to do. First, we've got to put this place in order. The way I see it, we need a program, teachers, leaders, people with brains, specialists.'

"'Know any?'

"'I've met a few in my day. We need a music program. Weasel can organize it. Yoga—I'll get Yogi Schwartz on that one. Philosophy. I'll teach it myself. Dance, cuisine, nature, religion, hiking—oh, it'll be quite a program. Folks will come here by the hundreds. You'll see, Owings, we'll turn this place around.'"

"'Sounds like horseshit to me, but—'

"'Can't you think about anything but turds, Owings? A little optimism, that's what you need.'

"'Easy for you to say, Catskill. Wait 'till you run this hotel for awhile.'

CATSKILL RAN PARADISE HOTEL for a year. But only two customers showed up. Then he went back to India to practice silent meditation. "I'll come back to Paradise some day," he said, "soon as I get this silence right."

REBIRTH IN
A MAJOR KEY

ALTHOUGH I EARN MY living as a nurse, I often take my caretaking work outside the hospital walls. My marriage to Roger is a case in point. I am truly his head nurse. This raises questions. Should I be nursing a thirty-five-year old man? When is it time to give up the breast? Is it *ever* time?

I shouldn't have married the bum.

Now I'm stuck.

But aah, the beginning, when he wooed me! The sweetness, the delicacy, the turbulence. . . .

I should have expected it. Mother told me about the universal plan by the World's Maker to keep women in darkness, only to be used by men—used and abused, then thrown away and forgotten.

My best friend tells me it's my own fault. *My* fault? Can you imagine? My friend puts Roger on a pedestal. She says his abuse of me is not abuse at all but rather a disguised form of deity worship. "You want to see abuse," she says, "meet my husband! He's an expert. His doctoral dissertation was entitled

Evolution of Abuse from Ape to Man. He lectures on the subject at the university. His practicum is our marriage. So don't complain, my dear."

So speaks my friend. But is she sympathetic? No. She's a boring creature who takes me to lunch once a week. But that doesn't explain why I got married, or why I choose to stay married.

Years of handling Roger have made me tough. When we first met, I was shy, withdrawn, docile, and sweet. I had a low threshold vanishing point. I think that's what he liked about me. My vanishing point attracted him.

That's why he chose me over all the other groupies who flocked to his concerts. "Why me?" I always used to ask. "Why me?" There would be ten, fifteen, twenty gorgeous girls waiting in line at his dressing room door. Long-haired blonds, brunettes in courtly dresses, girls in shorts, tight jeans, baggy balloon work pants, all styles of clothing. Fat, thin, tall, short, and all styles of bodies, too: Jewish, Black, Chinese, Italian, Irish, Hispanic, Russian, truly a mini United Nations at his backstage door, waiting for him to bestow a kiss, a compliment, a hello upon them, so they could go home with a memory of their god singing in their hearts. Why did he choose me? Why was I so "lucky"?

I organize him. That is why he chose me—out of weakness, and because, deep down, he knew he was nuts and walked at the edge of a cliff peering down into the dangerous fathomless abyss. He needed a tough hand and a guiding light. He sensed it in me.

I've always had a talent for organizing. Ever since I was three years old, I've organized. Mother said I started even earlier, in her womb.

An avid Marxist, my mother imagined my organizational vibrations hammering out the words "Fetuses of the world, unite!"—the opening words of the Fetal Manifesto, a document still to be written. When I squeezed out of her warmly heated, perfectly managed condominium and toppled into the world, my first cry sounded like "Organize!" The Good Samaritan Hospital nurse held me in her arms and wrapped a blanket around me. I screamed for the second time, "Organize!" I saw the doctor with his dangling stethoscope start moving to the right. Nurses and aides merged behind him, spread out in a semi-circle around me. I could *feel* them getting organized right in front of me! What a sales child I was, what a motivator of men and women! Not even a minute old and I organized the hospital workers on the spot, succeeding where countless union and professional organizers had failed. I even got the doctor in line!

Now that I am an adult and living the frantic life of a thirty-three-year-old sufferer, married to the most miserable of men, subjugated every day to the torments of marriage, I harken back to those incredible moments of infancy when I led with my love energy and aura. I'm proud of that past accomplishment. Still, the present is where I live—an okay place, but I wouldn't push it on anyone.

I shouldn't have married the bum.

When we first met, he told me how he used everyone in his life as a stepping stone to finding himself. For example, many years ago, when he was an unknown guitarist, he got a job washing dishes in Big Sol's, an Upper West Side restaurant. After two months of washing dishes and scrubbing pots, the boss, Big

Sol himself, put a tray in his hand and said, "Today you're a waiter."

Roger survived as a waiter for two months. Survived, I say, because he never really developed the skill of serving others. He was too interested in serving himself. His favorite question at the time was "Who am I?" Perhaps it is a question every twenty-three-year-old asks. When customers sat down to eat, rather than taking their orders, he asked, "Who am I?" Since they didn't know, he often lost interest in serving them and moved on to the next table.

At the time he was practicing the guitar five hours a day. Every spare minute, up in that broken down fourth-floor fire-trap walk-upon on Sixth Street he called home, he'd practice his scales, arpeggios, Fernando Sor studies, Guiliani, Carulli, and Carcassi studies, his Granados, and Albeniz, his Bach *fugues*, *gavottes*, and *bourrées*, and always hoped an agent would call him and put him on the star-studded road to wealth and fame.

In time, Big Sol, who usually sat at the cash register, wearing a suit with a white apron, realized he had hired a strange person. He liked my husband, probably because both of them were crazy in their own special way, and he supported him morally, mentally, and sometimes even financially through his dishwasher period, pot washer period, waiter period, and guitar period.

The most significant thing Sol said to my husband that year came in the form of a question posed late one night after all the customers had gone home and Roger was cleaning off the last table. As he hummed a Sevillanas and did some Flamencan dance steps carrying dishes into the kitchen, Big Sol said, "How can you become a famous Flamencan guitarist with a name like

Roger Brown." My husband stopped in his tracks.

Big Sol saw the effects of his words. "Roger Brown just doesn't work," he added. "It's not a name for a Spanish guitarist. It's boring. No romance to it. The public will pay for names like Andres Segovia, Carlos Montoya, Sabicas, or Mario Escudero, but they won't even read an ad for Roger Brown.

"You can practice forever, and no one will listen. I used to be in advertising, and I know. The public wants names, images, and dreams. Roger Brown is a good name for a hamburger, but for a Spanish guitarist, it's worthless."

So my husband went on a five-month name search. He couldn't get the topic out of his mind. He wrote down hundreds of names in a notebook, underlined some, crossed out others, followed many with question marks. Then he went to his favorite place of meditation, the Cathedral of Perpetual Renovation on 110th Street, where he sat in a pew staring upwards for hours at the groin-vaulted ceiling, trying to grasp the right idea, the right feeling, the right name.

Roger's father had emigrated from the Ukraine in 1905. At Ellis Island, he'd changed his name from Bogdanovitch to Brown. Family tradition held that the Bogdanovitch's great sixteenth-century forebear had run away from his village of Pereyaslav and joined the Zaporozhian Cossacks near the mouth of the Dnieper, far below the cataracts, to become a famous rider, horse thief, and boat maker—the mythic great-grandfather Roger most admired. He wanted to pattern his life after that wild, adventurous, freedom-loving man.

However, Big Sol reminded him, you don't find any Spanish guitarists with Ukrainian names. My husband then decided to study Spanish history. His name search brought him to

Jimenez con las Manitas de Plata y el Corazon del Oro. This he shortened to Jimenez del Oro.

WHEN MOTHER AND FATHER told me to get married, I knew it was a sign from above. At the time there were no real prospects. Oh, Tom, the banker from Connecticut, was okay, and we'd lasted three months together, but his snoring broke us up. I didn't mind it since I'm a heavy sleeper, but when he snored at breakfast, dinner, and even during the rehearsal of our choral group, that was too much. When I pointed it out, he defended himself by saying, "Sure I snore. And I'm good at it, too." It didn't seem like a quality worthy of admiration. He finally walked out on me, repeating his usual cliche: "I can't live with someone who can't appreciate my true self." That was Tom.

Now, Mike was better. He didn't snore. But he did belch a lot. And he went to the bathroom in the strangest places. I gave up on him after a month.

Still, I was sure someone would rush in to fill my marriage vacuum. I just felt it. Intuition, if you will.

Naturally, I thought about organizing the problem by doing a little research.

Next day I went to the library. I checked the sections on marriage, household goods, history of men, married life in the Middle Ages, ancient Rome and Greece, and modern America.

I was at it for months. When I got bored with books, I tried concerts, lectures, and museums. For weeks I walked the halls of the Metropolitan Museum of Art, checking the walls of the Egyptian section for available men, trying to decipher the hieroglyphics for exact addresses and phone numbers, checking out the mummy section.

I looked at statues of naked men in the Greek section. One I particularly admired: fine muscles, tapered torso, firm buttocks, strong forearms, curly hair, sloping powerful back. I touched him gently, felt the smoothness of his stone body, examined his shapely leg muscles, and was about to explore further when a museum guard hurried over and warned me not to touch. The guard's name was Arthur, and we ended up having lunch together.

We sat in the Metropolitan lunch room at a corner table. As Arthur closed his massive teeth around a tuna fish sandwich, he told me he was working towards his doctorate in astrophysics and writing his thesis on the hibernation of metaphysical principles within molecular defenestration. He said such a topic would not be commercially marketable, and, since he had no cash, would I treat him to lunch. I obliged. Money is no problem for me when I have it.

Arthur's long legs crossed and uncrossed as he spoke; the combination of his jaw crunching into the tuna fish sandwich, and the black-rimmed glasses slipping down his nose, made him appear sexy. I like a man with good crunch. I also like a man who can handle his eyeglasses. Eyeglasses remind me of medieval knights jousting on horseback, charging their opponent with their lances and risking their lives for a kiss from their beloved. You don't find any men dressed in full armor riding horses down Madison Avenue anymore, but you do find plenty wearing glasses. Arthur's turned me on. When they slid off his nose and he pushed them back in place, first with a flick of his powerful wrist, and then with a jerk of his head, I swooned.

Arthur told me how he hated his museum job and hoped to

turn the world of astrophysics on its head, make a name for himself, then retire to a stellar observatory on Mt. Kenya.

I talked about my research in libraries. Then I told him how, during the summer, I had lain naked on the beach in Cape Cod, hoping someone would notice me. His eyes widened behind his glasses, and, feeling I had his undivided attention, I went on to describe the wonderful warmth of the sun shining down on my you-know-what, how the Cape Cod summer breeze gently brushed against its hairs, how, after I turned over and lay on my stomach, this same breeze had touched my "you-know- here" while the sun tanned it. Several men had approached me to ask for my phone number. By then I had been so lulled by the heat, so caressed by that breeze, that I told them to leave me alone because I was too busy. So I didn't come back from Cape Cod with a man, but I did have a great tan.

I could use anatomical or salacious words to describe my body parts, but instead I use "you-know-what" and "you-know-where," to keep their mystery private. Instead of being direct, I use indirect language. I choose to *imply*. It's because of my Puritan upbringing. Although my Irish father, Patrick Mahoney, was a wit and charmer, my English mother came from a long line of Puritans. Her great-grandparents had come over in 1644 on the Cornwall Salvation and landed in the Massachusetts area near Plymouth. Not much is know about their rickety boat, which made a life-saving stop at Iceland, then went further off course, landing in Greenland, Newfoundland, and Martha's Vineyard before finding America almost by accident. The Cornwall Salvation was filled with Latter-Day Puritans, a rare sect originating in the countryside of Cornwall who believed in the beneficent power of the daisy. Men and women did not sleep together—even married ones. The epistemology of the Cornwall Salvationers held that women were created horrible, and men worse.

My Puritan background excited Arthur. Most men were attracted to it. It never threatened them, made no demands, and brought out the hunter lurking within the male breast.

After the beach story, Arthur liked me more. "Take me out again for lunch," he said. "We could go to a concert. Let's go to my apartment and check the concert listings."

"Why your apartment?" I asked.

He bent towards me and whispered, "Because my apartment has the best listings you'll ever find."

So we went.

The apartment turned out to be across the street from the Metropolitan. We walked through a carpeted lobby to the elevator and rode it to the 12th floor. Arthur's three-room domicile overlooked both Central Park and Fifth Avenue. He had, he said, a perfect view of the marathon runners as they ran through the park. He could also, with the help of binoculars, look at paintings and sculptures through the open Met windows. He liked peeking. It was his greatest pleasure, the ultimate art-viewing experience. Peeking fostered secrecy and mystery and kept the halo of significance at the highest level.

A strange person. Yet he told me flat out that his father owned fourteen sweat shops in the garment district, ten of which were legal, and that personally he was a millionaire.

"Let's see those listings," I finally said.

He took my hand and lead me to the living room sofa. "Sit down. Relax. I'll get them for you."

He disappeared into the bedroom. I waited, surveying the

expensive antiques, the Persian rug covering a baroque table, the parquet floor, the French masters on the wall, including, I believe, an original Courbet, a Fragonard, and framed manuscript pages of Balzac's *Père Goriot*. The bedroom door opened and Arthur appeared, carrying a guitar. He sat down on a caned nineteenth-century American chair. "I play guitar, too."

Then he began singing in the most atrocious voice I'd ever heard. I didn't know if he was gargling, coughing, or blowing his nose. The worse he sounded, the more his eyes fixed on me. I realized his primitive howling was aimed at my ears. Then he sang a version of "This Land Is Your Land" that made me want to emigrate immediately.

He smiled and started another song.

"Arthur, please."

I put my hands over my ears, got up, and marched to the window. If this keeps up, I thought, I could jump. His chimpanzee screeching filled the room; I realized I had a rich sadist on my hands.

I slipped behind him, put my hands around his throat, and started to squeeze. Slowly the sound of his voice diminished until there was silence. I loosened my grip, but his voice returned. I gave a final ferocious squeeze and, while he gasped for air, tore the guitar out of his hands.

"I play guitar, too," I said, carrying the instrument to the living room sofa, well beyond his reach.

Arthur seemed more subdued during the next hour. He didn't sing anymore but told me about his childhood.

"Ever since I was four years old," he said," I've wanted to play music. My dream was to become a musician. I loved music. When I played it, I drifted into a world beyond textiles,

beyond family squabbles. I took piano lessons, then cello, trumpet, even percussion. But I had no talent. That's been my
downfall. I saw how you hated my singing. Everyone does.
My gift—if you can call it a gift—is to bring pain to others
through my music."

Arthur looked sadly at the rug and became quiet.

I didn't know what to make of this sudden revelation.
"Why do you still play, then?"

"For several reasons," he said. "First of all, I like to inflict
pain. Second of all, there is the deep lingering hope that, perhaps someday, by a stroke of luck, I'll play well. Playing music
gives me a feeling of power, even though I know it's kind of
perverted."

"Well, Arthur, at least you're honest. But why did you pick
the guitar? It's such a quiet instrument—especially the classical
guitar you're playing on."

"I hate guitar amplification," Arthur hissed. "It's unnatural.
If I can't inflict pain through natural means, I'm not interested."

He got up, walked over to his collection of records, and
pulled a black record jacket off the top shelf. "Just listen to this.
It'll knock your head off."

"Spoken like a true sadist," I said.

Arthur pulled the record out of its cellophane wrapper and
put it on the record player. Then he sat down, gazed at the ceiling, and waited eagerly for the first notes.

I listened. From the first, I was swept away. Beautiful.
Magnificent. Unearthly. I had never heard such sexy tones
from a guitar. Each liquid arpeggio had fire and love behind it.
Delicate, pulsating, masculine, feminine, earthly, heavenly—all
mixed together. I sat transfixed.

Arthur saw my pleasure. He reveled in it. This was a side of him I didn't know. "Who is it?" I asked when side one had finished.

"He's my favorite guitarist," he answered. "I've been a fan of his ever since he came to America four years ago. I go to all his concerts."

"So who is he?" I asked.

"Jimenez del Oro."

"Jimenez who?"

Arthur squinted in disbelief. "You mean you've never heard of him?"

I shook my head.

"*Jimenez del Oro!*" he repeated. "He is the greatest guitarist in the world."

"I like him, too. I must admit I've never heard such guitar playing on a record."

"He's even better in person." Arthur looked at me eagerly. "Would you like to go?"

"Why, is there a concert?"

"Yes. He'll be in Alice Tully Hall next Friday. The concert's been sold out for weeks, but I happen to have two tickets."

"I'm free. . . okay, I'll go."

"Good." Arthur beamed angelically. "You'll love this guy."

That was how I first heard of Jimenez del Oro.

OUR TAXI GOT STUCK in traffic, so we arrived at Alice Tully Hall just as the concert was about to begin. An usher handed us a program and pointed to our fifth row seats. We hurried down the aisle. I looked over the audience. A packed house. International types, too: Hungarians, Chinese, Russians, Spanish, Nigerians, Finns, Swedes, French, Mexicans, Mongolians, and folks from New York, New Jersey, and Connecticut.

We got to our seats just before the lights went out. I sat down and opened my program. Blank. I nudged Arthur; he opened his program. Blank, too. "They gave us a misprint," I complained. "Now I won't know what he's playing."

"It's no misprint," Arthur explained. "Jimenez always prints blank programs. He doesn't want his audiences tied to a script. He leaves it blank so they can imagine whatever they like. Try imagining the program. Everything else will take care of itself."

The lights dimmed. Silence. Anticipation. A spotlight fell on the solitary stage seat. The stage door opened, and a tall man dressed in a black suit with red bandana tied around his neck stepped out. He strode across the stage, carrying a guitar in his right hand and holding it close to his body. Applause filled the hall as he headed for center stage. Scattered cries of "Jimenez! Jimenez!" rose from the audience.

Jimenez bowed as everyone cheered. He bowed when the cheering stopped. Then he sat down.

A short man wearing a white suit and sombrero emerged from behind the curtain. He approached Jimenez, swinging a bucket of mud. Standing before the guitarist, he asked, "Jimenez, will you play your guitar tonight?"

Jimenez shook his head. "I will not."

The man took off his sombrero, bowed ceremoniously to the north, south, east, and west, and repeated, "Jimenez, will you play your guitar tonight?"

Again Jimenez shook his head. "No, I will not."

"Jimenez, will you play your guitar tonight?" the short man repeated a third time.

"No, I will not."

The short man lifted his bucket and dumped mud over the guitarist.

The audience applauded. Jimenez rose and bowed to his assistant.

I elbowed Arthur. "What's all this about?"

"It's a standard Jimenez opening. Before every concert he's showered with mud. It's an old Cossack custom. The Cossacks poured mud over their chosen leaders to remind them to serve their community and be humble. Jimenez does the same thing."

"But why mud?"

"God made man out of mud," Arthur replied. "Mud is a symbol of humility. It seals you to your Maker."

I didn't quite understand what he was talking about, but I tried to keep an open mind.

The short man presented a towel. Jimenez wiped off the mud and returned the towel. When the short man walked off stage, Jimenez picked up his guitar and played the first note.

He played a second note, then another and another. . . watery notes rolling across the strings, floating out of the guitar, across the stage, across the air-waves, and into my ears—ear kisses. His notes massaged my mind. I could feel Jimenez's fingers plucking, not only the guitar, but *me*. Ah, how magnificently his guitar plunged into my being, into the enzymes of my soul. Jimenez was playing his guitar for me alone.

Then I knew he loved me.

Arthur was only a bystander; so was the rest of the audience.

I sighed audibly. Arthur elbowed me. "Shhh," he whispered.

Jimenez played on. Love all over his fingers, love all over his mind, love in the look of rapture and lust filling his face when he cradled his guitar, love in the rapier fingers drilling elegance into every note.

The fifty-minute first half passed like thirty seconds. I sat there dazed, my mouth open, drinking in note after note. My eyes stared straight ahead, prisoners of a hypnotic power.

The intermission lights came on. Arthur said, "Let's go to the lobby for some coffee."

We made our way through the crowd. "Do you like him, Kathleen?"

What a question, I said to myself. Yes, yes, I like him. I *love him!* He shot stars on guitar beams. Arthur, how can I repay you for giving me *this*? A primal experience. A Dark Age Anglo-Saxon vision. Jimenez is the Beowulf of guitar playing, a mighty behemoth wallowing upon the waters, rising like foam from the top-most wave peaks, ocean-flying chips of water spread against the sky. I open my heart to him. He fingers my aorta, my ventricle. I am tired—oh, Arthur, *tired* of being me, of holding onto myself, tired of researching, tired of my ego. I want to yield, to throw myself into the waiting arms of the giant Jimenez-Man. He speaks of the darkling steppes, the Eurasian prairies, flat, wide, and awesome, of riders pounding the face of the tundra, forest zone, and steppe—and what is Jimenez but Jimenez Khan personified, of Aladdin's immortal Jimenez in a bottle, the Gimenez factor, Ginez turned to Genius! Genesis of Jimenesis, the Bible gone to heaven, Yak-Yak gone wild, sun of the future rising out of the past, all topsy-turvy, unwashed, and unnamable. How can I speak to you again, Arthur? Your name conjures up legends of greatness, Arthurian tales of round tables and swords, and swordfish, and swordfish steaks, and Guinevere undressing, and Lancelot lancing and lacing himself to voluptuous maidens singing under windows while courageous knights floss their teeth. Arthur, your mythic name creates visions, legendary panoramas.

But, you, Arthur, are in yourself, ah. . . so *boring*. When you walk in, I fall asleep. You are a medicinal soporific, a good pill, but a pill nevertheless. I don't want to pop pills any more. I want panting and adventure; I want gears shifting in my shift, innards turning. I want the tall, walrus- toothed, Walloon-built flesh fortress crashing down on me. Tied by guitar strings, imprisoned, the genie-rubbing bottle guitar body of the Jimenez-Man. I want to devour, not simply munch. Certainly not sip. Arthur, you are, at best, a sip. . . . But how can I tell you all this? I am so polite.

Mad thoughts raced through my brain, surfboards lost and scattered on a raging sea. "Do I like him?" I asked. "Oh, he's all right."

"Only all right?" Arthur looked disappointed.

Why fake him, I thought. "Okay, Arthur, the guy is *good*."

"Good is better than all right," Arthur said. "Still, don't you think he's even better than that? Like sensational? Like a genius?"

I feigned the look of a burned-out critic. Yes," I answered in a flat tone. "I suppose you could say that."

"Say what?"

"Genius. Sensational. Both descriptive of the proper mood."

"But didn't you feel him in your gut? Deep down? Weren't you moved?"

"Oh yes, I was moved," I answered. "In fact, I'd like to meet the guy. Learn some of his tricks. I took a few guitar lessons once. I'd like to find out how he makes some of those sounds."

Arthur stirred the coffee in his styrofoam cup and shifted to his drinking foot. "Maybe we can go backstage after the concert. It'll be mobbed, I know that. We may not be able to reach him, but we can try."

"Could we?"

"Sure." He stirred his coffee again, then took a sip. "Yes," I crooned, slowly letting the air pass through my lips. "I love him."

"*Love* him? That's pretty strong stuff." Arthur shook his head. "You're not supposed to love him. You're supposed to love *me*."

"Oh, Arthur. You're so literal. I don't love him in *that* way. I don't even know him yet."

"*Yet?*"

"Don't be so sensitive. I only mean his music thrills me."

"*Thrills?* What kind of expression is that? Interests you, yes. Intrigues you, yes. Even attracts you. But *thrills*?" He shook his head again. "Thrills are reserved for sexual preferences."

"Arthur, stop it. You're reading all kinds of wrong ideas into what I'm saying. How can I express it to you? I'm glad you brought me to this concert. I never would have known what beautiful sounds the guitar can make." I reached for a less threatening way of putting it. "This concert is really a psycho-sensual experience of magnetic, psychophysical proportions. It moves me neurologically."

"That's better, Kathleen."

"Besides, Arthur, you and I have nothing going between us. Just art. I don't see why you should be jealous."

"*Jealous?* Jealous of whom?"

"I don't know. It just seems you're overreacting to this whole thing. All I've been trying to tell you is what you've been trying to tell me: Jimenez del Oro is really good!"

"I agree with that."

"Yes, Arthur," I went on. "He plays with such feeling and has such warm sensual tone. It just makes me so warm and wet all over, I—"

"*Wet?*" Arthur's face lost some color.

"Well, er. . . damp."

"*Damp?* Where?"

"Well, I drool a lot. In the mouth, I suppose. Also, well. . . you know where."

Arthur straightened indignantly. "I do *not* know where. Where?"

"I can't say, at least not here in the lobby."

"What? How private is this?" Arthur grabbed me by the collar and pulled me towards him. "Tell me. Now!"

He tightened his grip and twisted my blouse. I started choking. "Tell me!" Other people turned to stare.

I grabbed his arms and, using all the strength I'd built up in my karate and weight training classes, forced him away. "Get your hands off me!" I screamed.

"You need some help, lady?" a man behind me asked.

An usher rushed over. "What's the trouble?"

"No trouble," Arthur snorted.

"All trouble," I shouted to the usher. "But there's nothing *you* can do about it. Mind your own business." The usher backed off. I turned to Arthur. "Stop it, you creep! Never, *never*, lay your hands on my body. Not only is it impolite and unmanly, but believe me, my friend"—and I leaned into his face, breathing steam into his bewildered eyes— "it is *dangerous*."

He backed off—but not far. "Dangerous, eh?" he laughed uneasily. "How so?"

"You'll see soon enough if you keep this up, Arthur. Don't play games with me."

"We'll see how dangerous you are," he muttered, and bit into his Styrofoam coffee cup. Some coffee dribbled down his suit. "Damn! Look what you made me do!" He stamped on the floor. The rest of his coffee popped out of his cup and landed on his pants. Tears of rage trickled down his cheek. He almost started to cry, but the lights dimmed and he checked himself. "We'll talk about this later," he hissed. "First, we've got to survive part two."

"Survive" was a good word. What was happening? Was Arthur actually jealous? What's wrong with getting wet over a guitarist? I come to concerts to move my heart—and my other organs, too. Getting wet is a compliment. I guess I should have been flattered that Arthur liked me, though, frankly, he wasn't my type. But Jimenez turned on my switches.

Part two began. Arthur and I simmered next to each other. Our seats felt too close for comfort as steam came out of my shoulders and seared his arms, which he held, like a catatonic, close to his body. In this fashion, we survived the dimming of the lights.

Jimenez strode on stage again, sat down, and began playing.

He wooed me with his deep chestnut hues. Once again fire and oil sizzled.

Needless to say, the second half ended in a standing ovation. Jimenez gave us five encores before he waved goodbye. As he walked off, I'm sure he winked at me and whispered, "I'll see you backstage."

I turned to Arthur. "A superb performance," I said.

He mumbled something about pheasants, stood up, and started heading for the exit.

"Don't you want to go backstage?" I asked.

"I want to go home," he growled.

"You said we would go backstage."

"Too crowded."

"I don't mind."

"I do. You'll never get near him. He's got a fan club a mile long. It's a waste of time."

"I've got time. Besides, you promised."

"Look, Kathleen, if you want to see this guy Jimenez, then do it yourself. I'm too busy."

"Busy? I don't see you doing anything. If you won't go backstage with me, I'll go myself."

"Good."

"Arthur, I don't even have a ride home."

"Take a cab."

"To Bergenfield?"

"Sure, it's only eighty bucks."

I was indignant. "I can see we won't be seeing each other again."

Arthur agreed. He turned away and lost himself in the exiting crowd.

I was glad Arthur left me, glad to be alone. Slowly I followed the mob of fans through a side door, up a flight of stairs, and into the dressing room entrance. It was filled with women—beautiful women. But there were men, too. Also mothers and fathers with their children.

"Jimenez, open the door!" shouted an irate fat woman with black hair. She swung her hand-bag against the closed door.

A stocky man with a bulldog chest sprang forward. "We're not waiting here for our health, Jimenez," he snarled, pounding on the door with his fists. "Open this door for us!"

I hadn't realized that Jimenez's fans could be so violent. Worshipful, I could understand—Jimenez was excellence incarnate; excellence could be worshipped—but really, what was wrong with these people? Why Did Jimenez bring out the animal in them? Was it his tone? His rhythms? His ineffable charisma? Maybe. Often, during the concert, I'd felt like an animal myself, and even now, I wanted to claw down the door, hurl myself on Jimenez, and sink my teeth into his flesh. Only my training as a nurse kept me from doing it. I'd sometimes wanted to kill some of my patients, too. But I had learned restraint and patience. It was often the only thing preventing me from wringing their miserable necks.

Suddenly, the doorknob turned. The mob hushed. Out stepped Jimenez.

His dark eyes scanned the fans before him. I loved those eyes, and his sculpted face; the power of his gaze controlled and tamed the unruly mob.

Jimenez stood amid a sea of beaming faces. Majestically, and with a flourish, he reached into his vest pocket and withdrew a long, silver-tipped pen with an eagle feather on one end.

He gripped it in his writing hand, then held it aloft. Papers rattled as people reached for their autograph paper.

Jimenez signed for an hour. Slowly the crowd diminished. During all this time he hadn't looked at me once. He'd noticed everyone else, why not me? Was I not worthy? The fact he didn't notice me made him seem even more attractive. As soon as men react to me, I start thinking there is something wrong with them. After all, if they notice me, what does that say about them? To Jimenez's credit, he didn't. I could tell he knew how to handle a woman—especially *this* one.

Half a dozen fans left. Jimenez kept signing. Still, not a glance towards me.

Then I stood next to his elbow. As he signed his final autograph, I heard him say under his breath, "Let's go out for a drink."

Was he talking to me or to himself? As I later learned, Jimenez often talked to himself.

"How about it?" he asked.

I didn't answer.

By now the last fan had thanked him and left. I was the only one remaining backstage. He still hadn't looked at me. "Let's go," he commanded.

"Are you talking to me, Jimenez?"

"Who are you?" he asked, looking at the floor.

"My name is Kathleen."

"What do you drink, Kathleen?"

"Oh, anything. Mostly milk."

"That's good, Kathleen. I like milk, too."

"Do you like whole or skim?"

"I like *you*, Kathleen. Let's go." He took me by the arm and led me out the stage door.

We headed down Broadway, past video stores blasting tape cassettes, crossed against the green light, and entered Sam's Deli. We took a corner table.

Raising his hand, he summoned the waiter. "I'll have the left of the menu," he said. The waiter nodded, took the menu, and disappeared into the kitchen. Soon he returned with three plates piled high with chicken wings. I reached for a wing, bit off a piece, and chewed it slowly. "Not bad," I said. "Are you a good judge of food?"

"Of course. I know food better than I know the guitar." Jimenez took a chicken wing, broke it in half, and tore it to pieces with his teeth. "I've been eating all of my life," he said, swallowing his first load, "and I've become an expert. I understand my food by entering into each particle before I eat it. Understanding helps digestion."

"You impress me, Jimenez. I thought all you could do was play guitar."

"How little you know me. You don't even know who I am."

"I read the articles in the papers," I said.

"Those fictions. I write them myself, or with the help of my agent, Spider Wasserman, whenever he's out of jail.

"Fictions? You mean they're not true?"

"You naive thing. What do you know about music? What do you know about life? What do you know about business, finance, or the nether-world of concert promotion? What do you know about the building of a public character, or the creation of a career? You think that, merely because you see something, it is true."

"What is that mumbo-jumbo supposed to mean?"

"This isn't mumbo-jumbo, my dear. Mambo-jumbo, perhaps, in so far as it's got a specific Latin beat. And the mambo-jumbo deep within my mumbo-jumbo has been influenced by Nigerian upswells, the heights of Mt. Kenya, and African rhythms transported from Timbuktu north across the Sahara."

Jimenez bit into another chicken wing. I saw his two golden front teeth shining behind it. The sound of his crunching far exceeded Arthur's.

"If your press releases are fictions," I asked, "what *is* true about you?"

A strange smile formed on Jimenez's face. He kept smiling, looking into my eyes, but didn't answer.

"Tell me about Spider Wasserman," I finally insisted.

Jimenez's eyes lit up. "My agent? Now there's someone I can work with. Spider's dynamic, impressive, creative. A mind like a razor trap. Knows how to get in there and fight. He's a master of the nitty-gritty. Never went to college, or high school. Learned it all on the streets. He's a dirt fighter. Yes, Spider's my man. Without him I doubt I'd be where I am today. Spider's a master at P.R. and advertising. Never tells the truth. It's a religion with him. He simply doesn't believe in it. But beneath his tough exterior is a tender, sensitive, once-abused heart. He's got compassion for people, even though you wouldn't realize it right away. That's why he says that telling a lie never hurt anybody, but telling the truth can kill you."

"That's a strange twist."

"Spider's a strange man." Jimenez sipped his milk. "But as I say, without him I'd probably be playing guitar in coffee shops, or giving concerts in my basement to groups of chairs, or waiting tables and playing Albeniz, Sor, Granados, and Bach in my kitchen. No, I need a guy like Spider. He takes care of the practical world. We've got things divided up pretty evenly. He looks after the nuts and bolts; I do the soaring."

"The soaring?"

"Yup. That's what a concert is all about. Soaring. Flying. Reaching for the stars. Concerts aren't about playing notes. They're about soaring. I learned about soaring by accident. One day I was practicing in my room. My concentration was superb. I forgot about the notes; I forgot about my technique and trying to play everything correctly. Suddenly, I lost myself in the music. All my conflicts disappeared. I felt myself rising off my seat, transported and uplifted. A new experience. I never had felt that before. Higher and higher I went, through the ceiling, through the roof. I floated. I flew. Across New York City, across America, around the world.

"It all happened in a few physical seconds, but the experience seemed timeless, infinite. I had reached a new realm, touched a new world. I think my physical brain-size increased in that new dimension of *soaring*. Since that day, whenever I play guitar or give a concert, my only purpose is to soar. Pure and simple."

"Now I understand your concert a little better."

"I'm glad," Jimenez said. "Soaring is my business. It's also a tradition in our family. My ancestors worshiped at the feet of soarers. Those who couldn't soar worshiped at the feet of chickens. Probably explains my affinity for chicken wings."

Jimenez sipped his milk, then bit into another chicken wing. "As I said, I have to credit Spider Wasserman with much of my career success. But it hasn't been a straight upward path. Lots of bumps in the road. Lots of down times, too. Once I discovered soaring, I started looking for performing jobs. It was a long search. Most booking agents said no. The few jobs I did get were mediocre. My art was not appreciated. I got anxious, tense, even desperate. I practiced less and spent endless hours on the phone, writing letters, and trying to get bookings. Very discouraging. I received about thirty nos to one yes. And these were on the good days. Slowly, over a period of months, I lost my inspiration. I even forgot why I played the guitar. My sense of love, life, and meaning dwindled. During that time I thought of myself as nothing; soon I became nothing.

"What did I do?" There was a long pause while he chewed and swallowed his chicken. "When people lose their way today, they go to a shrink. But I didn't need a therapist. I knew my problem: I'd forgotten how to soar. Where does one go for that? To an ornithologist, of course. That's how I ended up in ornitherapy with Dr. Willian Tweederhopper. A brilliant man. He spent years studying how and why birds fly. Do they soar, he asked, or simply coast?"

"I'm a researcher myself," I said. "I do research in the hospital where I work. I never heard of ornitherapy. How does it work?"

"Hard to explain," Jimenez answered. "Dr. T emphasized flying, aeronautics, and wing-spread. Before you can become his patient, he tests your spread. He makes you jump from a chair, flap your arms, and try to fly. Obviously, in the beginning of your ornithological training, you can't soar. Out of the question. Soaring only comes when you are cured and blessed. In the beginning, however, you walk into his office with a broken wing or a sore throat—there are so many bird diseases afflicting mankind. Dr. T. then explains that man's purpose on earth is not merely to fly, but to soar. People are unhappy in life because their soaring potential is not realized. They fail to rise above the traffic jam of human existence."

I looked somewhat baffled. "Does soaring have anything to do with reincarnation?" I asked. "I mean, during your concert you talked about your many lives. Is that for real?"

"Of course it's for real."

"You mean you actually remember things that happened thousands of years ago?"

"Yes."

I shook my head. "How can anyone remember those things?"

"It's a talent I have."

"Well, it's beyond anything I've experienced. When did you discover this?"

Jimenez leaned back. "In college I studied history." He reflected a moment. "I found I had an affinity for many of the historical personages I studied, and also an affinity for certain historical periods. Upon further examination, I realized the affinity existed because I had once lived during those periods. Experiencing reincarnation meant I was actually 'remembering' my old moods and friends."

"You mean you just kept being reborn, going from one life to another?"

"That's right."

I looked skeptical. "There's no proof about reincarnation. One has to believe it on faith. Trouble is, I have no faith— especially in such hogwash."

"Hogwash?" Jimenez's jaw tightened. "Reincarnation is not hogwash; it is an absolute fact!"

"Well, at least it's good for your show," I said. "You sure keep the pace going. The audience likes it, too. Or at least they tolerate it."

"Tolerate it?"

"I mean, they *love* your guitar playing. When you played those sonatas and serenades, I fell in love with you. You've got charisma, power, *savoir faire*, everything, all expressed in those notes. When you told me about soaring, I understood simply by listening to your playing. But once you stop playing and start talking to the audience, then I think you're a bit lost."

"Lost?" Jimenez involuntarily smacked the table with his fist. "I am *never* lost. I'm in charge from the moment I come on stage."

"I wonder. There's a certain hesitation in your body language that—"

"What are you talking about?" Jimenez's voice rose in indignation. "You just met me, and you start tearing my program apart. You don't know the first thing about music."

I realized I had hit a nerve. "You may be right, Jimenez," I said softly, trying to push the snorting bull back in its pen. "But I do know about *people*. I take care of them at the hospital all day. It's my job, not only to read their medical charts, but to read the intangibles as well, and that means the looks in their eyes, their body language, their intonations when they speak. I'll admit I don't know you, but I still sense there's more to this reincarnation stuff than meets the eye." I paused and surveyed Jimenez' mood. He relaxed a bit. "Maybe you're shy," I added.

"Me? Shy? Ridiculous. How could I be shy when I stand and perform before thousands of people almost every night? Shy is the last thing I am. Commanding, powerful, towering—

those might be better words to describe me. Hypnotic, fascinating, charming, talented—that's my job. You've got to be a fighter to go out in front of those animals every night. Shy? Never."

"Maybe while you face the audience, you try to escape at the same time."

"Where do you get these crazy ideas from? Why would I go out in front of them every night if I wanted to escape from them?"

"I think it's your way of handling shyness—and that's good. But maybe your emphasis on reincarnation is a camouflage, a way of avoiding pain.

"Avoiding pain?" Jimenez laughed sardonically. "Now that's a new one. Sure, it's true that performing is tough, and that's I've got to psyche myself up before each concert. Still, when I play my guitar—"

"I'm not talking about your guitar. Your guitar is your strength. I'm talking about how you relate to the audience and to people. I'm saying that talking to people is hard for you. Why, look how hard it was simply to look me in the eye."

Jimenez fell silent.

"I can understand that," I continued. "Every night you face a new audience; every night you have to start all over again trying to deal with them. Falling back on the past is one way of avoiding the conflict. What is reincarnation but an escape into the past?"

"Reincarnation is no escape," Jimenez protested. "It is the noble growth of mankind through a progression of learning experiences."

"Perhaps it is. But overemphasis on your many lives can

lead to a fragmented personality, poor concentration, and other dangers."

"Absurd!"

"Facing your pain might help you. Think about it."

"I *am* thinking about it, and I think you're crazy. You're just jealous of my talent."

"Giving up reincarnation might help release more of your talent."

"There you go, wrong again. My talent is released *through* reincarnation, not in spite of it."

Jimenez ate another chicken leg. Then he started feeling *my* leg under the table. His fingers felt warm, sure, and strong as they crawled up my leg. I recalled the arpeggios he played on stage. Sure enough, he was playing "Recuerdos de la Alhambra" just beneath my knee. Now came a Spanish roll of fingers across my thigh. True to his word, Jimenez never stopped practicing.

"What are you playing?" I asked.

"Recuerdos," Jimenez answered as he tremoloed his way up my thigh.

"Is this part of soaring?"

"It's the introduction."

He kept talking as he practiced, first on my right leg, then on my left. "Soaring lessons with Dr. T. took place in his Broken Wing Factory, an aviary where patients sat in nests with an ample supply of worms. While they nested, Dr. T. walked among them, lecturing about the meaning of life. He examined my head and told me I had brain arthritis—a common disease among professionals. This sickness had overtaken me two years before, when, during a bout of depression, I gave up risk taking and challenge, and started looking for a safe way of performing. Gradually my bird-soul had been drained of all soaring hope. I had lost sight of the mystery and adventure of life."

During Jimenez's monologue, his *rasgueado* and tremolo had advanced up my thigh.

"Your tremolo and *rasgueado* are warming my leg too much," I said. "Please, slow down."

Jimenez withdrew his hand. He continued his *rasgueado* and tremolo on the delicatessen table top.

"My training with Dr. T. began with Socratic questioning. 'Are you an eagle or titmouse? A condor or sparrow? A robin or crow? Are you an ostrich or hawk?' Telling questions, especially for the neophyte soarer. 'Are you willing to give up the transient glamor of anxiety attacks? Are you willing to give up your petty angers, the luxuries of self-hate, self-loathing, and self-analysis? Yes, even self-analysis. The intellect that analyzes often creates a new form of slavery. By building new, higher, and thicker walls of intellect, which can, in turn create new barriers and excuses that keep you from soaring."

Jimenez looked into my eyes. "Dr. T. spoke about sexual energy as couple soaring. Perhaps, Kathleen, we can soar together."

"I find your story about him charming," I said, "but unbelievable."

"Unbelievable to your limited mind. If you cannot imagine reincarnation, you cannot imagine Dr. T. But he is real nevertheless, because he is a fiction. Fiction is the true reality." Again Jimenez looked into my eyes. "I am looking behind your eyes, Kathleen, into your soul. I am looking past your history, into the history of your ancestors. I see everything you are, were, and will be. I know you, Kathleen. I know your totality."

He leaned back, and crossed his legs. "Okay, Kathleen, since I know you so well, I'll tell you about me. My real name isn't Jimenez. It's Roger Brown."

"Roger Brown? Such a dull name?"

"It may be dull, but it's mine. Maybe I'm a dull guy. Maybe I do outlandish things to impress you. But you have such a kind face, such tender eyes, such compassionate breasts, such a fine nose. Plus, I like your legs—"

"Oh, Jimenez, you're just trying to impress me again."

He straightened. "You're right. But my name *is* Roger Brown. You can go to my house in Bergenfield, New Jersey, and research me." Jimenez held up his hand. "But enough of this chatter. I have more important things to ask. Kathleen, will you marry me?"

"What?"

"Will you marry me?"

"Are you joking?"

"No, I'm serious, Kathleen. I'm thirty-five years old. Time to get married."

"But you don't even know me."

"Of course I do."

"What makes you think so?"

"I looked at you."

"Oh, that again. Just because you look at me doesn't mean you know me."

"Kathleen, I know you. It's just that you don't know I do. But even if I don't know you, so what? Knowledge and marriage have very little to do with each other. My parents, for example, have been married for almost forty years, and they still don't know each other. Hasn't stopped them from staying married. I know another couple, good friends of mine, who claim to know each other intimately. They spend most of their hours together getting to know each other even better than they knew each other before. Last month they got divorced. They said they knew too much about each other and couldn't stand what they knew. Now they're both looking for people they don't know so they can start all over again. I think the idea of knowing each other in marriage is overrated. What you need is knowledge of the higher forces, not knowledge of each other."

Such eloquence by Jimenez made me think. What kind of nut was this man? And he questioned the sanctity of my domain—knowledge, analysis, intellect, rationality, research, the areas where I shone. But as I reflected, I realized Jimenez had faith. That's what made him strange to me. Behind his zany camouflage lay a serenity and faith that nothing could shake. His certainty with women, with his career, even when ordering chicken from the waiter, all derived from that inexplicable, mysterious faith. I didn't understand it. But I could sense it was there.

"So you want to marry me?"

"Yes."

I shook my head, not knowing what to say. I knew Jimenez was serious, yet I couldn't take him seriously. I couldn't laugh either. It was just so strange: I was twenty-nine and ready to get married, too.

We finished eating. Jimenez signaled the waiter, who brought our bill. He paid it, left a big tip, and we walked out.

"Let's walk around town awhile," Jimenez said. "I think better when I walk. Cool air lubricates my brain. How about your brain? Do you like cool air?"

"Sure."

"While we're walking, I'll think about our future, and you can tell me about yourself. Your future looks very good."

"You think so?"

"I know so."

"I like a man who is so definite."

"So do I."

"You don't suffer from false modesty either."

"Of course not. Shall we set a date for our marriage?"

"Hold on, I'm not marrying you."

"Okay. I understand you don't want to be rushed. We'll walk around town awhile. Then we'll decide. Personally, I envision a small wedding, just a few close friends. And perhaps dinner in an Italian restaurant, followed by a honeymoon."

"Jimenez, why do you want to get married? You've got a good life already. And what about children? And freedom? Get married, and your freedom will fade away. Once kids come, it will disappear completely."

"The question is not one of freedom, Kathleen, or of knowing each other, or of getting along, or even of liking each other. Those feelings come and go, floating by like clouds. I'm sure our marriage will have clouds, but freedom is shining behind the clouds. The question of freedom does not concern me."

"What question does concern you?"

"The question, 'Can we *travel together*.' I believe we can. I *know* we can. To prove it, we'll start off by walking around town tonight. Walking is one of my favorite ways of traveling together."

We headed south along Third Avenue. The buildings became smaller, more personal. By the time we hit the Village, I felt better. I liked the sprinkling of tenements, boutiques, and mom-and-pop stores we found along the way. By Wall Street I was full of energy. Finally, when we arrived at the South Street Seaport and walked along the East River, I agreed to get married.

"Will that be to me?" asked Jimenez.

"When I'm ready to get married, the right man will appear," I answered.

Jimenez looked around. "There is no other man in sight. *I* have appeared." He took me by the arm. "Let's go."

Two weeks later we were married in City Hall. We signed a few papers, then went off to an Italian restaurant to begin our honeymoon.

As we strolled down the street Jimenez said, "Of all my wives, you're the best."

"*What?* I never knew you were married before!"

"There is much you don't know about me, Kathleen. That's why we got married, so you can find out."

"That's a dirty trick, Jimenez. You've been lying to me all along."

"I did not lie. You never asked me about my other wives."

"It's not fair! You should have told me!"

"Why? What's the difference? I'm not married to them anymore."

He noticed me boiling. "Don't worry," he said, kissing me on the cheek. "Don't be jealous. My other wives were just for practice. You're for real."

"That doesn't make me feel any better. You used them. Maybe you'll end up using me, too. Is this part of your reincarnation philosophy? Am I just another woman, just another life?"

"Indeed you are. You are another woman *and* another life. And of course I will use you. I use all my women. They use me. It's mutual. Without being used, they'd feel useless, and so would I. As for another life—my wives all welcome another life, especially with me."

"Sounds like a lot of rhetoric to me."

My anger slowly softened. Jimenez did love me in his way. Otherwise, why would he marry me? "What were those other women like, your other wives?" I asked. "Were they as good as I am?"

"No one compares to you, my dear. You are incomparable. On the other hand, my other wives were incomparable, too. All four of them were jewels in their own right."

"*Four* of them? You were married *four times?*"

"Five. But my first marriage was annulled by my mother. I was only eleven years old when I eloped with Maria de la Castendenda and her little dog, Pepe. We spent a weekend at the seashore—then Madre Gansa found us, and we had to go home again."

We headed uptown to our apartment on East 13th Street. As we passed a fruit store, I wondered if marrying Jimenez had been a mistake.

"Is it right to be married four times?" I asked.

"Kathleen, there's nothing wrong with being married many times. It's an education. My marriages were milestones in my path to artistic freedom. But you're my girl now. I'm always faithful to the girl I'm with. I never stray. I just get divorced."

"This is not a good beginning, Jimenez. I can't trust you."

Jimenez kicked a bottle that had fallen out of the overflowing trash can on the corner. "It does not matter if you trust me, Kathleen. We did not get married to trust each other, but to travel together."

Jimenez stopped, looked at me, then towards the Empire State building up ahead. "Our goal is to create—and in the process, to meet God."

"How did God get into this?"

"He's is the one who keeps pushing me. He's the one who got me to practice the guitar every day. He got me into concert work, even got me an apartment on the East Side. When I was younger, before I knew about Him, He worked with Madre Gansa. They worked together until I realized they were all part of the same person. One day, they took me to a concert of the German classical guitarist Ludwig Heimenblotter. I realized, while squirming in my seat through Heimenblotter's dull rendition of the Bach 'Lute Suite in A minor,' that I could play the suite better. At that moment I knew I had been part of His Celestial Team all along. Only my thoughts separated me. So I changed my thoughts. Since then things have been okay."

"That's a lovely story, Jimenez. I'll go along with it, even though I'm an atheist."

"Atheists think more about God than anyone else. Rejecting is a form of acceptance."

A car ran a red light, then screeched to a halt just before the corner. Pedestrians scattered, and cab drivers shook their fists. We stepped up our pace.

"Whatever you think, Jimenez, this God stuff just doesn't sit with me."

"And why should it? With your limited imagination, how can you know? How can you be introduced to these energy

forms? But with me it's different. When I was four years old,
my mother told me the world was created out of guitars. Ever
since then I've known that the guitar is a holy instrument.
Through guitar, I talk to God. We have a personal relationship.
We're buddies. We talk about anything that's on my mind.
Also, stuff that's on his mind. He worries about his creations.
He especially worries about me. He often asks why he put me
on earth. I try to sooth him, tell him it's not a mistake, and that
I'm really not so bad. Sometimes this makes him perk up a bit,
but usually he just looks at me and groans. Sure I feel bad when
he does this—who wouldn't? When your whole existence is
questioned, you tend to lose self- confidence. But then I give a
great concert, and he feels much better. It reminds him he put
me on earth with a purpose."

"You have a friend," I said.

"I do," Jimenez answered. "So do you, but you don't realize
it, since you don't play guitar."

"I know a few chords."

Jimenez looked pleased. "Good," he said. "Then you'll be
meeting sooner or later."

Jimenez took my hand. We swung our arms as we walked
uptown.

"Let's travel on our honeymoon!" I finally said.

"Good," said Jimenez.

He squeezed my hand and picked up the pace.

The Art
of Bonality

Introduction

HISTORIANS CALLED IT "The Age of Rubble." The worst
was accepted as the best. The best was rejected as the
worst. People did not respect their artists and wise men, but
bowed to their fears and hatreds. Genius was feared, but imbe-
ciles were well treated. An imbecile was provided for by the
state, but a genius had to get along by himself. Geniuses were
a threat: They lived above the popular mediocrity of the day.
People resented their lonely existence. Somehow it reminded
them that they too might be lonely if they paused to think of
what they were doing. However, most were too busy earning a
living, watching television or bowling to consider bothering
about the direction of their lives.

It was the age of the airplane and astronaut. It was the age
of flight. And although a great deal of flying was done in
every direction, the greatest flights of all were the flights from
self. These flights from self caused the personality of the
country to be split down the middle. This personality split
was considered a physical split by the census takers who,
when counting, doubled the population of the country. The
census was accepted by the President, who claimed that if a
man's body could be in one place while his mind was in another, he could work in two places at once, thus doubling his

work output.

The music of the period fell into three categories. First was music of the Deep Beat. This was the music of teenagers and children who ran the country through their parents' earning power. Next was Classical music which was governed by electronic gadgetry. Finally, there was Folk Music, which was no longer played by the folk, but by serious classical musicians who could not make a living in their field.

During "The Age Of Rubble" music had lost its deep philosophical meaning. It had become merely a means of earning a living, a quick road to success, fame and fortune. The true roots of the living tone had been forgotten and nobody was interested in finding them again. The search for meaning had stopped. The country was united by its indifference.

The teaching in the schools was absurd. Any expression of interest by a student was squashed by the teacher. Any interest by the teacher was squashed by the principal, and any interest by the principal was squashed by the Board of Education. There was a continual inflow of squashed educators and outflow of bored, restless students who hated school and only wished to graduate to be free. The only goal the teachers and students had in common was the three-o'clock bell. An inspired student was a threat to the class because in his enthusiasm for learning he might go berserk, thereby destroying the monotony of the classroom. Pupils prone to inspiration were put in a special class held in the basement where no one could hear their screams of delight.

Creativity was being destroyed by the system. It was into such a system that Thomas Repent was born.

Youth

THOMAS REPENT WAS BORN in Humble Hospital. The ten months he had spent in his mother's womb gave him more brain power and physical zing. Thus he came out boisterously singing, and his parents realized a musical son was born.

Thomas started piano lessons at the age of five. He quickly learned and mastered the simpler works of Bach and Mozart, and by the age of ten had mastered the music of all the great composers. He then began composing short musical pieces. His first work, "The March of the Vitamins, "was performed in his health education class in public school.

Soon Tom was not satisfied with piano playing. He wanted to learn other instruments. In fact, he wanted to learn every instrument man had created. He began studying the oboe, clarinet, trumpet, flute, bassoon, cello and French horn. When these instruments were mastered, he tried singing. When his voice gave out, he learned guitar, banjo, musical saw, sitar, Chinese Huhu flute, and South African ground hole drum. He learned many more instruments but still he could not express his deepest feelings; still he was not satisfied.

This dissatisfaction led him to the invention of new instruments. He drew up plans for a Musical Holland Tunnel, a Guitaroplane, and Tuba Vacuum Cleaner. He then created the Stone Xylophone consisting of a circle of stones hit with a divining rod. The stones produced different tones giving him much pleasure, but causing the neighbors to move. He invented the Egyptian Tomb Tuba, the Medieval Windbag, the Razorophone which consisted of a razor cutting into a telephone line causing buzzing, fumes, fires and finally a visit from the local fire department and telephone company. He invented the claraviol by sticking a clarinet into a violin and bowing one while blowing the other. Then came the Melodic Meat Grinder, the Organ Exhaust Pipe, the Dog Drone where three dog teeth were brushed against a cinder block. Finally came the Fly Glassophone, where a glass filled with flies was held against your ear in order to hear the musical buzzing.

Every week he would invent another instrument, but still he was not satisfied.

Tom graduated from elementary school and passed the test to enter the special High School of Music and Moneymaking. The purpose of Music and Moneymaking (M and M as it was called) was to combine the "spiritual aspects of music with the practical aspects of moneymaking." Once a year student graduation programs were performed in the New York Stock Exchange.

Tom's first lecture was given in class by his music teacher, Mr. Barker. "Today's subject is music. Music has two aspects, the beautiful, and the financial. These qualities merge when you sell a song.

You may ask, what qualifies me to teach the sweet mysteries of this heavenly art? Let me tell you. First I worked with the Secret Service before deciding to devote myself to the stock market. Here I developed my deep love of music by listening to the ticker tape. In 1929, when minor chords accompanied financial music, I lost all my money and had to earn a living playing the violin in the street. I played the best side-

walk music including Bruckner Boulevard Serenade and Long-
horn's "Short Steer Boogie." I saved my pennies and went to
college. With my varied background I was quickly hired by
this school.

"Today I am going to show you my new method of music writing. In it the treble clef has been changed to a dollar sign, while the
bass clef is a decimal point. This method teaches you to write music
(like a bank account). Every note has a definite time and monetary
value. The longer a note is held, the more interest it gets."

Tom took notes furiously for the next four years enabling
him to graduate Summa Cum Sumac.

After graduation there was a party in the Repent house.
"You're going to love Plop Tech." said his father. "It's one of
the finest colleges in the East. Life begins at college, new ways
of doing things, new people, and new ideas. College is fantastic!
Wish I could go."

"Why don't you, Dad? I'll stay home and watch Mom."

"Now Tom, don't make jokes. Save your regressing for retirement when you can do it on Social Security. Now is your
time to carve a place for yourself in the world."

"But I'm scared, Dad."

"Of course you're scared, Son. You wouldn't be a true Repent
if you weren't. Every Repent is scared. In fact, the prime qualities
of a Repent are fear and misanthropy. These are tempered with
the redeeming qualities of obsequiousness and hypocrisy, which
are glossed over by the higher qualities of universal love and
brotherhood for which our family is best known. We always
make it a point to treat all men as brothers, unless of course they
are in the family. But best of all, ours is a singing family. 'Sing
your troubles away by passing them on to another.' Yes, the Re-

pent code of ethics gives one strength to go on in life. These are my best words to you, my son. Now please go to college!"

And so Thomas went off to college where new worlds opened and old worlds closed. When four years had ended he received his degree in Musical Protoplasm.

He then looked for his first job in a local night club. "I'm Thomas Repent," he said to the owner. "Do you have a job for me? I've just received my degree in Musical Protoplasm."

"Musical what?" asked the owner.

"Musical Protoplasm," replied Thomas. "Such a degree enables me to play any instrument, compose any kind of music and lead any orchestra. It makes me the embodiment of a living musical tone."

This question made Thomas realize the value of his college degree. As he walked out of the club he thought, "Years of practice, years of study, years of scales and arpeggios and what do I have? What's it worth? People do not understand my degrees. People do not understand me. How will I communicate to them? I have played every instrument and none of them satisfies me. Perhaps I must invent a new instrument to express my own feelings. Perhaps that is my mission, to invent a radical new instrument, a new music, an anti-failure pro-growth music." He thought about this as he walked. He had to do something constructive with his life.

The Discovery of Bonality

THOMAS RENTED A CABIN in the mountains for the purpose of study and meditation. He spent three years listening to the sounds of nature around him and wondering how he would express his feeling for these sounds. During this time he never exercised. His joints became stiff.

One morning while sitting under a tree a strange thing happened. He leaned back and suddenly heard a crack coming from an unused joint in his neck. He liked the sound! He turned his neck to the left. He got the same sound only with more bass! He turned his head to the right, same sound only with more treble! *If I can get such sounds from my neck*, he thought, *why can't I get them from the other bones and joints of my body?*

He cracked his knuckles and heard an A flat come out. He cracked his elbows. Out came an F sharp. His shoulders cracked out an A, his hips a B-flat, his backbone a D sharp and his jawbone a G. Soon he was cracking out entire melodies on one arm.

"This is great!" he shouted. "At last I've found the sound I want!" He called this new art form "Bonality."

Every day he practiced bonality. He would warm up with scales on his knee cap, thigh and wrist. Then he moved to broken chords on his knuckles. Soon he could play melody on his right arm and accompany himself on his left. This opened the possibilities of performing sonatas on his vertebrae, and crunching out passages on his elbows.

"Bonality is a revolutionary discovery," he said. "I must now create a musical literature for it." He thus began work on such compositions as "Bonality Breakdown," "Fantasy for Backbone and Knuckle," and "Sonata for Left Hand Alone."

Finally after two more years of practice and composition Thomas felt ready to leave his cabin retreat and return to the city. Now he would work to popularize his new Art of Bonality.

Return

WHEN THOMAS RETURNED TO the city, the first place he went to was the Mammoth Booking Agency in New York.

"May I speak with Mr. Mammoth?" he asked the secretary.

"You'll have to make an appointment," she said. "What instrument do you play?"

"I play my bones," said Tom.

"Bones? Huh, why do we get all the nuts?" the secretary muttered to herself.

"Yes, I play my bones." repeated Thomas, and he cracked out a few measures of the "Star Spangled Banner" to demonstrate.

The secretary stared in amazement. "I've never seen anyone do that before," she said. "Wait here. I'll get Mr. Mammoth."

A few minutes later Thomas was invited into Mr. Mammoth's office. A sign hung under a picture of an elephant, which read *Buy Mammoth on the Sabbath.*

"Good morning, Mr. Repent," said Mr. Mammoth leaning back in his chair and squinting through his eyeglasses. "I hear you have an exciting new act for us."

"It is not an act, sir," replied Thomas. "It is an art."

"Oh, don't worry about that," said Mr. Mammoth. "We book that, too. Where have you performed before?"

"I do not perform, Mr. Mammoth, I concertize."

"Well, son, go out and get some experience in the field. Then come back and we'll talk some more."

Thomas began to redden with anger. "How dare you insult me! I did not come here to ask you for work. I came here because I have chosen you to work for me. Consider yourself and your organization fortunate that I have chosen them to help further my career."

Mr Mammoth started to get angry, but then his anger turned to laughter. "Mr. Repent, your approach to management is certainly unique. Before I throw you out, let's see a little of what you can do."

"I do not concertize under threats of violence," replied Thomas. "However, in this case, since I need a job, I will make an exception." He then began cracking out his own arrangement of Beethoven's *Fifth Symphony*.

When Thomas finished, Mr. Mammoth looked stunned. "I must admit I've never heard that kind of sound before. Very original, very original indeed. I think we'll be able to work together. We'll begin planning your debut in Town Hall at once."

Concert

THOMAS HAD BEEN PLANNING his debut concert for years. Now his great moment was to arrive. All over New York he saw posters..., "First Bonality Concert in History." The newspapers were filled with ads. Many critics had called the Mammoth Agency asking, "What's Bonality all about?" Interest was stirring in underground music circles. Musical journals were trying to get interviews with Thomas, while many music schools were thinking that if Bonality was a successful new sound they would have to find bonality teachers.

The concert was scheduled for March 21st, the first day of spring. This day symbolized both the rebirth of nature and the birth of bonality. Thomas got to Town Hall early that night to warm up. He went through his exercises while the hall began to fill up. By 8:30 there was standing room only.

The lights dimmed. The spotlight threw a white circle of light on the center of the stage. Then Thomas walked out, bowed, and began his concert by cracking his neck. Then he played a rondo on his right arm. This was immediately followed by the Backbone Concerto. As the melody was being crunched out on his vertebrae, he added luscious harmony on his ankles and flowing counterpoint on his shoulders and knees. The mellow tones of his joints filled the hall. His bone cracking penetrated every ear.

When the concerto ended, there was absolute silence. The audience was too stunned to move. Not a hand clapped as Thomas bowed. Undaunted, Thomas launched right into his biggest piece, the "Messiah Sonata." Its crunching melody, grinding harmonies, and trills on the rib cage brought the audience to a new emotional low. Many walked out, though some were still too stunned to move. Thomas then cracked out his own arrangement of "Tubas Forever," by Mortimer Beethoven. More people walked out. He tried a Lawrence Haydn quartet on his knuckles and a rock song on his neck, but people kept leaving. Boos sounded from both sides of the hall. He heard a woman in the first row say, "Disgusting!"

"Belongs in an asylum," said another.

"Drug addict," said an elderly gentleman.

By the end of the concert only three people were left in the hall, and two of them were janitors.

No one came to the post-concert reception, not even the Mammoth Agency. Thomas went home and cried for three days. He wanted to commit suicide but was afraid of the pain. Once he stopped crying however, a terrible rage began to consume him. "My bonality is so revolutionary that no one understands or appreciates it," he shouted as his fist tore through his pillow. "Every artist who is ahead of his time must fight public ignorance and indifference. Why should I be an exception? I must find a few brave souls who dare to open their minds and appreciate bonality. I must find the chosen few who dare to bare their true feelings and express their true selves. The public is used to hiding its innermost thoughts. I stood before them in Town Hall, stripped away all falsity, gave them real emotion in music, and they responded by running away. They were afraid to feel. They are weak and frightened. But there is hope. I must educate them, teach them to conquer their fears, show them the emotional release of bonality. My real work now is to educate the public. I must find an audience for bonality. I will begin a bonality school. Books must be written, teachers must be informed, an advertising campaign must be organized. A campaign must be waged against public ignorance. People must learn to feel again. Their bodies and minds must unite. Bonality is the music of the body. It is the music of feeling. People must learn to hear and feel again.

" Most adults are fixed in their ways. I must begin with children. They are open to change and new approaches. They can feel their bodies and have not yet been closed off from themselves by demands of parents, schools and community. Children hold the future for bonality."

Thus Thomas felt a new hope rising. Though both public and Mammoth Agency had dropped him, he nevertheless felt stronger. He wouldn't be pushed around by what others expected of him. He wouldn't be a prisoner of approval. His new hope in bonality had given him a cause, and this cause gave him guts, built his character from an egocentric, arrogant, self-proclaimed genius, into a more selfless man totally devoted to his new art.

First Grade

FRIEDA GILFRY BROUGHT HER son to a tomb-shaped building called Public School 8. "This will be your daytime home for the next eight years," she chirped. They went down some dark steps and entered the classroom.

The teacher introduced herself as Mrs. Toad, guardian of morality and self-proclaimed leader of children. Thomas sat down in a seat which was still wet from the leaky pen of a previous pupil. "That is your new seat," said Mrs. Toad. "You should be proud to have such a seat. Many brilliant pupils have used it in the past."

Mrs. Gilfry left the room and the class began. The first topic was the birth of Mrs. Toad. She explained, "You see, children, life is created by the combination of sperm and egg. However, there have been certain exceptions to this rule. Our Lord Jesus Christ was one of them, and I am the other. Instead of being impregnated by another man, my mother was impregnated by God. She would never let another man touch her, and neither would I. All my children will be born through this virgin birth as it is called. I wouldn't have it any other way. Now, how many children in this class have been born like me?"

The children looked at her blankly. Thomas yawned, then stretched. His hands rose high in the air as he did so.

"So, my boy," said Mrs. Toad to Thomas, "you too are a product of virgin birth. I am glad someone here didn't need a father. The world would be a better place if less time were spent in bed."

Then Mrs. Toad pointed to some letters along the top of the blackboard. "Today we will learn the alphabet. When we speak or write, we use words. They are made of letters. All the letters are part of the alphabet. There are 26 letters. I want you to re-peat them after me.'

The class spoke the letters together. Then they learned a song to help them remember it.

Thomas went home after school excited about the alphabet. He practiced writing and saying the letters until he knew them perfectly. At supper time he recited the whole alphabet to the surprise of his family.

I see your first day at school has been a success," said his fa-ther. "Do you know the Chinese alphabet is different from ours? Their letters look like pictures. They sound like singsong. When we hear a Chinese person talk it sounds strange. But when a Chinese person hears us talk he laughs because we're so strange.

"Then there's the Greek and Russian alphabet whose letters are still different. When you go to the museum you'll see an-cient Egyptian letters which were actually pictures of things. There's just no end to the number of alphabets you can make."

Thomas went to his room after supper, his head swimming in alphabets. He lay down on his bed and dreamed about strange letters and foreign sounds. He thought about all the things he couldn't say because he didn't know enough words. He felt frustrated. No matter how many alphabets he learned he still wouldn't be able to say everything he wanted to say.

Then he had an idea. Why should he use other people's faulty alphabets? Why bother with their faulty creations?After all, he had nothing to do with writing their alphabet. Why should other people force him to use their alphabet? Why should he say things *their* way? He had his *own* way of saying things. Therefore, he would make up his own alphabets.

He began by collecting sounds. First there were human sounds such as burps, gargles, bone cracking, coughs, and singing. Then there were the sounds of human beings relating to one another such as silence, purring, screams, stomach rumbling, heartbeats, pulse, the hissing of osmosis, the growing of capillaries, the shouting of sperm cells and the gossip of ova.

The non-human sounds followed, such as sirens, honking, airplanes, roaring, pile drivers banging, shopping bags swinging, wind groaning, trains moaning, plants growing, and rivers flowing.

Thomas gathered forty-two pages of sounds. Slowly the magic of synthesis was taking place in his mind; slowly the sounds were combining into the Gilfrian alphabet. That night he sat down to compose it.

Aump
Blub
Crapblab
Dlump
Eept

Floop
Greetch
Hablebable
Ish
Jujaw
Klab
Lupf
Mumpf
Numpf
Ompf
Pumpe
Queg
Reltch
Skreltch
Tubble
Umpf
Vɪyap
Weetch
Xeblehoffle
Yeeps
Zeebeeskrootchenbufflebierberg

Gilfry Meets His Ancestor Tobias

ONE EVENING AT THE end of a Gilfry concert, a skeleton jumped on the stage and said, "My fellow skeletons, I am the great grandfather of Thomas Gilfry. Three cheers for Thomas. He has brought the art of bonality to the public. He has turned the human skeleton into a concert instrument. He has given skeletons a place in the world. He has given the dead a chance to express themselves. If not for him I could not be here tonight. The living have forgotten the dead. But the dead shall inherit the earth with the living. Because of Thomas Gilfry it is no longer a crime to be dead. He has given the dead a respectable place in society. Death is in every person. When they know this they will begin to dance. The death dance is the most beautiful dance ever created. (It is a monument to life.) No living person should be without it."

When Thomas Gilfry heard this, he rushed back to the stage. "Are you Tobias?" he asked.

"I am," replied the skeleton. "I have been in the grave many years waiting to be resurrected. Who would have thought you would be my savior? When your grandfather died, he told me were an idiot. You just can't trust a person who has died."

They walked to the wings of the stage as half the audience fainted.

"By the way," said Thomas, "have you ever seen New York City? Most of it had not been built when you were alive."

"That's true," said Tobias, "but I've heard a lot about it-from the corpses (boys) in the cemetery."

Thomas and Tobias walked down Fifth Avenue. Although the streets were crowded, few saw the odd couple since most people refuse to see the living and the dead walking together.

"When were you alive?" asked Thomas.

"My years were 1816 to 1871," replied Tobias. "In those days musicians really had a hard time. No free training schools and no jobs. And if you cracked your bones you'd be jailed."

"We have many music schools now," said Thomas.

"I'd like to see one."

"Fine. We'll visit the Fewbard School of Music. It's just three stops on the subway." Thomas bought a token and went through the turnstiles, but Tobias got through for nothing since he had no body.

They arrived at Fewbard and saw two bonality players practicing scales on their elbows and knuckles. When they walked past, one of the players looked at Tobias and said, "There's a man who really practices.

"Yeah," said the other. "Just shows what a little hard work can do for the figure."

"This school has two floors," said Thomas. "The second teaches only bonality, whereas the first is for more conventional music."

They walked in. The first floor was lined with practice rooms. They opened one of the doors and found a student practicing on a coffee pot.

"Can you play a Gregorian chant on your pot?" asked Tobias.

"I don't play Communist songs," said the student.

Tobias was about to ask another question when suddenly a gong rang. Students rushed out of their practice rooms to lunch. In the emptiness of the hall the gong spoke.

"I am the school gong. Students run when they hear me clang. Our purpose in this school is to turn students into instruments. We do this by using instruments to teach our students.

"All our music has been written by the dead. Therefore all

our music is dead. Even I am getting tired of ringing. These are tired times. Long ago a student would roar before he would snore. Now he snores and never roar. Return to the grave Tobias. There is more life there than in this music school."

Just then the director of the school came storming down the hall. He grabbed Tobias by the arm. "How dare you come into s school like this!" he said. "I'm going to call the police and have you arrested."

Thomas Gilfry groaned, "Will the living and the dead *ever* come to understand each other? Sir, this is Tobias Gilfry, one of the great names in music history. He composed the Turnip Serenade which all your students are required to play before breakfast."

"Oh, is that right?" said the director. "Then, if he is so successful, why did he die? Where is his body?"

"Tobias was taken away in 1871," replied Thomas. "You see sir, Tobias is dead."

"I'm sorry about that," repented the director. "I didn't mean to speak so harshly. It's just that he looks so alive."

"I think big thoughts," said Tobias. "It keeps my figure trim and keeps me hopping around."

"Well, we've never had a dead person visit our school," said the director, "although many of our visitors have been close to death. Some have died after visiting our school. Between you and me, it's a miserable place to learn anything. The bonality section on the second floor is our only hope for the future."

"Bonality will save the world," said Thomas.

"I certainly hope it saves *me*," said the director. "If I don't produce a good student soon the board of directors will fire me."

Bonality Marches On

THOMAS RETURNED TO HIS mountain cabin to meditate and also to write. After three months he produced the one literary work on bonality, entitled *Tone or Drone*. In this work he expounded upon the philosophical foundations of the art. ". . .bonality fuses the banality of tonality with the finality of musicality resulting in reality." The book goes on to describe ideal bonality children's workshops, a history of bonality, a few bonal beginner's pieces, and the relationship of people to music. In the words of Thomas Repent, I quote from the last chapter:

"For centuries civilization and its taboos have pushed people's feelings into the gutter. People whose feelings are in the gutter can stand no higher than the gutter. It is the work of bonality to free people to climb out of the gutter...."

After his book was completed Thomas returned to the city. He traveled from house to house trying to find parents willing to send their children to his school. The only ones who would consider it were parents who wanted to get rid of their children. In the beginning he only had three students. Then something happened which was to change the course of his life.

Disc jockeys throughout the country had been working and looking for a new sound. Thomas had recorded the Backbone Concerto, with Knuckle Rot on the flip side and sent it to one hundred radio stations, One jockey, as a joke, played it on his program. Almost instantly his telephone began ringing as hundreds of listeners called. Who was the composer? Who was the recording artist? What was that sound? Other disc jockeys picked it up. Soon the Backbone Concerto was number one on the music charts. Radio stations played it countless times a day. Thomas began to receive phone calls. TV specials wanted him on their program. Colleges were asking for bonality concerts. Record companies and agents were calling for exclusive rights to his bonality compositions, performances and lecture appearances. Soon he didn't have a moment to himself. He was besieged by fans, agents and businessmen looking to sell their products through his name.

The next years brought one success after another. His concerts were given to thousands of cheering fans. His bow brought a mellow A flat from his backbone. Then he would open with the popular Backbone Concerto, followed by Variations on an Empty Knee Cap, Bonality Break-down and Knuckle Rot. After each concert he spoke with the audience about "Repent University," a school he was starting to teach up-and-coming bonality players. The leading music critic of the New York Grimes now said of Thomas, "Thomas Repent was once ugly, but today he is beautiful. He has changed himself from a squeaking runt into a musical prince through his art. Bonality purifies the mind and body by emptying them of the garbage of everyday existence. No longer does he walk through the streets like a trash can making ugly and empty noises. Music makes your body beautiful. It is true that Mr. Repent's face has changed little since the old Town Hall concert. But today, when people look at him, they are in reality listening to him through his eyes. And when they hear the beautiful sound of his bones cracking they can't help but love him."

This life force had surged through Thomas Repent from the day he was born. It was so great that words alone could not express it. From his vital center came a force which caused his bones to crack. And his bones were extensions of the world around him. They were hard, strong, and yet they could sing and dance. They were the highways over which new thoughts traveled from his body to his mind. They sent blood messages to the tiniest islands of his body. No cell remained uninformed. Always the message came, "I must come through. I must speak!"

When Thomas Repent reached the age of ninety-six his eyes were hollowed by years of bone cracking. The time had come to return to the true father of bonality, the maker of cosmic tones and maker of all bones. He felt at peace with himself. "His life had been a success. Not the simple-minded success of mass worship and financial riches, but a success in the deeper knowledge that he had experienced great music and shared it with others. He had left a legacy behind him: those who knew him would continue to develop bonality after he died.

Thomas sat in his armchair remembering the original vision. He wanted to see everyone cracking their bones, laughing and dancing together. He now knew this vision had driven him all his life. He had been the first to speak through his bones. He expressed a deeper reality. His music was earth music. Were not the volcanic fires of the earth caused by the friction of the earth's unexercised joints? Did-

n't the earth crack when it quaked? Were not the earth-
quakes expressions of earth bones fighting to speak the
essence of the earth? They had been trying for mill"ions of
years. The urge for self expression could never be destroyed.
Human beings were no different from the earth in this respect. Rivers poured, rocks melted, seas withdrew, then returned to flood continents, and always the great life force
unseen behind each mammoth minute kept saying, "I must
come through. I must speak!"

Business

Depressions Can Be Fun

TOM LOCKWOOD KICKED THE wall. Why wasn't he getting more out of his depressions? Whenever Jack Blotnick got depressed, he went to Florida; whenever Sarah and Sidney got depressed, they ate deli; whenever rich Harry Fosnut got depressed, he bought a new car—or a new business. Even Toots Lint, when he got depressed, went to bed.

Everyone Tom knew got benefits from depressions.

Couldn't he?

He wanted to talk out his problem with his therapist, Dr. Jones, but Jones had just run himself over with his car. He wanted to tell his mother, but she was too busy with her own depression. Uncle Nat was out of town collecting seashells in Montana, and Ronda, Tom's back-rubber, spent most of her time dissecting frogs.

"I'll take a walk," he sighed. "Maybe I'll feel better." He wandered through the business section of town. As he passed the Small Business Administration, a door opened and a man dressed in a gray business suit stepped out. He took Tom by the arm and helped him into the cluttered office.

"I'm looking for small businessmen," he said. "Won't you sit down?"

Tom slumped into a chair.

"What's the matter?" the man continued. "Perhaps I can help you?"

"Oh. . ." Tom sighed. "I'm so depressed. I don't know what to do."

"Do you feel bad?"

"Bad? Are you kidding? I feel terrible."

"It could be your attitude. Depressions can be fun, you know."

"Ha, that's a laugh!"

"Yes, but only if you know how to handle them."

"Well, I'd sure like to know how to do that."

"It's simple." The man poured coffee for Tom and himself. Then he explained, "Here's what you do: Instead of using your depressions to depress yourself, use them to depress other people."

"Huh?"

"You could make a business out of depression. Call it *Depressions Incorporated*. The Small Business Administration would gladly get you started with a loan."

Tom sat up in his chair. Was this guy nuts? "Business?" he asked.

"Of course. You've already got the product—depression. You just need to get customers by promoting and selling."

"That's all very well," Tom said, "but I don't know how to promote things. I'm a lousy salesman."

"You must be joking," the man scoffed. "You're an excellent salesman. Why, ever since you walked into my office, I've felt depressed. Do you realize you have the power to depress others?"

"I hadn't thought about it like that—"

"Well? Not everyone can depress others. It's a talent. You should develop it."

"But don't you think people want to avoid depression?"

"Absolutely not. Depression is the prelude to creation." The gray-suited man started to cry.

"I'm sorry I'm making you cry."

"Don't be sorry. I thank you for sharing your talent with me. When you start your new company, I'll be your first customer."

Tom knew the man was right. All his life he had managed to depress people. Now he could do something constructive with it, build a nationwide—even worldwide—organization. By advertising on TV he might even be able to depress the whole country! What potential! Suddenly, he began to see thousands of dollar bills in the coffers of his new company. He might even become a millionaire! And all he had to do was be himself—his good old miserable depressing self.

"Thanks for your help," Tom said. "I'm going to start my own business." He rose to leave. "Funny," he added as he reached the door, "I feel better already."

"Watch out for that," the man warned. "You'll never make any money that way." Tom caught himself. "What I meant was, I feel bad about feeling better."

"That's better. It's good to feel bad, but it's better to feel worse. Guilt can be a powerful sales tool."

Tom left the SBA office filled with hope.

Paying Off a Loan

I CHARGED INTO THE BANK Monday morning, frantically looking for money to pay off the loan shark swimming behind me. The teller said, "Go downstairs to the vault." I took the steps three and four at a time with the shark snapping at my heels. Luckily the vault was open. I raced in, tripped over a bag of coins, and fell headlong into a pile of cash. Feeling relief, I gathered the piles together and stuffed them in the loan shark's mouth. His huge jaws snapped greedily on the greenbacks. When he'd had enough, he swam clumsily out of the vault, up the stairs. His fin got stuck in the revolving door, but he wrestled free and escaped down Ocean Avenue.

I sat in the remaining pile of cash, sweating. That was a close call, I thought.

Then I saw a beautiful woman coming towards me. She had long blond hair down to her waist, a slender lithesome figure, and tight skirt with cash receipts printed all over it. Her legs were so close together, I could easily tell she was the bank mermaid.

"What are you doing here?" she gasped. "Help! Help! A *robber!*"

"*Please* don't shout," I said. "My ears are very sensitive to pressure. I'm not a bank robber. I only came in for a loan. I had to pay off a debt in a hurry. Now that I have, I feel much better. Perhaps you can sit down and we can talk?"

She looked me over. Slowly, she calmed down as she realized I was harmless. "We've had several robberies lately," she explained, perching herself on a stack of hundred-dollar bills. "I guess I'm a bit jittery."

We sat for half an hour discussing the banking business, foreign currency, and the falling value of the dollar. "Imagine," I laughed, "soon those hundreds you're sitting on will be almost worthless."

"Yes, it's a real problem," she answered. "Sitting on dollars won't keep inflation down."

Her name was Esther. We left the bank together and I took her phone number.

We saw each other during the next few days. I was so happy to be free of debt! Now I could love again. And what a beautiful woman I had to love! It made me realize that banks can offer more than just money.

On Friday afternoon, I went to the bank to meet her. Suddenly, I saw the loan shark swimming down the street and coming after me again.

"What do you want?" I growled. "I just paid you off!"

"Like hell you did!" said the shark angrily. "Those dollars you gave me ain't worth nothin' no more. I wanna be paid off in gold. Ain't you heard about inflation?"

The old panic returned. I started to run. The shark chased me. How could I repay him? I ran ahead of his ferocious snaps. I headed towards the bank. It was my only hope. Charging through the revolving door, I dashed down the stairway, leaping three and four stairs at a time. Luckily the vault was still open. I raced in, tripped over a bag of gold coins and fell headlong into a pile of cash. "Take the coins," I yelled. "Take the coins!"

I picked up handfuls of coins and shoved them into his greedy mouth. I could hear his sharp teeth grinding them into dust. As he swallowed, I knew his digestive enzymes would compact all the coins it into gold bars. Finally, the shark had had enough. He swam clumsily out of the bank and down Ocean Avenue. I sat in my pile of cash, waiting for Esther.

She arrived looking concerned.

"What happened?" she asked. "I was worried about you."

"The shark was after his money again," I said. "But don't

worry. I gave him the gold in the vault. He's satisfied now." I wiped my sweating brow with my handkerchief. "Let's go out to supper together?"

"Good idea." She took my hand. "You've had a rough day."

I agreed. We headed for a nearby seafood restaurant, entered the back room, and sat down in a quiet corner.

"Relax," said Esther in a soothing voice. "It's all over now. Put your mind at ease and eat your fish."

The waiter brought out their seafood orders. She looked closely at my plate. "Hmm," she mused thoughtfully, "looks like shark."

I studied my plate. "You're right," I gleefully jabbed my fork into the fish. I ate with a vengeful smile of satisfaction.

Hell Travel

HI, MY NAME IS RUTH. I'm in the travel business. For three years, I struggled when I opened my own travel agency. During these dry business years, not one customer came through the door. That's why, even thought my name Ruth comes from the Hebrew-Anglo-Saxon etymological root meaning "pity" or "compassion," I didn't feel much of either.

Those were down times.

Finally, I got so frustrated I fried myself. It didn't work. A month later, I tried boiling. No success. Over the year I attempted other methods of suicide but none worked.

That's when I realized I was immortal.

After that I didn't mind being kicked around and vilified by friends, relatives, and the local press. Rejections by the unions and family didn't bother me either. After all, rejections are merely temporal. In a hundred years or so, all my critics will be gone. But I'll still be around forever. That's something to be proud of. Not many business people can say that.

Speaking of business, I started a new travel agency. It all began when one of my friends answered my request for funds by saying: 'Go to hell!'

This gave me an idea: Why not do it?

So I went to hell.

The visit inspired me. I created a new form of travel! It shows how helpful friendship can be. My friend told me to go to hell, and I went.

After my first trip, I decided to lead a tour to the underworld.

Then I renamed my travel company Hell Travel. Pain professionals loved the name. As the public learned more about this hot new destination, I was amazed at the positive response we got. There was a huge market for this kind of travel.

Remember, if anyone tells you to "go to Hell!" inform them about our services. We'll bring them straight to hell—and at a low price, too!

Our ad in the *New York Times* reads: 'Go to Hell with us!'

Economy tours start at $995. They provide the basic itinerary of fires, but offer only one pitchfork; stabbings are all performed by professionals from a Hieronymus Bosch painting.

Clients often ask: How do we decide on prices?

Here's how it works: Hell has many levels or "circles." Prices depend on how many circles you want to visit. For example, Economy Hell tours give you only one circle. Although not as in-depth, you nevertheless get a general picture of life below. Travelers meet the condemned, burn with the natives, and acquire an overall view of what their future might be.

We also offer extra portions of torture for those who register early!

Hell Travel doesn't limit tours to the living. We promote among the dead as well. But we charge them a lower fee.

Luxury Hell Tours start at $4,995. These trips explore every level. Dante only wrote about nine circles. But he never really went to Hell himself except in his imagination. The poet added Purgatory and Paradise to attract more readers and soften the blow.

On the other hand, our company softens nothing. We're proud to say our tours are just plain hell. We visit more circles than Dante. Twenty-six, to be exact. We've also added root canal and psychotherapy at no extra cost!

The introduction to our *Travel Manual of Infernal Travel* states our simple business philosophy: *Rejection presents a hell of a challenge. Welcome it!*

My travel career has been built on rejection. I've turned it into a flourishing business. So can you.

One final suggestion: Don't go to hell alone.

Come with us!

Success Story

FERNANDO DEFECTIO LOVED FAILURE. Every morning before he went to work, he fell down on his knees and prayed: "Oh, Great One, fill my days with shortcomings."

When his boss told him he was incompetent, he smiled

proudly and said "Thank you." When he read a letter from his estranged wife condemning him, he felt fulfilled; when his friends tasted his soup and spat it out, cursing his cuisine, his day was made.

At the beginning of Fernando's career, he had been satisfied with ordinary mistakes. But soon he tired of these. How could his art grow? he asked. What about self-improvement?

His first attempt at improvement had been to develop a limp. In this manner, he had been able to trip over himself and fall on almost anything. He had lurched into a china shop once, breaking priceless cups and dishes. When the owner called the police, Fernando had thanked him by falling into the window display.

Since he had no previous record, the arresting officer, a student of political history specializing in the decline of Rome, had dismissed him with a simple warning: "If I catch you claudicating around here anymore, I'll pummel your *pupick*!"

Out of a job and a spouse, Fernando found himself with a lot of free time. Determined to develop himself, he went to the library to study failures of the past. Now he was no longer satisfied with just ordinary failures—only Great Failures would do. He wanted to become a model for future generations. "Some day, parents will tell their children about me," he proclaimed.

After months of study, he learned to botch up answers to any question, misinterpret information, and speak incomprehensibly.

During the next few years his failures began to achieve recognition. Jobs started coming in.

His first professorship came from a university in Indiana. Hundreds of students attended his lectures, carefully trying to misunderstand everything he said. The "success" of this course was overwhelming. A poll taken at the end of the semester disclosed that not one student knew what the professor was talking about.

The following semester, Fernando, in an attempt to eliminate all efficiency from his classes, presented a new series of lectures entitled, "Achievement Through Error." Many students, registering by mistake, flocked to the wrong room in order to miss his course.

By the end of the semester, Fernando's classes were moving rapidly—both clockwise and counterclockwise. His amazing progress in no direction convinced the university president to award him with the Medal of Defection.

Today, Fernando is proud of his past mistakes and hopes to make more in the future. His advice to his admirers is simple: "Success is not easy—but neither is failure."

Jones Corners the Water Market

IT WAS A NEW DAY in the life of If-The-Shoe-Fits-Wear-It Jones. As President of First Caterpillar Firm, he had created the motto "Down the Pillar!" which helped turn Greek columns into delicatessens.

First Caterpillar banked on the Danube where water flowed into its coffers. Indeed, its currency was neither the Franc, Forint, Deutschmark, or dollar, but the silver liquid of water. As First Caterpillar's vaults filled with hydrogen and oxygen, Jones watched his water empire grow. As he watched water banks rise everywhere, he dreamed about someday cornering the water market.

That's when the staff realized Jones was a madman. Everyone knew except his water-worshiping wife, Penelope. Jones not only had his eye on the river sources of Europe but cast an acquisitive glance on the Atlantic and Pacific as well.

"If I can corner those markets, I'll be Water King of the world!" he roared. "No one will ever dump on me again!" His eyes filled with tears as this vision of perfection gathered in his loins. That morning, he visited his therapist, Dr. Eyehav Urine.

"Doctor, what is my prognosis?" he asked in a watery tone. "Will I be able to conquer the water markets of the world? Or will I be forced to sit in my closet all day drinking bottled water?"

The good doctor rose: "I have to go the john," he said.

Language

A Tense Mood

I REMEMBER WHEN PLUPERFECT CAME to visit Conditional. After dining on a mixed clause and verb grill, Pluperfect said: "Conditional, I love dependent types like you. Do you love me?"

"Love you?" Conditional considered the matter. "That would depend…"

"Depend on what?"

Conditional paused seductively on a morsel of would, and whispered: "That would depend on your clause."

"I have an independent clause," Pluperfect boasted.

As soon as he spoke these words, he recalled his best friend Future Perfect, and how he had asked him for help in his quest for Conditional. "With your help, I might marry Conditional," he had said.

"Might?" Future Perfect had asked.

"Oh, no!" Pluperfect had shouted, nearly jumping out of his sentence. "I'm beginning to sound as moody as that creep Subjunctive." He had straightened his tense, paused, and continued, "I'll be more definite. If I were to ignore Subjunctive, I would marry Conditional."

"Much better," Future Perfect had replied, nodding his auxiliary in agreement. "I'll help you."

"Thanks."

Pluperfect had felt encouraged. When he met Subjunctive on the following day, he had punched him right in his Mood, shouting, "I don't mind an Indicative Mood, or an Imperative Mood, but I can't stand a Subjunctive Mood!" Then he'd kicked him in his If.

Subjunctive had fallen to the ground, his verbs leaking. Gasping, he'd said, "If I were you, I wouldn't do that again."

"Spoken like a true Subjunctive," Pluperfect had sneered.

"You may be right," Subjunctive had replied before lapsing into unconsciousness.

Pluperfect cried out: "Had, had, *had, had!*" as victorious Pluperfects have done for ages. Then he marched off to meet Conditional.

When he reached her home, he knocked politely and entered. Kneeling humbly on a verb, he asked: "Will you marry me?"

"I'm so glad you finally asked," Conditional cooed, flashing a smile.

Next week, at the wedding ceremony, Pluperfect said: "Conditional, I'll always love you."

"And I'll always remember when you would love me," Conditional answered.

And Subjunctive, who was worst man at the wedding, said: "If I had known all this would happen, I never would have come."

What Are Friends For?

TOM WAS SUFFERING FROM writer's block. After three weeks, he said, "I'll visit Jack. It will relax me."

Jack lived on the other side of town. Tom needed exercise, so he decided to walk.

On the way he passed trees, homes, children playing on the sidewalk, and a tunnel. Two trucks drove by. Finally, he saw Jack's house up ahead.

What a magnificent Dutch colonial structure it was! Richly decorated shutters hung from the side of each window; a red brick facade shone in the afternoon sunlight; a slate roof crowned the spacious second floor, and white smoke was rising from the tall, stately chimney.

Then Tom noticed smoke coming out of the *windows*. He saw more smoke creeping along the walls; it started to seep through the bottom of the front door.

Jack's house was on fire!

Tom smashed open the front door and rushed into the living room. He ran down the hallway and found Jack in the bedroom, suffocating from smoke and coughing out his guts. Grabbing his friend by the hand and collar, he managed to drag him out just as the roof collapsed.

The two friends sat safely on the front lawn.

"That was a close call," gasped Jack. "Thanks for saving my life!"

Tom sighed as he wiped beads of sweat from his brow.

"But am I worth saving?" Jack continued. "I've been so down and depressed ever since my novel was rejected for the sixteenth time. I appreciate your effort, but it would have been better to save the sofa."

"Cut it out, Jack," Tom said as one of the walls started burning. "Any life is worth saving, especially yours."

They watched as the roof caught fire. "How did this happen?"

"When you hear why," Jack replied as sirens screamed in the distance, "you'll know I'm a true friend. *I lit it.*"

"*You?*"

"*Yes, me.* I love the sound, smell, and warmth of a fire. But the real reason I lit it is cure your writer's block. I did it to give you a subject for your next story. I did it for *you!*"

"Me?"

"Yes, Tom. After all, what are friends for?"

That was Jack's last utterance before the fire engines and ambulance arrived.

Tom waved goodbye as the medics took Jack away.

"What a friend!" he said, before heading home. "The embers from Jack's house will fire my mind. I'll dedicate my next story to him."

A-Muse-Ing

I WAITED FOR MY MUSE to show up. I like her. She always runs around naked when she comes. But I can't seem to catch her. She's light-footed, lighthearted, and full of fun. There's something devilish about her. Maybe it's her enigmatic smile.

One day, she appeared again.

"Muse, you beauty," I said. "I hope you stay here forever."

"I'll do as I please."

I couldn't stand her independence.

Suddenly, I had an idea: Chains! That's it! I'll chain her to the computer. She'll never escape.

I took a chain out of my desk drawer. When her back was turned, I grabbed her, threw her against my keyboard, and chained her to the keys. Now, beautifully bound to letters A and R, she was mine!

I gazed upon her. Longing and desire flooded my mind. I waited for her to give me an idea. . . .But nothing happened.

She laughed. "You idiot! Chains can't hold me. You're wasting your time. Let me go. Keep trying this and you'll never catch me!"

She was right. A chained muse means nothing.

Sadly, I released her. "Is there anything I can do to keep you?" I asked.

She smiled seductively. "One thing."

"Yes?"

"Forget me."

"How can I forget you? I need you."

That enigmatic smile again. "Forget me," she repeated, and strolled out the door.

For a week, I felt depressed. I shopped, read, jogged, watched TV, and took walks.

Months passed.

One morning, I awoke feeling fresh and alert. I went straight to my desk. Voilá! She was standing by my chair, naked and beautiful as ever.

"I never expected to see you again!" I said. She was so alluring. How could I have forgotten her?

She pointed to the blank screen on my computer monitor. "Sit down," she commanded. "Get to work."

"Yes, ma'am!"

I sat down and wrote this piece.

Mr. Olby Through a Wall

HARRY OLBY LOVED WORDS. He loved collecting them and taking them to work in his car. At the office he filed them in a separate drawer. He played with them during lunch break; he even spoke to them.

That's why, one evening after work, he said to Clara, "I need a room where I can play with my words in private."

His wife nodded slowly, then fell asleep in her armchair.

The next day she was surprised to see her husband working in the back yard. "What on earth are you doing?" she asked.

"Building my new room."

"But why are you building it like that?"

"It's the only way to build a room nowadays," Harry replied. "Inflation is pushing up the price of lumber, bricks, plumbing, and insulation; heat and electricity are going up, not to mention skyrocketing labor costs.... Nowadays, the most economical way to build a room is out of words."

As construction of his room proceeded, Harry's neighbors began eying him strangely.

"He's half-cracked," Mr. Parsnips muttered one morning,

walking his dog past Harry's house.

"Poor guy," Freeman Jones said to his wife as they drove by in their new Ford. "Might be 'cause he's so overworked at the office."

The neighbors' comments didn't disturb Harry. "My room will be the best in town," he affirmed, and he began raising the north wall with clauses. He filled in the cracks with spare letters and roofed it over with a paragraph. For added insulation, he put two run-on sentences between the walls. Then he made a desk and chair out of spare commas, cut out a bay window with hyphens, and laid down a period rug.

Stepping aside, he surveyed his work.

"Sure looks good," he said, smiling in satisfaction. "Just what I've always wanted."

He named it Personal Playpen.

Harry was happy in Personal Playpen. Every day after coming home from work, he would eat supper, take a hot shower, and relax in his room.

One day Harry and Clara received an official letter from the State, announcing that a new highway would soon be built right through their house. The entire block was scheduled for demolition. Naturally, they would receive payment for their home and subsequent relocation.

Clara was terribly upset. The neighbors were furious. They signed petitions against the highway, picketed the governor's office, and tried suing the state. But in the end they were defeated. Everyone had to move to make room for the highway.

Strangely, Harry was not too upset about the pending demolition of his house. Mild annoyance was about all he felt. When they bought another home on the other side of town, he simply transferred his word room and attached it to the dining area.

Once they settled in, Harry discovered his Personal Playpen was so portable he could take it on weekend vacations. He even took it to Europe on a business trip. It helped him at work too. He attached it to his desk, and whenever he felt overwhelmed or tired, he relaxed in it, and would soon come out feeling refreshed and confident.

The managers at the office liked the room because it helped Harry work better. Clara liked it because it made Harry easier to live with. Even Harry's neighbors liked it. Harry often invited them in to play with his words. The kids made up all kinds of funny sentences, and old Mrs. Grumply even invented a new word called "Gurch," which made Harry Olby laugh so much he rolled through a wall.

Dan and the Hebrew Letters

DAN SUFFERED FROM STUPIDITY. Stupidity bound him to Earth. Feeling ashamed of his condition, the lad decided to find a teacher. He wanted a guide to lead him up the Self-Improvement Ladder.

One morning, he visited Mrs. Mitsvah's Landslide Academy of Torah, Talmud, Calligraphy, and Hebrew Letters. This kind teacher took him by the hand and taught him to draw the Hebrew letter *aleph*.

Dan drew the first diagonal line of *aleph*, then added hooked curves on the upper right and lower left.

Suddenly, the *aleph* burst into flame! Smoke and fire shot in all directions. The letter rocketed skyward, zoomed in concentric circles around a cloud, then turned around and headed straight for Tom's head! In a flash of blinding light, it entered his left ear, inflamed his cerebellum, and lit his eyes with fiery passion.

"Good for *you*, Dan!" Mrs. Mitzvah encouraged. "Now you understand what *aleph* is all about."

She gave him three cookies. "These sweets are your temporary reward, a small pleasure. But no pleasure can compare to the joy of learning a Hebrew letter! Next we'll try *beth*."

Dan painted *beth* on the schoolyard pavement. When he finished, *beth* burst into flame, rocketed into the sky, somersaulted on an American Airlines route, and suddenly, turned around and headed straight for Dan's head! *Splat! Beth* landed in his mouth! The letter burned his tongue, then peppered his stomach with hot ash before heading to his brain, where it vibrated next to the *aleph*.

Next came *gimel*. But after Dan drew it the *gimel* didn't catch fire. It froze, hardened into iron, sank and disappeared under the schoolyard. Dan heard a rumble. An earthquake! The schoolyard burst. *Gimel*, covered with molten lava, shot skyward, and rocketed in circles. Searching for a place to land, it spied Tom. Like a falling star, *gimel* shot earthward, smashed through Dan's right eye, filling his brain with molten lava, electricity, and magnetism before settling quietly next to *aleph* and *beth*.

Every day Dan drew another Hebrew letter.

After twenty-two days he had mastered the entire alphabet.

At night, the fire from the Hebrew letters shining through Tom's eyes illuminated the town.

Mrs. Mitzvah felt pleased with her student's progress. So did Dan, who had gone from dumb to smart in twenty-two days.

Tommy Types His Way to Cold Turkey

THE WINNER OF THE typing contest got a free trip to Turkey. Tommy entered. He'd always wanted to see the poppy fields. When the gun went off, forty contestants began typing. "Thumbs" Goldberg flew at incredible speed; "Thirty Fingers" Halligan pulled into the lead at three hundred words a minute. Content was superfluous; only speed counted.

Tommy won by kicking out Halligan's electric typewriter plug, turning over Goldberg's table and pouring glue on the keys of comma virtuoso Luke Looseness.

"Congratulations, Tommy," said Mr. Keys, who organized the contest. Using the pantomime techniques perfected at University of Serif, he handed Tommy two imaginary stubs. "Here are tickets to Turkey via Typing Carriage. Just put your clothes in the roller and you'll be off."

"What?" said Tommy. He pushed aside the proffered hand." I want the real thing! Give me a real trip, or I'll turn you in for pushing dope."

Mr. Keys drew back. "Call in the Lettermen!" he cried.

Four Letters entered the room. "Put this young man on the first plane to Turkey," Mr. Keys ordered. "He wants the real thing."

"North Turkey?" asked the short Letterman, dressed like "o."

"Exactly," answered Mr. Keys.

What a surprise when Tommy's plane landed in the Pontic Mountains near the Black Sea. Snow fell and a chilling north wind shook the needles on the pine trees.

His teeth chattered. "I'd better slow down," he said.

Tommy stayed in northern Turkey one month. That's when he kicked his fast-typing habit cold turkey.

I Go for the Cuneiform

THANK YOU," KARL SAID, relieved that he would be so easily able to escape the predicament he was in.

"Nothin', Karl." The Basher looked mean. "Gimme more information."

"More information?" Karl bit his lip. "I just don't have it."

"Get it, or your life won't mean a damn!"

"You're very clear."

"I mean to be." The Basher twisted his moustache. Then he twisted Karl's moustache. "You'd better get that info quick!"

"Yes, sir! I'll run as fast as my leg will carry me."

"Good, 'cause if you don't my boys'll fix it so your leg'll never carry you again."

"You mean—?"

"Right!"

Karl hopped out of the room. Minutes later he returned, carrying a ledger book under his arm. "Here it is," he panted. "I dug it out of the cellar floor, next to Jackson."

"Good. Jackson thought he had all the answers. That's what happens to wiseguys."

"I'm not wise, Basher. I swear."

"Yeah, kid, I know. You're real dumb." Basher's iron fist opened. "Gimme the book."

"It's all I got, Basher. I swear."

"You ain't got it no more. You got nothin'." Basher grabbed the ledger. His thumb pushed page one open. Greedy eyes combed the debit and credit columns. Information in Babylonian cuneiform writing was scribbled on every line. A hint of a smile crossed his face. "Good stuff," he muttered with satisfaction. "I go for the cuneiform."

Handfuls
of Air

The Man Who Thought He Was a Chicken

ONCE THERE WAS A young man named Clem who thought he was a chicken. He spent his days sitting under the living room table and clucking. His father sent for doctors and psychiatrists, but none could cure him.

One day a wise neighbor came to the door. "I think I can help your son," he said. "May I try?"

"Please," answered the hopeful father. "Come right in." The neighbor entered. He crawled under the table with Clem and began to cluck.

"Hey! Who are you?" Clem asked. "Why are you clucking?"

"I'm a chicken," the neighbor answered.

Clem looked the neighbor over. "You sure don't look like a chicken."

"Looks are deceiving."

The two soon became friends. They compared beaks, gossiped about hens, shared grain, and smoothed each other's feathers.

Towards evening, the neighbor crawled out from under the table. He walked around the room.

"Hey! What's the matter with you?" Clem clucked. "You're

walking like a man!"

The neighbor reassured him. "Just because I'm walking like a man doesn't mean I *am* one. In my heart I'm still a chicken."

Clem thought it over. He had to agree the neighbor had a point.

The next day Clem crawled out from under the table. He stood up and walked like a man.

That evening the family ate supper in the dining room. "Can I have a salami on rye?" asked the neighbor.

"Are you crazy?" Clem protested. "You're going to *eat* like them too?"

The neighbor smoothed Clem's ruffled feathers. "Just because I sit at a table and eat like a human being doesn't mean I cease to be what I am. I'm still a chicken." Clem looked puzzled. "Don't worry," the neighbor went on, "you can imitate human beings and still remain the chicken that you are."

Clem thought it over. He was convinced. Pushing his table into a corner, he picked up a ham-and-cheese sandwich and started eating. He spread his beak to imitate a smile. The next day he returned to his job at the Pathmark check-out counter; a week later, he registered for business courses at the University and was accepted into their MBA program.

Eventually Clem became successful in the field of grain marketing. He kept his secret identity as a chicken while working with others.

He lived a long fruitful life.

Only his closest friends knew he was a chicken...and they didn't care. They liked him for what he was.

Tough to Tender

ONCE UPON A TIME, there was a hen named Peckerella. Could she peck! She could peck a walnut until it cracked; peck a rose bush to shreds; peck a fence until it broke.

And she could peck a rooster's ego full of holes.

Farmer Florentine's favorite rooster was a bright bird named Roy. He was a bold cock, and had a way with chicks. Even the old hens loved him. Some laid eggs just to get his attention or be mentioned in his morning crow.

Roy Rooster was a rare combination: kind yet strong, tough yet tender. And when Roy heated a hen's fire, you could see the hen changing from a tough old layer to a tender cooker.

That's why Farmer Florentine decided Roy should marry Peckerella. It was the only way to soften her.

When Roy cast his eye on Peckerella it was fright at first sight. And for Peckerella, that meant war!

But Farmer Florentine's orders had to be obeyed. They dutifully stood side by side for the wedding ceremony while the cows, dogs, geese, goats, pigs, and fleas of the barnyard gazed at them in abject silence.

The next day, Roy Rooster and Peckerella settled into a coop on the fashionable north side of the barn. There, on top of a hill overlooking the orchards in the valley, they spent the early days of their marriage at war with each other. Every day you could see feathers flying out the window and bits of grain rolling under the door, or hear frantic cackles and the sound of wings beating against the inside walls of the coop.

Finally, Peckerella drove Roy right out. As he left, he cried, "We've been pecking in circles. Can't we find better things to do than peck at each other? We must have more in common than that. After all, we're both fowl." He shook his craw. "Maybe someday we can walk quietly in the barnyard, or eat chicken feed together." Then he marched through the door, turned, and crowed back, "I'm through with the way we've been doing things. It's got to change or we're finished!"

This said, Roy Rooster flew the coop.

Peckerella felt terrible. She *needed* to fight. Without Roy around to blame things on, what would she do?

She paced around the coop, angrily pecking her breast. "I'm a good fighter," she declared. "Why should I waste my time fighting that scarecrow? He's not worth it. I'd be smarter fighting the best. And *I'm* the best! From now on I'm fighting myself!"

Right away she started to peck herself. At first, she pecked her feet. When they were bloody red and swollen, she pecked her legs, belly, and chest. She even pecked her neck. What a pain!

And yet, through the pain, she felt proud. She was *good*. The best! No one could peck like Peckerella. The pain just proved it.

Proud of herself, yet writhing in agony, she pondered her destiny. What should she do? Pecking was fun—but it hurt so much. Should she keep it up, or take it out on others?

Then a frightening question arose in her mind: If I can't take my own pecking, she wondered, who can?

She slid her beak over her feathers and patches of bare skin. Suddenly she noticed that, where it had once felt tough, it now felt tender. Her hard muscles did, too.

She couldn't understand it. This wasn't like the tough Peck-erella she had known. A new self, born of mortification, was slowly emerging.

Peckerella had tenderized herself.

She started to cry. Tears rolled down her beak like Mama's chicken fat.

She stepped outside the coop. A breeze caressed her skin; the sun warmed her. She felt herself opening to the world around her, yielding, giving in. . . . She took a deep breath, opened her beak, and clucked. It seemed that, by giving up her pecking, she had gained an even greater power.

She hopped around the coop, clucking happily. Then she headed down the path towards the barnyard.

When Roy Rooster saw Peckerella, he hardly recognized her. "Who are you?" he asked. "Are you my wife?"

She rubbed her tender skin against his. "Yes," she answered. "I'm ready. Let's try again."

"I knew," he declared. "I just *knew!*"

They walked quietly through the barnyard. And that night, as the moon shone over the farm, they ate chicken feed together.

Twins

THERE'S NO WAY OUT of this place!" Andy shouted. "I can't find a door or window anywhere." He beat his fists against the white wall in helpless frustration. His legs were red from pounding and scratching.

"We'll never get out, never!" Phyllis whined. "I'm really

scared, Andy. We could starve here if we don't find an exit soon."

"Are you kidding?" he asked, shaking his head. "There's enough food in here to last for months. There you go again, Phyllis, always giving up. The slightest problem comes along, and you fall apart. Why don't you just quit worrying for once? Stand up and fight!"

"You think you're so tough, but I don't see you doing too well either. All you do is shout and scream. And it gets you about as far as it gets me."

"Well, maybe you're right." Andy's eyes surveyed the walls. "I'm gonna try again though. I've been in tight spots before, and I've always found a way out. Don't worry. I'll find a way out of this one."

He started feeling his way along the smooth walls and dome-shaped ceiling. Some faint light was shining through, but that was all. He searched for hours but found nothing.

"Let's wait," he said philosophically. "Sometimes waiting can clear your mind. Waiting may reveal an opening we don't know about."

So they sat waiting. Every noon the heat rose. Then one day in the early afternoon, just as the heat had subsided, Andy noticed a small crack in the ceiling. The crack grew larger every minute.

"Hurray, we'll be out soon!" he shouted.

"Hurray!" Phyllis cheered.

Suddenly there was a tremendous cracking sound. The domed ceiling broke open; the walls fell to the side; air and sunlight burst in. Andy and Phyllis stood blinking in the brilliant light.

When their eyes adjusted, they looked around. Two hundred yards ahead of them was a barn with a farmhouse next to it. A brook flowed to their left, and in the distance were pastures and meadows. On their right stood a chicken coop, and before them, a big brown hen. She clucked happily as the other hens came running out of the coop. They gathered around the newborn twins, clucking wildly. After twenty minutes, the clucking subsided. The hens lost interest and drifted off.

Then the big brown hen picked up Andy and Phyllis and brought them into the coop to teach them how to cluck.

A Session with Dr. Megamouth

DO AS YOU'RE TOLD!" Voice commanded with a terrible authority.

"I won't!"

"You will!"

"No! No!" Breath was adamant.

"You will, or I'll strangle you!"

"Never!"

Realizing that force wouldn't work, Voice got softer. "Look, just do as you're told and don't ask questions."

"I can't stand it when you talk to me like that," Breath hissed. "It makes me want to *strangle you*."

"Just do as you're told."

"Stop kicking me around, Voice! I'm not your slave. I'll do what I want, *when* I want."

As Breath crossed the room, Voice watched her supple movements. He sensed his own desperation. Without her, he was silent and helpless; without her, he was nothing.

He tried once more. "Breath, without me no one will know you're around. You need me to proclaim your existence."

"That's not true!" she snarled. "Anyone can live without *you*, but no one can live without me."

"Look, honey, we've got a problem."

"Don't honey *me*."

"What I mean is, we've been fighting together too long. We need some help, some guidance. Perhaps we should see a social worker or therapist—someone who can help us work things out."

"And who would you suggest?"

"Dr. Megamouth."

"Megamouth! Are you kidding? He never shuts up."

"He does talk a lot," Voice agreed. "Still, he's the best in the business. He helped Tooth and Gum with their marriage. . . ."

"Yeah, but he sure messed up Tongue. Now all he can do is twist all day."

"You're exaggerating. It's not that bad. Tongue was a nervous wreck before he went in. He kept beating on Velum, kept accusing her of being too soft. Tongue was so squirmy, even Saliva had a tough time living with him. I think Dr. Megamouth did a good job with Tongue."

"Well, maybe you're right," Breath sighed. "I guess a session wouldn't hurt us."

"Atta girl."

"Don't give me that 'girl' stuff."

"Okay, okay."

The next day, Voice and Breath went to visit Dr. Megamouth. His office was spacious and comfortable, with rows of teeth hanging from the ceiling. Voice sat on a molar in the corner, while Breath lounged on a bicuspid.

"What brings you two here today?" Dr. Megamouth asked, flashing a canine smile from behind his desk. "You're both looking well."

"Looking well, but feeling awful," Voice replied. "Aaa-haaa*haaa*." The doctor nodded sagely. "Then I'm glad you've come." He leaned towards them. A fatherly smile crossed his face. "What seems to be the trouble?"

"We're always fighting," Voice grumbled. "Breath just won't give me the support I need. I want to sing, but without her help I can't even cough."

"Is this true, Breath?" Dr. Megamouth asked.

"Why should I help that slob?" she hissed. "What has he ever done for me? He just plays with his larynx all day—or wiggles his uvula. His idea of communication is to make up big words and ask me to help him say them."

"What would you like him to do?"

"I'd like some support."

"What kind of support?" the doctor asked, dentalizing hard on the final "t."

Breath sighed. "I'd like him to ask me how my lungs feel; I'd like him to be concerned with all the pollution I inhale. He doesn't care about what I want. He just uses me."

Dr. Megamouth leaned back in his rocking molar. "This is a common problem among couples," he remarked. "But, as with most common problems that seem complicated, the solution is quite simple."

"Yes?" Voice leaned forward. "What is it?"

"Yes, what is it?" Breath asked.

"What is it?" Dr. Megamouth answered. "What is it? That is the question. The question to your problem is, what is the answer? The answer to your problem is, what is the question? And since the question is, 'What is the answer?' then the answer to your question has to be, 'What is the question?'"

Voice looked confused. "Is that your answer?"

Dr. Megamouth smiled back wisely. "You mean, is that my question?"

"I still don't understand," Breath said.

"Splendid!" Megamouth rubbed his hands. "Many of my patients have been helped by my methods. Now I want both of you to go home and think about what I have said."

Voice and Breath thanked the doctor, rose slowly, and left his office.

"Did you understand what he was talking about?" Voice asked as they walked home along Tongue Road.

"Not a word," Breath replied.

They pondered the unanswered questions and unquestioned answers raised during the session. By the next week, they were so confused by the previous session they couldn't even fight. The second time they entered Dr. Megamouth's office he said, "You both look awful. Haven't you been sleeping well?"

"We feel very confused," Voice answered.

"About what?"

"I don't know."

"You mean you're confused, but you don't know what you're confused about?"

"Right."

"Then why are you both here?"

"I don't know."

"If you don't know why you're here, then get out!" Dr. Megamouth pointed to the door.

"Megamouth's methods certainly are unique," commented Breath a few days later as they lay side by side.

"Yes," Voice answered. "He has a way of turning confusion into chaos. After leaving his office, you feel glad you're just confused again."

"True," Breath added. "Confusion starts you thinking; it makes you examine yourself. It's just a matter of accepting it as a temporary friend—someone to work with."

Breath kissed Voice. "Goodnight, honey."

"Goodnight."

As they drifted off to sleep, Voice could hear Dr. Megamouth saying, "The answer lies in the question."

Overwhelmed

LARRY WAS OVERWHELMED. THOUSANDS of shoulds, have tos, and musts rained down on his head: He must do the laundry, wash the car, earn more money, phone the children, sell his stocks, buy his stocks, sell his mother, wash his father, paint his clothes, deliver his wife, dress his chicken, clean his rabbit, fire the furnace, fire the maid. Yes, Larry was overwhelmed.

He went to Dr. Wilhelm Helmut, the local psychiatrist, to find a cure for his ailment.

The doctor spoke in dulcet tones sweetened by M&M candies rolling in his mouth. "Larry, your problem is that you are overwhelmed." The doctor blinked in satisfaction.

Larry thanked Dr. Helmut, paid him $80.00, and started to leave the office. "Not so fast," the doctor warned as a hook descended from the ceiling, catching Larry by the seat of his pants. "The fee is $95.00." Larry coughed up another $10.00, then gave the doctor one of his shoes as collateral for the remaining $5.

The realization that he had been overwhelmed relieved Larry. He danced down the street and clicked his heels. But, all at once, he realized that the realization he was overwhelmed in no way freed him from being overwhelmed. This realization startled him, especially when it occurred to him that he had paid the doctor for nothing.

Enraged, he raced back to the doctor's office for a refund. But his intense anger made him forget what he had been overwhelmed about, so when he reached Helmut's office, he ended up paying the doctor another $35.00 for a short consultation.

Poorer but wiser, he went home and kicked the wall.

The Depression

GEORGE BUMPER WAS FEELING really low. Depression fogged his mind and chased away the sun. It gave him a headache, and soon it gave everyone around him a headache.

He didn't know what to do. He was afraid to take pills or drown himself. He put cannons in front of his house to shoot himself, but was afraid to fire them because he knew the police would come.

George was an indecisive coward—and he knew it.

One day, at wit's end, he went to his mother's house, sat down on her sofa, and began talking to the four walls. They came up with four unusual answers to his problem. The ceiling offered him a further solution, which was followed by a proposal from the floor.

At this point George walked out.

Who else could he ask?

Maybe there was no answer.

Just as he hit bottom, an idea struck him. Of course. So simple. Why hadn't he thought of it before? Who would know more about depression than...a depression? Why not go straight to the source?

He laughed softly. How simple things where when you knew the answer.

George knew a depression that lived in a hill at the edge of town. A rather deep depression. You could estimate a depression's wisdom by its depth: The deeper a depression is, the wiser it is.

George drove to the edge of town and parked his car in front of the hill. Then he walked over to the depression. Peering down into its unfathomable black maw, he asked, "Who are you?"

No answer.

"Why do you bother so many people?"

Still no answer.

"Why do you bother me?" George growled. "Why don't you stay in your hole where you belong?"

The depression grunted.

"Tell me!"

The depression turned over and opened an even bigger depression in the hill.

George banged his fist on its edge. "Who are you?"

"*Uuuuh . . .* leave me alone."

"Tell me!"

"I'm too depressed to answer."

"Tell me—or I'll fill you up!"

"Oh, no, don't do that! You'll kill me if you do that."

George ran to his car and took out a shovel. He ran back, dug up a chunk of sod, and held it aloft. "You'd better answer— and quick, or I'll fill you up."

"Okay, okay."

"Who are you?"

"Put that shovel away."

George lowered it. "I'm listening...."

The depression grunted and sent up a noxious odor. Then it belched: "I'm a hole."

"A hole?"

"A hole."

George was disappointed. "You sure you're not lying to me?"

"I never lie. I depress."

"You mean that's all you are? Just a hole?"

"That's all I am. But it's enough for me."

"Then why do you feel so bad?"

"I don't feel bad. *You* feel bad."

"But why do I feel bad when I *have* you?"

The depression laughed. "Because you stole a part of me."

"Hmmm. . .I never thought about it like that."

"Well, start thinking about it! And in the future, don't bother me. I just want to sit in my hole and rub on the rocks. Being a depression can be fun, you know."

"I never knew that."

"There's lots of things you don't know. That's because you're stupid."

George felt ashamed. "I'm sorry I bothered you."

"So am I. And tell your friends to stop bothering me, too."

"I'll tell them." George pulled his old depression out of his pocket and threw it into the hole. "Here, take this. It belongs to you."

"Thanks," the depression sighed. "I can use them." George went back to his car and put the shovel in the trunk. As he drove away the sun was shining on the hill.

The Flight of Stairs

STAIRS WAS TIRED OF everyone walking all over her—tired of her two-story house, tired of kids, tired of adults, tired of friends and neighbors running up and down.

Stairs had had enough.

One day she decided to leave. Early in the morning, before anyone was awake. . .she ran away.

The family was heartbroken. The second floor almost collapsed without Stairs' support.

"Where are those Stairs?" Father cried.

"She's never around when you need her," Mother complained.

"We can't get to our rooms," the kids whined.

Finally, after several days of searching, the police found Stairs hiding on the first floor of an empty warehouse.

"We missed you so much," Mother said tearfully. "Please come back. We really need you."

"I want to come back," Stairs answered, "but I can't stand being trampled on all day. I can't stand the heavy footsteps. Every night my steps hurt. Will you be more gentle when you walk?"

"Of course," Mother replied. "We're glad you spoke up."

"We just didn't know how you felt," Father added.

"We'll be careful and walk softly," the children said. "Things will be different from now on. Please come back."

And now each year, on the anniversary of her abrupt disappearance, the family performs the Rite of Stairs, walking up and down her in solemn procession.

It is their way of remembering the flight of Stairs.

Crankyville

WHEN THE SUN ROSE in Crankyville, locals wept. When the sun rose higher, filling the blue sky and warming the Earth, they wailed. When the sun set, they sat in their backyards before charcoal grills with sizzling steaks with rich wines and delicious desserts on tray tables, and groaned.

Crankyville residents were not a happy lot.

One day, after 9.3 months of incubation, Emily Cranky gave birth to Sam, her first child. "He is strange," noted Emily's husband, Lawrence Cranky. "See how his eyes shine."

Sure enough, Sam's eyes lit up when he saw the sun rise. Every morning he crawled around his crib singing. Noontime he giggled. Every evening, the sound of his happy breast-fed gurgles and parade of burps could be heard for blocks.

Puzzled, Mrs. Cranky shook her head. She agreed with her husband. "A strange child, indeed. What's wrong with him?"

"We can't have him *smiling* all day," warned Mr. Cranky. "What will the neighbors think?"

A pleasant panic warmed Emily Cranky's stomach. "What should we do?"

"Let's bring him to Leslie Pissencure, the sad therapist."

"Excellent idea, Lawrence. It's a sad day in Crankyville when you see a child smile. And our own son! How embarrassing! It's just too much to *bear*."

Sobbing, Mrs. Cranky broke down in a grin.

Mr. Cranky held her hand. Holding it tenderly, he said, "Don't worry, dear. Dr. Pissencure uses the 'heel and crush' method. It's a powerful healing technique. She'll fix our Sam, so he'll never smile again."

"That's wonderful, Lawrence," sighed Mrs. Cranky. "What would I do without you? If there is one thing I can't stand it's a happy child."

The Crankies took Sam to the Teary Wing of Lachrymose Hospital, where the staff specialized in cases of public happiness. For two years, they treated the child with miracle misery drugs coupled with depression therapy. But even these powerful techniques could not stop Sam from smiling. He gurgled and giggled when his doctors arrived; every morning he still rocked with excitement when the sun came up.

"He is a danger to the community," said the hospital's chief surgeon, Dr. Wilbur Chronickrank. "If he keeps this happiness and laughing stuff up, we'll all be out of *business*. He needs something more drastic. It's time for the scalding rag. Let's dip it in boiling oil and wipe that smile off his face!"

Dr. Chronickrank wiped Sam's face with the scalding rag.

But Sam kept smiling. Then he started to laugh.

Dr. Chronickrank panicked. He dropped the scalding rag, grabbed his black bag, and ran out of the hospital. Panic gripped the hospital staff. They ran after the doctor.

That's when the earthquake began. The walls of the building started to shake. The happy vibrations shook the hospital until it finally collapsed.

Sam's parents rushed to the site. After a short search among the rubble, they found him near the remains of the latrine.

Relieved, Emily and Lawrence Cranky began to cry.

The sun rose.

Sam sat smiling in his crib. He played with a brick and giggled.

Bayonne Bernie Visits Dr. Opto

BERNIE WALKED DOWN THE street in Bayonne, looking at the blurred Broadway street signs. My vision is not what it used to be, he thought. Once I could see a tree in the desert. Now I can hardly make out the cars parked at the curb. He headed south along Broadway and bumped into a door whose sign read: *Improve Your Vision Through Revelation. Dr. Opto. By Appointment Only.* Bernie straightened his transit uniform, checked the polish on his shoes, opened the door, and stepped inside. A tall man in a suit and tie said, "Don't loiter around here, son. Make an appointment first."

"I'm looking for Dr. Opto," Bernie explained, "but my vision is so poor I probably couldn't see him even if he were standing in front of me."

The tall man smiled. "Your vision has improved already, son. I am he."

"I see," said Bernie.

"Of course you do," said Dr. Opto. "Do you have any other problems?"

"I get headaches, doctor. Also, I'm afraid of success and failure."

"Small problems," said Dr. Opto. "Nothing that corrective surgery cannot cure." He looked Bernie over. "Tell me, son, what business are you in?"

"I'm in transit," said Bernie.

"Well, aren't we all?" The doctor stroked his chin. "But aren't you looking for something more stable? Vision improves with stability. Have you tried gazing at clouds?"

"Huh?"

"Might also be because you're average," the doctor went on. "Average height, average weight. You can't expect to have good vision if you're average. What size shirt do you wear?"

"Medium."

"I thought so." Dr. Opto felt Bernie's forehead. "How do you feel?"

"So-so," Bernie said.

"An average answer, too. Son, I see your problem: Your life is too dull, too average. You need some pain. Real pain." Dr. Opto pointed to the door of his office. "Come in and sit down. We'll solve your problem in no time."

Bernie entered Dr. Opto's office. He sat down on a comfortable sofa, stretched out his legs, lay back, and gazed at the ceiling covered with stars, a crescent moon, and patches of blue. "How serene," he thought. But Dr. Opto bashed his beatitudes by shining a flashlight in his eyes and asking, "Where does it hurt?"

"Everywhere," Bernie answered. "But mostly in my head, lower back, and knees."

Dr. Opto uttered a psychic "Hmmm," followed by a soothing "Aaaah." He placed a hand on Bernie's brow. "Gaze at your lower back, son," he said. "See the back pain coursing through your spine. See the spiders crawling in your skull, building webs behind your eyes, weaving pain across your temples. Make friends with your pain," he repeated. "It's your best teacher."

Bernie relaxed. He watched his spiders turn slowly into stars. The flood of pain in his lower back dissolved into crystal water. Bernie fell asleep.

An hour later Dr. Opto reached into Bernie's pocket, pulled out his checkbook, and scribbled some figures on a check. "Sign here, son," he said.

Bernie looked at the check. "A thousand dollars!" he cried. "That's outrageous!"

"Don't be angry, son," Dr. Opto said patiently. "Pleasure costs money, but pain costs plenty more."

Bernie gritted his teeth as he left the doctor's office. He headed towards the center of Bayonne. He was about to kick a lamppost when he noticed the street signs were clearer.

The Broadway street sign on the road ahead of him was clearest of all.

The Laughing Turnip

TOM LAYGOOM PLANTED A vegetable garden in his back yard. In late August, he harvested his crop, filling his basket with tomatoes, carrots, cucumbers—and turnips.

"Ha, ha, ha!"

Tom looked up. "Who's laughing?" he asked. Seeing no one, he shrugged his shoulders and picked more cucumbers.

"Ha, ha, ha!"

Puzzled, Tom looked up again. No one was around.

"Ha, ha."

Tom looked down. The laughter was coming from his basket. He leaned down, put his ear to the vegetables, and listened. At first, nothing. Only silence. Then suddenly, he heard it again.

"Ha, ha, ha!" The turnip was laughing at him!

Tom couldn't believe it. No turnip every laughed at him before. He picked it up, examined its smooth skin, stem and underside. The turnip looked totally "normal." Maybe he was wrong—

"Ha, ha."

Nope, he was right. Tom Laygoom had grown a laughing turnip.

After the shock wore off, he wondered. "What should I do with this strange loquacious vegetable?

The next day, he decided to take it to Pathmark. At the check-out counter, when he placed it besides his other purchases, the turnip laughed again.

"Young man, are you laughing at me?" snarled the check-out man.

"No sir," answered Tom.

"Wise guy, eh?"

"No, no," Tom apologized. "I'm not wise. I didn't laugh, sir." He pointed to the counter. "It was my turnip."

The man's face was turning red. "You think I'm stupid?"

"Ha, ha, ha."

"Watch out, kid. I'll smack you in the head."

"It's not me. It's my—"

The turnip laughed again. The check-out man grabbed a broom, crouched in a batter's stanch, and swung it as Tom grabbed his turnip and ran out the door.

Next he went to the hardware store to buy electric plugs. As he was paying, the turnip laughed again.

Tom apologized to the owner, "It's my turnip."

The bald, white-haired man sighed in resignation: "Just pay for the hammer, kid." Then, under his breath, he muttered, "Why do I get all the nuts?"

As he walked down the street, doubts began to cloud Tom's mind. "Who will believe me?" he asked.

He trudged on for blocks deep in thought. Finally, after three hours of mental churning, an idea came to mind. His mother and father owned Laygoom Cleaners. Due to increased pollution controls, their business had been failing; they needed cash to survive. Perhaps with proper promotion, his unique laughing turnip could make some money.

People would want to *see* a talking turnip. And of course, *hear* one, too. As Tom considered the media possibilities, he realized the best venue would be to put the turnip on a TV talk show.

Filled with renewed inspiration, he headed to local WBTB-TV station. Introducing himself to the secretary at the front desk, he told her about his idea. She immediately called Station Manager Sigmund Papsquirt, Programming Director Bobo Boncelles, and Lesly Beauswitch, Head of Sales.

When these executives heard their first "Ha, ha, ha." they fell in love with Tom's idea.

"No other station has a turnip," crowed Papsquirt.

"Our ratings will soar!" Boncelles exclaimed, then purred softly, rubbing his hands with glee.

"I like the idea," Beauswitch added. "But we can't put a naked turnip on TV."

"Good point, Lesley," Boncelles agreed. "Let's dress him up."

They fitted the turnip with a shirt, bow tie, tweed jacket, black pants, and polished Florsheim shoes.

Sigmund Papsquirt examined the colors and tailoring of the outfit. "Nice," he concluded. "The vegetable looks quite handsome."

"He needs a name," said the secretary.

"How about Ted Turnip?"

"I like Laughing Turnip better," Boncelles put in.

"A combination name will sell better," claimed Beauswitch. "How about Ted Turnip the Laughing Turnip?"

The executives all agreed.

Two days later the turnip was given his own talk show, *A Turnip's Turn*. The show premiered on September 3rd.

Audiences loved it. Ted Turnip answered all questions with a laugh. As he improved and mellowed, he began laughing about environmental politics, human relations, health foods, vegetable and human sexuality, and the weather.

Over the following years, Ted developed an international following. He made so much money he eventually gave up talk shows altogether. After buying the TV station, he used his leftover funds to plant a garden of fertilized human seeds in his back yard.

Then he gave up laughing altogether.

Naturally, the laughing Turnip didn't need Tom anymore. The grateful vegetable gave him one million dollars for his service as a talent scout.

That's when Tom saved his parent's business with a quick infusion of cash.

Leif Ericsson Meets Lord Berserk

LEIF ERICSSON TAKES HIS adventure across fiords, over mountains padded with growling grass and poison trees. Unafraid, Leif trudges among bandages and gnarled knee trunks bent at the hip, plopping his way to America.

Discoveries are never easy. But what choice is there?

Leif has no friends. Who else is crazy as he? He cannot relate to mere sanity. He craves adventure, striking out across lonely, dangerous seas for unknown lands fraught with danger and hard beauty—that is the beatific life of a crazy man.

And none are more masterful of crazy life than Lord Berserk. Leif kneels before his master, Lord Berserk, dressed in bear skins. Shaving cream drips from his beard. The nobleman Norseman crowns the bare head of Leif, his first and only subject.

"Leif," he declares in a deep fjordian voice, "Sail on, my child. Let no whale or bloated walrus dent your enthusiasm for madness, let no lackey of dripping blues besmirch your belly-busting visions. You will conquer the world. Your tools will be blindness and foolishness.

"Let dried hags of village politics vent empty rages upon you. Let empty-nested, brain-barren creators of thatched roof philosophies rail against you.

"These winds are meaningless when a man is on quest, crawling and flying on permanent search for spirit gold. My Leif, you shall wander and find it far beyond the seas.

"I give you my bear blessing. Go forth. Conquer your black waves of fear. Beat the winds of worry with your iron fist. Let your new world rise on the pine ashes of the old."

"Thank you, Master Berserk," Leif answered gratefully. "Though I sink into murky dreams and the robust camouflage beyond tree tops makes no sense, I will nevertheless clear the road beyond Norway, and reach for a path beyond the stars.

"Bless me, father, with your bearskin tunic. Burning desire and fiery attachments shall carry me to the edge.

"My journey is long and endless."

Theseus

THESEUS GRABBED ARIADNE'S THREAD. "It's better under-ground," he said. "Labyrinth walls protect me from sun-stroke but not from the paws of the Minotaur. If I dance the *syrtos*, will his savage soul be soothed? Can't be sure. He may prefer Egyptian *dance du ventre,* or *Getae horas* from not-yet Romania." Theseus paused a moment to inhale the fresh Cretan air. "Well, maybe he's not as bad as they say. Minotaurs have problems of their own. Living in a labyrinth can take quite a chunk out of your mind.

"He may need someone to talk to or some peaches from Rhodes. I won't prejudge him, even if he has horns."

Theseus gripped Ariadne's thread. Then he danced *syrtos* straight into the labyrinth. Fours days later, he met the Minotaur at a bend in the tunnel. "Dance *hasapicos!*" the monster roared.

Theseus obliged. After an hour of sliding feet, the Minotaur spoke: "You know, I want to retire in Constantinople. With social security kicking in, I could do it within three thousand years."

Theseus and Minotaur argued about *hasapicos* versus *syrtos,* then laughed over the Misirlou dance competition in Pittsburgh.

Theseus thumped his chest with pride. "I'm a *syrtos* man," he boasted.

"I favor butchering a *hasapico,*" the Minotaur drawled, raising a horn.

After two days of dancing *syrtos,* Theseus finally shouted: "*Hasapico* creates *hasapicosis!*"

Then he piled *syrtos* upon *hasapicos,* slew the Minotaur, and threaded his way back to Ariadne.

Adam

I N THE BEGINNING GOD created Heaven and Earth. And it was good. Then He created Adam as a solo dancer. And it was better.

All folk dances come from Adam and Eve, claims Blobbo the Elder, research assistant at *Byblus Times* from 1146 to 1105 B.C.

He explained: "The Lord tired of solo dancing. 'Partner dances are best,' He said. Then He created Eve for couple dancing."

Adam and Eve waltzed and Hamboed for years in their garden. With his special fondness for Bulgarian rhythms, Adam also danced *ruchenitzas, pravos,* and invented the *kopanitza* using his hands to kopan (dig) up the earth in 11/16th time.

Eve played the flute.

Dr. Kirby Bentworth, greatest grandson of Blobbo the Elder and Chairman of Dichotomous Studies at Bladder-on-Tyme University, believed Adam's dance notations were inscribed (chiseled) on clay tablets in the Garden of Eden and passed down from generation to generation straight to the present.

That's why dancers say they're in paradise.

Blood Flow

"BLOOD FLOW IS CONTROLLED through metaphors," said kindly Dr. Breathdare to Jason Peabody, who lay under the Thirty-third Street sign. Blood oozed from the wound beneath his sixteenth vertebra, forming a puddle on the sidewalk.

Jason remained calm. While watching his blood flow south towards Thirty-second Street, he meditated upon the Danube and its smooth flow past Slovakia, Hungary, Bulgaria, Romania, through the Dobruzhian Delta, and into the Black Sea.

A dark stream now trickled past bankrupt Macy's, the IRT

subway station, and Madison Square Garden.

Dr. Breathdare kneeled beside Jason. "You've made your point, Jason," he said with quiet assurance. "People are beginning to stare at you. Time to give up this attention—getting device and get back to your office." Then he commanded: *"Stop this blood flow: Now!"* Jason concentrated on the command. He placed the clamp of his mind on his arteries and slowed his heartbeat. The wound began to clot.

"Thank you, Jason," said the kindly Dr. Breathdare. "You have performed an outstanding public service. Better to speak up than bleed in public. People *will listen* to you."

Jason rose. "Thank you, Doctor," he said, picking up his briefcase and heading towards his travel office in Penn Plaza. "Now I can finish writing my Eastern European guide book."

Waiting for the Mail

"I SURE HOPE I GET some mail tomorrow," Lancelot said as he fed his pigs. He shoveled slop into their trough and continued to glance at page 63 of Ovid's *Metamorphosis*. Holding the book open with the heel of his work boot and letting the sun illuminate the text, he read the luxuriant hexameters.

How he loved Latin! Every morning before feeding his pigs, he'd spend a meditative hour sitting at his desk under the cozy light of his table lamp; coffee in hand, he pored over each word, checked meanings in his Latin dictionary, then consulted Webster's dictionary for Indo-European roots or other connections between ancient and modern tongues.

Lancelot believed a thorough understanding of etymology both enriched his life and provided innovative ideas needed to run a successful pig farm.

Not that his farm was successful. Far from it. Pigs often died, especially when he wanted them to produce beef. His innovative feeding methods were questionable: often when he ran out of cornmeal or slop, he tore pages out of Dante's *Inferno*, or even *Lives of the Saints*, and threw them in the trough.

One morning, as he strolled across his farmyard, pondering important problems while stroking his chin, he spied his favorite pig pen on the right. As he entered it, he continued questioning himself: Was he wasting his life as a pig farmer? Should he become a Latin scholar?

He squatted beside a sleeping hog. "Tell me," he demanded, "what is more worthy? To place pork chops and ham on the dinner tables of distant city folks, or read Virgil and Cicero in the original?"

The pig snorted, grunted, wiggled its ear, and turned over. As its snout widened, it rumbled a soft reply: "Lance, I'd think it over a bit more. Mid-life changes take time." Then, snorting again, the pig closed its eyes and buried its snout in the mud.

"You think so?" Lance queried. "But what do you know? You're only a pig. Besides, I work by consensus. I'll ask the others."

He trudged across the pen. "I feel foolish asking pigs for answers," he grumbled. "They're not as smart as they look. What do they know about life beyond the pen? Better for me to leave this farm, see the world, expand my horizons, and become a credit to the human race. Besides, I want to read Virgil in the original."

So Lancelot started making plans for the future. The very quest that had convinced him to buy his pig farm was now pulling him away from the security of his pens and propelling him into the world of men, women, dogs, and commerce. Would he be able to study Latin or read Virgil and Ovid in such a world?

On Tuesday morning, Lancelot Hogsfeld packed his suitcase, put the farm in the care of his aged parents, locked his front door, and marched down the dirt country road.

He soon passed a farmhouse. An old man sat in a rocker on the front porch. Although Lance remembered seeing the old man before, now. he looked so much older.

Lance came closer. Stopping five feet from the rocker, he inspected the torn shirt, baggy overalls, gnarled fingers, and white beard.

"Who are you?" he asked.

"I am the god of tooth-fillings," the old man explained.

"My teeth are fine," Lance said," but my *life* is full of holes. I worry and hardly slept last night. How did you sleep?"

"I never sleep. I watch the stars. My cousin was a star. So was my uncle. But now I'm a professional Old Man. I make house calls, visit hospitals, and pick up the mail."

"I don't get mail," Lance complained. "People only write my pigs."

"Hire me," the Old Man advised. "You'll see mail pile up to your ceiling." He hitched up his suspenders. "Tell me, son, why do you want to get mail?"

"I'm looking for a goal," Lance answered. "Maybe I can find it in the mail."

"You need a commitment, son." The Old Man raised his

arm, swatted Lance across the face, and sent the pig farmer flying off the porch.

"What the hell'd you do that for?" Lance yelled, rubbing his backside as he got up.

"I want you to pay attention to your pigs."

Lance rubbed his chin. "I feel like punching you in the mouth."

"I wouldn't do that, son."

Lance clenched his fist. "Okay. What do you have to teach me?"

"I already taught you," the Old Man replied. "There's more coming." He pointed in the direction of Lance's pig farm.

"Go back home," he said. "Wait for the postman. You'll find your answer in the mail."

Frogs

ONCE, AS A TADPOLE, I sat on the highway, waiting for a Great Fourwheeler to crush me into flattened insignificance. Indeed, I was a run-over child lost on the super highway of Frogdom. While my friends graduated into frogs, I sat in a pool of lard undulating beneath Mother Elm Tree, swimming for months in our backwater Pond of Illusion.

But I was a happy tadpole. What did I know of suffering? Only undulation. Yes, these subtle movements of pond moss caused my only pain, plus an occasional smack on the ear from a falling pine cone, dropped on our pond by a hapless chickapea bird.

But soon I grew into a frog.

One day, sitting on my bench under the pond, dining on grass blades, I spied the forbidden unctuous piles of His Royal Sauciness. Who was this giant urchin? Why had he visited my pond?

Then His Royal Sauciness spoke. His resounding voice filled our pond with positive vibrations.

"Oh, holy tadpole, son of frog," he said. "Suffering is good for you. Your duty is to feel its transformation pain. Let it fill your belly and fry your soul. The obstacles it creates help you climb your inner mountain, raising ashes to the stars and bringing a bolting rush of heaven down to your webbed feet.

"Yes it hurts to spring upon webbed feet. Why shouldn't it? How else can a frog attain higher vision? Spiked toes and nails in your heels push you heavenward where your reptile mind can mingle with the stars.

"And mingling with the stars is its own reward."

Carlos the Cloud

CARLOS FLOATED ACROSS A Spanish sky. Father Sun rose in the morning, dressed him in a moisture suit and sent him out the east door to travel across the heavens.

Carlos played with the other clouds. At the close of each day, he settled above a tree. There he gathered moisture and slept as stars passed over him.

Every morning Carlos ate a moisture breakfast.

He grew larger and stronger.

His nebulous muscles bulged until, one day, he burst, feeding hundreds of the plants, trees, and rivers below him.

Carlos looked up at Father Sun. "Raining is fun," he said. "Can I do it again?"

But one day Carlos understood the downside of his cloudy condition. "Father, I was once so big and strong. Now I'm small and weak. Why grow, if this is what happens to me?"

"You have just watered the Earth and made hundreds of plants, trees, and rivers happy," answered the Sun. "You have helped them grow. When they grow, you grow, too. Next time you have your moisture breakfast, think about plants, trees, and rivers. Then, when you grow, you'll grow in wisdom, too."

"Who cares about wisdom?" said Carlos. "Who cares about plants, trees, and rivers? I want *muscles*. I want to be big and *strong* again."

Father became angry. "Listen, lad," he sizzled. "Stop pestering me. Filling and emptying is a cloud's job. That's the nature of a cloud."

He pointed a ray at a group of men below him, standing in front of a hardware store. "See those people? Filling and emptying is their job, too. They pass across the land gathering their talents and giving to others. After many years, I call them back home for a short rest. Then I send them down to work on Earth again."

The next day Carlos drifted across the early morning sky again. Darkness blanketed the earth. The smell of trees wafted up to him, and the cool, fresh morning air brushed against his nebulous body. Father Sun appeared in the East and saluted as morning rays lifted the night. Carlos felt his vision expand.

"Where were you last night, Father?" he asked. "Did you die?"

"Of course," answered Father Sun. "I die every night and come back the next day. Dying is part of my nature and my travels."

"That's easy for you to say, Father. You're an old man."

"You can die at any age, Carlos. And at any age, it's an expansion."

"I want to expand, too," said Carlos. "I want to accumulate and become a *cumulus*. I want to be Carlos the Cumulus, the biggest and strongest cloud in the sky!"

"Naturally, Carlos. Most clouds want to get bigger, stronger, and expand and float across the sky. But it is also a cloud's nature to burst into rain and disappear. Clouds are temporary and limited by nature. Carlos, you will certainly grow bigger and stronger, and perhaps even attain your wish and become the biggest and strongest cloud in the sky. But don't think about size too much. Think rather about *giving*. That is the nature of both sun and cloud."

"Carlos, you are learning what it is to be a cloud. Learning too, is a form of giving. Travel with your cloud friends. Play. Grow. Expand.

"And float over the Spanish sky."

Jack and Jill and the Big Bad Wolf

ONCE UPON A TIME there was an eleven-year-old boy named Jack. At thirteen feet tall, he wore a size forty shoe, and a right foot six miles long.

On walks, his right foot often demolished cities.

One day Jack decided to visit California.

Starting in New York City, his first step landed on Cleveland. Clump! That was the end of Cleveland. Then St. Louis and Albuquerque: Clump, clump! Finally, he arrived in San Francisco and took a stroll on the beach.

There he met an eleven-year-old girl with braids named Jill whose right hand was six miles long.

Jack liked her.

"Let's be friends," he said.

"Sure," she said, extending her right hand. "Shake hands."

"Hold on," said Jack. "Friendship takes time."

They surfed in the ocean and frolicked on the beach for two years.

One day they received an urgent phone call from the mayor of Santa Fe. The Big Bad Wolf had retired from the book he was living in and taken up residence in the Sandia Mountains. Every Wednesday at midnight, he came into Santa Fe to snack on a person or two. Santa Fe's population was diminishing.

Townspeople got annoyed. After three months of visits, real estate values fell; the threat of becoming a midnight supper was terrifying.

"Come right over, Jack!" the mayor pleaded. "Bring Jill, too. We need all the help we can get."

Having read in the *San Francisco Kabbalah Beach Book* that every mitzvah creates an angel, Jack and Jill immediately agreed to go. Holding hands, they clumped towards Santa Fe.

Wednesday night found them waiting for the Big Bad Wolf in the town plaza. Sure enough, at midnight he arrived, big, hairy, gray coat streaked with black, and mouth salivating for his upcoming midnight snack.

Jill walked straight up to him.

The Big Bad Wolf faced her, bared his teeth, and growled ferociously.

Jill shook her head. "Bad manners," she said. "That is *not* a civilized greeting. A civilized person shakes hands."

The wolf, hit by this sudden identity crisis, answered, "I don't have a hand."

"A foot or paw will do," said Jill.

The wolf put out his paw. Jill shook it with her six-mile hand. And that was the end of the Big Bad Wolf.

Jack and Jill became local Santa Fe heroes.

Zane's Brain

WHAT'S IN ZANE'S BRAIN? Yesterday I had a chance to examine it with my magnificent microscope. Here's what I saw:

There is a giant fire burning on the right side of Zane's Brain. It must be a hundred feet, a thousand, or a million miles high; it's shooting flames into the sky and burning up many planets, the Milky Way, and several galaxies.

On the left side of Zane's Brain is a great lake. It must be hundreds, thousands, even a million miles wide. Peaceful and beautiful, it sits there quietly absorbing the sun. Like all other lakes, this lake is full of water.

One day, the Fire on the right side of Zane's brain had an

idea. "I'm dynamic, creative, innovative, adventurous, curious, expansive, and smart," it said. "I like to experiment and try out new things. Today I'll do something different. I'm going to make some money."

The Fire scratched its hot head thoughtfully. "Should I steal it or borrow it?" it asked. "Well, borrowing is just plain boring. I'm going to *steal* it! That's exciting and fun, especially if I don't get caught.

"I'll start off by stealing a dollar. I'll get a slice of pizza with it. Then I'll steal $10, then $20, $100...$1 million! I'll soon be the richest fire in the world! I'll steal more and more until I steal the whole world.

"And what will I do with the world once I steal it? I'll burn it, of course. Ha, ha, ha! That's what fires do!" The Fire kept laughing diabolically for fourteen days. Then it stopped and thought:

"Wait a minute. I'm part of the world. If I destroy the world by burning it up, I'll destroy myself! That's not a good idea. I like to have fun, but I don't want to die!"

The Fire sat down on a hot stump to think it over. Meanwhile Lake heard about how Fire wanted to steal things, and how his uncontrolled desire might eventually destroy the world.

"That hothead!" said Lake. "I'm part of the world, too. I don't want to be destroyed. I don't want to die. I know Fire gets carried away with himself sometimes. He doesn't know what to do with all that extra energy he carries around. I'd better stop him before it's too late."

So, beneath her calm surface, Lake started making waves.

"I'm going to take my water and dump it on his stupid fire-filled head! I'm going to dampen him real good! I won't let him destroy me!"

So Lake dumped 50 million buckets of water on Fire. It made a sound like *SSSSS*. Soon Fire's desire to steal a million dollars fizzed down to $1,000, $100, $20, $10, $1, and finally to nothing.

Fire's flames relaxed.

"Thanks, Lake," he said. "I'm feeling much better. I don't know what came over me. I just got too hot, I suppose."

Then Fire took Lake by the hand, and they went out for pizza.

Wow, Look at That!

ONCE THERE WAS A little girl who said, "Wow, look at that!" She went outside, saw the sidewalk, and shouted: "Wow, look at that!"

She saw a car passing by, pointed to the cement, and shouted: "Wow, look at that!"

When she saw a bird, mouse, dog, or cat, a flower, tree, man, woman, and child, she'd point and shout in amazement: "Wow, look at that!"

One day a bad fairy came to her house.

"You're a stupid moron!" said the bad fairy. "Don't you know that it is impolite to shout: 'Wow, look at that!?' Worse, it is wrong. The things you point at are ugly and bad and it's silly to think they aren't. Be suspicious. Things are not the way they seem. Dogs rot. Cats die. Chickens get roasted. Flowers fade. Children age. Old men and women die. Cars break down. Planes get rusty. Mice get run over by cars and rot on the street. The world is full of misery. Remember it next time you want to say, 'Wow, look at that!'"

The little girl felt terrible. How could she have been so wrong?

She started seeing the world differently. Soon she said nothing, her smile faded and her eyes grew dead. Her face looked like a pancake run over by a bus. She got sadder but couldn't even cry because she thought smart, sophisticated little girls didn't do that sort of thing. Finally, she hit bottom, lay down on her living room floor and fell asleep. A dream reminded her that once upon a time the world had been filled with awe and wonder.

Suddenly, another fairy appeared. "Hello," it said, "I'm the good fairy. The bad fairy and I work together teaching little girls about life. We're really the same fairy, but we wear disguises and try to fool you by looking different. The bad fairy teaches you to feel sad, see misery and hardship everywhere, hit bottom, and go to sleep."

"Why does it do that?" asked the little girl.

The good fairy touched the little girl with her magic wand and answered: "So that when you wake up, you'll know for sure the best thing to say when you see the world is, 'Wow, look at that!'"

Snoring

JACK JOCK SNORED. EVERY morning before the alarm sounded, a nightmare originating in his lungs rose, wreaked havoc in his trachea and produced an emission of Series A snoring gas.

Now completely awake, he saw the wraith Irving Incubus, arm in arm with his wraith, Sarah Succubus. This couple had been together since the 8ᵗʰ century and were spending their declining years frightening dreamers with bone-chilling nightmares.

Terrified, Jack drew the bed sheets over his head.

"Jack Jock, thou art a churlish curl," Irving growled. "But for the kindly protection of thy blessed mother, this secret snoring would be stiffly punished. I condemn thee to fill out government forms for thirty days!"

Sweat jiggled on Jack's forehead. "Oh," he groaned, "anything but that!"

"I'll not joke with thee, Jack Jock," Irving cackled. His jowls jingled. "Beware! In the future, no mercy for the likes of thee will I show."

Succubus nodded in agreement. Irving took her hand and both departed.

Jack Jock panicked. What would he do? Filling out government forms was a punishment worse than an accounting course. As he paced the floor, his heels dug into the wood, turning it to pulp. Glancing at the *New York Times* headlines, he read: "Interest Increases in Incubus-Succubus Income Teams: Income Incubating Schemes Now A Thriving Business."

This shocked Jack Jock. Could Incubus and Succubus be a hoax headquartered in Washington? Had they been hired by his mother?

Suddenly, he heard footsteps outside his bedroom door. "Mom?" he called.

A high voice from behind the door sighed, "Yes, dear?"

"What are you doing out there?" Jack cried.

"Just putting a couple of my medieval puppets back in the attic, dear," she answered sweetly.

"At 5:00 a.m.?"

"Yes, dear."

Jack felt soothed. Mom often did strange things. He relaxed, turned over, and went back to sleep. An hour later he was snoring "Til Eulenspiegel" in utter satisfaction.

The Shoe

THE FIRST MAN TO appear on earth was barefoot. He ran around feeling the grass beneath his feet. All men were connected to the earth by their feet. Thus, the foot became a symbol of the unity of mankind.

One day a leader asked: "Why ruin our feet by walking on them? Let us protect ourselves with shoes."

Foot purists objected. "By wearing shoes, the art of foot feeling may be lost. The easy way is not necessarily the best way."

But once people wore shoes and found they could go anywhere without foot pain, they no longer wanted to go barefoot.

Foot purists were soon purged by shoe lovers.

During this period, a fear of the foot developed. Soon no one dared to go barefoot anymore.

People began to sleep and even take baths with their shoes on.

Soon many were afraid to remove their shoes at all. When a shoe became worn out, the shoe dealer, rather than remove it, put a new one over it instead.

Shoes began getting bigger. At thirty a man would have about fifteen pairs on his feet. At forty he could hardly walk, and at fifty he could only sit. Production in the country was slowed, but as the president said, "We must make sacrifices to preserve our way of life."

Today, hiding the foot has influenced thinking in many ways. Scientists who thought the earth was round now claim it is shaped like a shoe. Places of worship, once towers of beauty, are now built in the shape of a shoe. Even the President lives in a shoe.

Several doctors have banded together to write legislation that would prohibit the birth of barefoot babies. Many claim if this law is passed, the shoe problem will be permanently solved.

Pure Mind

A PHILOSOPHER SAT IN his chair thinking about the problems of life. "I am imperfect," he complained. "My mind is impure and I am disgusted with myself. I am not moving from this chair until I reach a state of pure mind."

Thus he began to sit. After several months of sitting, his legs wore away. He broke off the useless bones and tossed them out the window. The following week, his ribs and liver fell out. At the end of a year, his vertebrae turned to dust. A worried look crossed his face when his nose fell out, and his cheeks caved in. Finally, three months later, his skull crumbled into a heap of powder.

Pure mind at last ...and he disappeared.

The Philosopher and the Turtle

A PHILOSOPHER SAT ON the roadside wondering about the truth. One day an old man passed in front of him. "Truth is in the eyes of the turtle," said the old man. "When it comes out of the bushes, look into its eyes and you will find what you want."

"Thank you," said the philosopher.

A few minutes later a turtle appeared on the road.

"Here is my chance," said the philosopher. "Now I will find the truth." He was about to look into the eyes of the turtle when suddenly a thought crossed his mind.

"Which foot shall I move first?" he asked. "If I move my left foot first, this would be awkward and break the rules of etiquette. If I move my right foot first, I might offend my left foot. Besides, my right foot is stronger and such a move might frighten the turtle. According to Boswick Biatz' *Principia Ethica*, "the right foot precedes the left foot except in cases where the left foot precedes the right." Also we must consider that my left foot is pivotal and cannot be moved except after my right, which cannot be moved because it is too strong and will frighten the turtle."

By now the turtle had passed the philosopher. The philosopher thought faster.

"The left foot is progressive, while the right foot is reactionary. Therefore, I would be making no progress at all by moving them since my left would take me forward and my right would bring me back to my original position."

The turtle approached a bend in the road.

"If I combine the efforts of both my left foot and my right and jump," continued the philosopher, "I would be violating the rules of locomotion set down for civilized man. Besides, both feet have fallen asleep from sitting so long."

By now the turtle had disappeared around the bend.

"Surely another turtle will be coming soon," said the philosopher.

When Jonny Comes Home

WHEN JONNY WRESTLED THE other fifth-grade kids in the park, his black hair flew wildly about; when he pinned them to the ground, you could hear his victory scream from the sandbox to the trees across Barnard Park.

The park was a second home to him. He liked playing there after school and on weekends. Often he lay down in the tall grass just north of the brook and dreamed about airplanes, hunting in Africa, Antarctic icebergs, and space flights to Mars. One Saturday morning, he was playing in the park when two urban archaeologists drove up in an old sedan. They parked near the gate, stepped out of their car, and started examining an inclination in the tall grass. Even though Jonny was only a few feet away, they didn't say hello to him; they didn't even look at him, but kept their eyes fixed to the ground. Their foreheads were wrinkled in concentration.

"It could have happened here," said the short, bearded man.

The other adjusted his glasses and squatted down. "Possibly." He pushed over a stone, then scooped up a handful of dirt. "Let's get the equipment and start digging." Jonny looked at the inclination. Intriguing. What was under the ground that these men found so interesting?

The archaeologists came back two hours later with shovels, pick-axes, and a bulldozer. By then, Jonny had fallen asleep in the tall grass. The men bulldozed away a deep layer of topsoil. Then they went to work with pick and shovel, scooping up chunkfuls of earth, examining them carefully with their hands, and scooping out some more.

"Nothing yet," said the bearded one.

"We've got to go a lot deeper," asserted the other.

The bulldozer tore deeper into the earth, scooping out masses of dark brown soil. The operator didn't see the boy sleeping in the tall grass. He piled the soil right on top of him. And as the hole got deeper, he piled the rest of the earth on top of Jonny, too. The archaeologists dug and searched all afternoon. Having found nothing of importance, they gave up the site for the day—maybe even for good. They bulldozed the pile of earth back into the hole. Jonny wound up at the bottom, completely buried under eight feet of soil.

Strangely, it didn't bother him. It felt serene underground. The air coming through crevices in the rocks above his head enabled him to breath. He didn't panic. In fact, he wasn't even worried. He liked the quiet. He couldn't hear people yelling; he couldn't hear radios, planes, cars, or honking horns. All he heard was a soothing silence.

Hours passed, days passed, months passed, years passed. Jonny didn't know how many years, but he knew he was down there a long time. Sometimes he thought about his mother cleaning the kitchen, or his father coming home from work; occasionally he remembered the kids at school. But most of the time he lay passive and peaceful, enjoying the cool quiet of his underground home. He liked eating earthworms—though, as time passed, he found his appetite diminishing. Still, he always enjoyed a good meal or the cool water seeping through the earth after a heavy rain.

One day he heard the earth rumbling. Stones and soil scattered around him; things seemed to be coming apart. People were digging above his head. Suddenly, the head of a steam shovel tore through the earth. Someone was building a house and they were clearing Jonny out with the rest of the foundation.

Sunlight broke over his head. He blinked at its brilliance. Clouds floated by. A bird circled above the brook. He heard the shouts of a construction crew and the hum of motors as cars sped along the road nearby. The air was clear, and a breeze rustled the leaves of a maple tree.

Just as the steam shovel was about to demolish his old underground home, Jonny stepped out. He passed the sand-box and started down the road. He saw a billboard advertisement of a man with a smile on his face, holding a mug of beer. The large white letters read: Drink Budweiser. The sign made Jonny thirsty. He saw a bar up ahead, entered, and sat down on the barstool in front of the counter. The TV in the corner had a baseball game on it. The customers sat nursing their beers and talking about a possible Yankee victory. The bartender was carrying a mug of beer to a customer. "I'd like some water," Jonny said. The bartender walked right past him. Jonny tried again. "I'd like some water." The bartender slowed down, took out a towel, and cleaned the counter in front of Jonny. "Water!" Jonny nearly shouted in the man's ear. Not a blink. Maybe the guy was deaf. He kept cleaning the counter. Then the bartender raised his eyes and looked straight into Jonny's face. His expression remained completely blank. "I'd like a . . . aw, what's the use. They don't even *notice* me around here! I'll get some water in the bathroom."

He slid off the barstool and headed down a dimly lit corridor in search of the men's room. When he got there, he walked straight to the sink, turned on the water, cupped his hands, and was about to take a drink when he glanced at himself in the mirror. All he saw was the green wall behind him. He leaned across the sink, stuck his nose an inch away from the mirror, and looked again. Nothing. A fly landed on the mirror. He saw its reflection perfectly. Disconcerting. Where was he?

Maybe the mirror was broken. He tried other mirrors. All were the same. He looked for his face—nothing. He looked for his neck, shoulders, chest, arms. . . . Where had he gone?

Then he understood the bartender's blank expression. His new condition surprised him, but didn't bother him much. He accepted it, realizing he would make adjustments in his concept of self. The water in the sink was still running. He cupped his hands to collect it for a drink, then laughed. Hands? What hands? And why should he be thirsty? Or hungry? Or tired? He had no mouth or tongue with which to be thirsty. Thirst must be a remembrance, an old habit, like picking your nose or sleeping, a habit he could easily get rid of. Jonny laughed again. He was free of such things now.

When he left the bathroom, he didn't bother pushing the door open but chose the window instead. He passed through the window pane and glided towards the center of town. Traveling the busy sidewalk, he began to see ad-antages to his state. He thought about Africa—and there he was, suddenly, in Nigeria, visiting an oil well. He changed his mind: The Arctic might be more interesting. In an instant, he stood beside a penguin. He jumped from a glacier in Greenland to the mountains of Nepal . . . to a seaside resort in Argentina . . . then back again to New York City.

Yes, there were advantages to his condition. It felt so free. No restrictions whatsoever. Exciting, yet strangely peaceful. He could go anywhere, see any place, do anything. What power. What fun.

Fun! Suppose he jumped into someone's mind for a few moments. What would happen?

He saw a man walking along the sidewalk. Anger, fear, sadness, ambition, greed, and desperation all registered on the fellow's contorted face.

A good candidate, Jonny thought. He jumped into the man's mind, sat there, and waited.

The man stopped in his tracks. A look of incomprehension crossed his face. His pace slowed down. His contorted features relaxed. He blinked, then began walking gracefully and slowly with a new sense of dignity. He smiled.

Jonny questioned himself. What kind of new power did he have? Was it *his* presence that had changed the man? He decided to try someone else. He jumped out of the man's mind. Immediately the fellow sagged; his face contorted in a mass of contradictions.

Jonny's question had been answered. He realized *he* had done that. His presence had brought joy; his absence, tension and sorrow. How about his parents? When he disappeared long before, how much pain and sorrow had they felt?

How long had he been away from home? Months? Years? He glided along the street until he came to his familiar Dutch colonial house. The shutters were gone; aluminum siding had replaced the old shingles on the walls. He passed through the door. A young family now occupied the house. Three children were playing on the living room floor.

He went to the drawer where the mortgage papers had been kept and saw his father's faded obituary in an old *New York Times*. He also found an official-looking letter stating that his eighty-eight-year-old mother had been living in the Manor View Nursing Home for the past three years.

I'll visit her, he thought. He passed through the wall of the house and headed north past a shopping center, an apartment building, and some empty lots until he arrived at a building with a new lobby. He passed the receptionist and went upstairs to the second floor. The halls smelled of old skin, urine, and death. Haggard, half-dead bodies lay on bedsheets or sat immobile and expressionless in chairs, staring at the wall with unseeing eyes.

He found his mother propped up in front of a TV set. She was white-haired, frail, and very thin, and her eyes were staring blankly at a soap opera. Jonny moved closer to her and jumped into her mind. She straightened. Her eyes lit up, and her lips parted in an unaccustomed smile. She rose from her chair, walked to the door of the TV room, and strolled down the hall, singing to herself. A nurse saw her and was about to bring her back to the TV, but something about the old woman's face made the nurse stop, and she let her pass.

Jonny decided to stay with his mother. The old woman's

health and disposition improved. By the second week, she read books, took walks around the nursing home grounds, told the doctors stories about her past—including a few off-color jokes— and chatted with the nurses. During the third week, she sent a letter to New York University for a correspondence course in the Great Books; a few days later she asked the head cook out to see an off-Broadway play. Jonny remained. Five years later, when her physical body wore out, she was buried smiling, in her coffin.

That day Jonny left the nursing home. He headed down the street towards the center of town. He thought about his power to make others feel good. He liked the feeling. Suddenly, a tree blocked his way. He pushed it, but as it fell, one of the branches struck his head. The blow made him gasp. He grabbed the branch, but it turned into a mouthful of grass. He shook his head, opened his eyes, and looked around.

The archaeologists were still digging in the grass.

Grendel the Nightmare

I N THE LAND OF Mesopotamia lived Abraham and Sarah Cyclops and their three children, Bi Cyclops, Multi Cylops, and Grendel the Nightmare.

They were a family of monsters all over four-hundred feet tall with nine arms, with feathers on their legs, and scales covering their bodies. Abraham and Sarah had one giant eye in the center of their head, Bi Cyclops had two, and Multi Cyclops had six-hundred scattered all over his body.

Grendel had thirteen eyes—three in her head, four in each ear, and one on each knee. She also liked to eat whole whales and fried trees, and she had a dreadful scent.

Papa and Mama Cyclops were a friendly and responsible couple. They made sure their children had good manners, ate enough, played well, and went to school on time. Papa liked to tell the kids bedtime stories.

One weekend, Grendel went with her class on a school trip to visit the Dead Sea in Israel. After a long hike in the Judean Desert, she returned exhausted, and sat down beside the Dead Sea.

She relaxed, lay back on the beach, covered her body with sand, and fell into a deep sleep.

Then she overslept.

Grendel slept by the Dead Sea for four thousand years.

In 2010, she woke up, rubbed her head, yawned, then cried, "My alarm didn't go off! I'll be late for the party!"

She rose to her full four hundred and forty-five feet and

stretched her seven arms. As she turned to face Egypt, three hundred feet of matted hair tumbled down her back. The muddied feathers covering the giant quadriceps of her left leg stiffened under the morning sun.

Worms she had eaten during her last meal, ordered from the Akkadian menu at Hammurabi's Restaurant two-hundred-fifty years ago, crawled out of her belly.

Chewing on a tender triceratops bone while simultaneously scratching her hairy armpits with her blue claws, she watched her rotted green incisor tooth fall out and land on the fortress of Masada.

Grendel smiled. The thunderous vibrations of the crashing tooth echoed wildly across the Judean desert.

The monster roared her hideous Cyclopian laugh. The sun trembled in the sky as four hours passed. Then she bent her malfunctioning, gigantic, disgusting body toward the Dead Sea.

She looked straight down into the Dead Sea. Salty bubbles from seismic shifts rose from the depths as images of reflected clouds passed above.

Suddenly, Grendel saw her face in the water!

"I look *awful!*," she cried. "I can't go to the party like this!"

Reaching over the Jordan river, she tore a tree from an Amman suburb, rinsed her mouth with Jordan water, and brushed her six remaining teeth. Then she dug under the beach, grabbed a few ancient dental remains, and stuck them in her gums. "I like implants," she giggled as sand and rocks dribbled down her throat. Her stomach crushed the remains into enzymes to improve her digestion.

Leaning over the Mediterranean and looked at herself again in the water. Not much improvement. What a mess! The centuries underground had ruined her face and figure. Her nose hung from one cheek; pushing it back to the middle of her face, her eye fell out. She grabbed the cornea before it hit the ground and was about to stick in back in her head when her ear fell off.

"I'm falling apart!" she screamed. "No one will dance with me at the party."

Looking north to Galilee, she spied a giant sack lying in a landfill. She grabbed it, cut out holes for eyes, nose, and mouth, then pulled it over her head.

Grendel the Nightmare looked down at her claws. "I'd better hide these, too," she said.

She picked some leaves to weave an eighty-five-foot pair of gloves. Then she scooped sturgeon, flounder, and catfish from the Mediterranean and sewed a new dress from the dead fish.

A giant Euphrates eel slithered out of her mouth.

Once again she looked at herself in the Dead Sea.

"Not bad," she burped. "I'm ready to party!"

She lifted her left foot out of the mud creating a cavernous hole. She grinned as Mount Sinai fell into it. Then she walked across Europe, jumped into the Atlantic, and swam to America.

Two hours later she arrived at the Jersey Shore, grabbed a hot dog stand to eat, strode down route 35, and headed for Morristown singing her favorite song:

> *I'm the wicked witch Witch-Hazel,*
> *I'm the one that everyone fears;*
> *I'm the wicked witch Witch-Hazel,*
> *I got legs coming out of my ears.*
> *I'm the wicked witch Witch-Hazel,*
> *I wear ceramic tile;*

I'm the wicked Witch Witch-Hazel,
And I like to smile-
Hee, hee, hee, hee, heeeeeeeeeeeee.

THE PARTY

MEANWHILE, AT THE PARTY, Grandpa danced on the living room floor, Grandma stirred a pot of stew, Jerry climbed out the window, and Jack hammered the wall. Everyone was eating, drinking, singing, laughing, and having a great time.

Aunt Martha brought a pool stick into the living room and shot pool on the living room floor. Pop said, "You can't play pool without a hole," so Sue and Larry chopped one into the floor. Everyone shot pool except Ma and little Janie who spray-painted pictures on the wall instead.

Suddenly, outside it grew dark. Lightening flashed and thunder rolled.

"Look, look outside!" Uncle Jack screamed. "What's that thing?"

Everyone ran to the window. Frozen in fear and wonder, they saw Grendel the Nightmare clumping down the road singing her song.

She arrived at the house and knocked on the door with her toe. "Let me in," she cried. "I want to join the party!"

She lifted the roof off and stepped inside.

"Get off my new rug!" Ma screamed. She charged Grendel waving a frying pan. But Grendel paid no attention. She picked up Grandpa and held him close as they danced together.

Grandpa pounded her with his fists. "Put me down!" he shouted. "Get a partner your own size!"

Grendel took a few drinks, loosened up, and started stripping. First, she took the bag off her head. When the folks saw how ugly she was, they ran for their lives.

"Why are you running?" Grendel asked. "Am I so bad?" She stopped dancing. "They hate me!" she wailed. Rejection made her sad, then mad, so she ate the house. She washed it down with the Hudson River but that didn't work, so she burped it up again, then headed for town searching for new adventures.

GRENDEL MEETS DAN THE GLOP MAN

DAN THE GLOP MAN flew to the moon to look for a bride and to purchase real estate. Locating neither, he returned to Earth, landed in the Atlantic Ocean, and created a tidal wave that washed the streets of New York.

Dan still wanted to get married. After centuries of rejection, he finally met the woman he loved sleeping under a mountain.

Here's how it happened.

One night, Dan saw the mountain shake in the moonlight, and rise like the lid of a colossal coffin. From its lava center, he saw a giant witch head emerge. Green teeth shone in the moonlight and a hideous laugh bellowed throughout the valley.

Awestruck, Dan stared at the beauty before him. She unfolded herself into full monster height and roared a hideous cackle of introduction: "I am Grendel the Nightmare. I slept under this mountain but now I'm fully rested. I'll brush my teeth and have a good time."

Grendel's bones cracked. Her four hundred ingrown toenails squirmed while sixty-three fingers dangled from her nose.

When Dan beheld Grendel, love filled his heart. "At last," he sighed, "the girl of my dreams!" He stamped over to introduce himself. "I am Dan the Glop Man. I love you."

Dan gargled his tender love-laugh, "Ho, ho, ho, *hoooo-ooooo.*"

Grendel's cornea, still on fire from the molten lava beneath the earth, winked back. "You love me?"

"Yes," said Dan. "I want to marry you."

"Marry me? Why, you don't even know me. Let's have a picnic first."

"Okay. I'll pack some sandwiches for lunch. Do you like human-on-rye sandwiches? I use oak trees for toothpicks."

"You're a disgusting animal, Dan. Only animals eat people."

"I've never eaten anything else."

"Well, it's about time you did. Even though I've been sleeping for centuries, I know more about manners than you do. You need some education. In fact, I wouldn't marry you unless you had a college degree."

"But I love you," Dan insisted. "I love the way your eye shines in the moonlight. I love the feathers on your legs. I love your claws and the way your hair curls under all your arms. I love—"

"You may love me, Dan, but love is not enough. You have

to have brains to make love work. Only when you get your degree and do some graduate work will you be worthy of my charms."

So Dan decided to go to school.

He started in kindergarten. Grendel acted as Dan's mother and took him to register.

"Sorry, we don't accept giants," said the school registrar.

"You will today," said Grendel. "My son is a fine, healthy boy. He will be a credit to your school. Besides, he's learning how to play basketball."

So Dan started kindergarten. That year, with his blocks, he built three new cities for America.

Dan liked school and finished elementary school, high school, college, and graduate school in just one year. He graduated Summa Cum Sumac with a degree in Cloud Blowing.

One day he sat with Grendel on a delicatessen. "Will you marry me now?" he asked.

"Yes, my dear."

"Where shall we live?"

"Good question. I want to live where people like each other."

"Me, too."

"People who stick together make a good community," said Grendel.

"Let's move to Stickyville. All the people there are stuck together."

"Sounds good."

After three years in Stickyville Dan and Grendel had a son. They named him Mark.

But Mark didn't look like Grendel or Dan.

So they renamed him Question Mark.

GRENDEL LEARNS
TO PLAY GUITAR

ONE DAY GRENDEL WENT for a walk in New York City. She walked from Greenwich Village to 65th Street. Passing Avery Fisher Hall, she heard the beautiful sound of the New York Philharmonic giving a concert. Grendel sat down in the middle of the street to listen. Traffic backed up for miles. When cars honked, Grendel simply put her finger to her lips. "Sssh," she whispered. "Listen."

When the concert ended, she reached into Avery Fisher Hall, picked up the conductor with her claw, pulled him off the podium and out the window.

"How do you make such beautiful music?" she asked.

"Put me down! Put me *down!*" the conductor shouted.

"Will you tell me?"

"Not until you put me down."

"Not only will I put you down, but I'll give you a kiss."

"Oh no, not that!"

Grendel put the conductor on the sidewalk.

"All right, now tell me."

"You must practice," said the conductor.

"Practice what?"

"An instrument."

"But what instrument?"

"There are many to choose from. But which instrument would be good for you?" The conductor reflected as he leaned against a parked car.

"An oboe is too small. So is a trumpet. You'd probably swallow any woodwind or brass. Perhaps a stringed instrument, cello or bass. . . . No, I don't think so. As I see it, you need an instrument you can play solo, a piano or. . .I know, a guitar!"

"What's a guitar?"

"A wooden stringed instrument. It sounds beautiful especially when you pluck it classical style. Of course, you'll need a special guitar, one big enough for you to play on. I'll bring you to Flores del Torres, the best guitar maker in New York. He'll know what to do."

Grendel and the conductor went to a guitar shop off Bleeker Street in Greenwich Village. She stood outside a window filled with guitars. An old bearded man emerged, greeted the conductor, then embraced him.

"*Buenas dias,* Maestro."

He looked up at Grendel. "What is this, Maestro? A new instrument you have brought me?"

"No, Flores," said the conductor. "This is Grendel. She wants to play the guitar. I want you to make one for her."

"I only make for professional players."

"Think about the challenge, Flores. You would make the biggest guitar in the world. One of a kind. It would have the biggest sound. You'd be more famous than Caballo del Mara."

"More famous than del Mara, eh?" The old man smiled through his beard. "I like that. I like you. I'll do it."

He looked up at Grendel. "First we must get some wood."

Grendel carried Flores del Torres to the lumber yard. They couldn't find wood long enough for her guitar so she carried Flores to the Redwood Forest in California. Grendel uprooted the tallest redwood tree, sawed it into boards with her fingernails, and dried the wood with her hot breath. Flores set up his shop in a forest clearing.

Grendel bent the sides of the guitar into S curves, cut out the face and back, and sliced up a giant oak for the neck. Using sap and dead fish, they formed a glue lake, then glued all the woods together. Finally, they strung the guitar with half a mile of nylon fishing tackle.

Grendel ran her claws over the six strings. She listened, eyes half-closed with pleasure. Her first beautiful guitar tones floated through the air.

Flores del Torres smiled. "Yes, my instrument is a masterpiece," he said.

Grendel remembered the conductor had counseled her to practice.

"I want to take guitar lessons," she said.

"I will send you to Andres Salovia. He is the greatest guitarist and teacher in America."

One week later Grendel found herself in Andres Salovia's back yard. She sat on top of a mountain, right foot on his lawn and left foot on Pittsburgh which she used as a footstool. Holding the guitar in her lap, she looked down at Andres Salovia.

Maestro Salovia looked up at a his new student, his black eyes peering from behind black-rimmed glasses: "Now, my child, hold the guitar like a baby. Love it, kiss it, caress it. Relax your claws. Place your left claw on the strings beneath the frets; brush lightly with your right claw: Listen to the sound."

Grendel brushed the strings. A lush, resonant chord rolled across the East Coast, stopping at the Appalachian Mountains. "It's soooo beautiful," she swooned.

"This is only the beginning," Andres Salovia said. "You must live with the guitar for many years before you can bring out its true tone. Be sure to practice every day. Make it sing."

Grendel fell in love with her guitar. She rented Howe Caverns as a studio where she practiced every day, slept, and imagined winged notes flying through the caverns. Decorating the subterranean walls with pictures of the great guitarists, she dreamed of the day she could play like the maestros she gazed upon. Her lessons continued for thirty-six years.

GRENDEL GIVES A CONCERT

GRENDEL DECIDED TO GIVE her New York debut in Yankee Stadium. In preparation, she picked up the Ramapo Mountains, placed them on top of the stadium pitcher's mound, and put her chair on the mountaintop and prepared her New York program.

She publicized her program by playing a C chord in the south Bronx.

Ten minutes later the stadium was packed with guitar fans and police.

Grendel stood on her mountain, bowed, knocked a Boeing jet out of the sky, sat down, and, using the left field wall as a footstool, placed her left foot upon it, cradled her guitar, and began playing "Sonata in C" by the 18th-century Spanish composer Fernando Sor.

Her sweet guitar tones filled the stadium. Pigeons stopped in flight, hot dog sellers swooned, and fans went crazy.

The vibrations from her guitar were so powerful that, after fourteen notes, Yankee Stadium collapsed.

Thousands of fans, still mesmerized by the music, ran into the streets singing. Despite destruction of the stadium and the piles of rubble, many guitar fans begged Grendel for lessons.

Grendel agreed. Soon word about her desire to teach began to spread. Throughout America, guitar lovers jumped in their cars, on buses, trains, or planes, and headed towards New York City for "Eastern guitar lessons." Grendel rented the State of New Jersey for a studio. She organized her lessons by placing beginner students in South Jersey, intermediates in Central Jersey, and advanced players in North Jersey. While the Vineland South Jersey area practiced scales, central Morristown worked on arpeggios and northern Bergen and Sussex Counties played the Vivaldi guitar concerto. After two years of practice, the entire state toured Europe, spreading the guitar gospel.

Grendel became so popular that during the November election, a write-in campaign elected her President of the United States.

On inauguration day she sat on the White House roof playing "Recuerdos de la Alhambra," a guitar masterpiece by Francisco Tarrega, a 19th-century Spanish composer. With the rapid fire of her sixty-three finger tremolo, Grendel soothed all her fans at the Inaugural Ball. When the applause had died down, she rose to announce her new program: "A guitar in every home, two in every garage."

This new federally funded program created over 247 million American guitarists. Three months later a referendum to change the country's name to the United States of Guitars was narrowly defeated by a bagpipe-leaning Senate. Nevertheless, at the end of each working day, people played guitar solos, duets, trios, quartets, and even joined guitar orchestras. Under the new ethos, young and old, fat and thin, played together in harmony.

Harmonious Tones, Inc. became a growth industry, as America exported music notes throughout the world.

Years passed.

Grendel sat on the Rocky Mountains surveying the country. She listened to Bach fugues in Oregon, Renaissance *pavanes* in Texas, and Fernando Sor sonatas in Michigan. Strains of Enrique Granados's "Spanish Dance Number Five" rose from river boats on the Mississippi, and the sound of "Leyenda" by Albeniz spread through Massachusetts.

"Today, people are playing better than ever before," she exclaimed. "Beautiful music sweeping the country. It's a renaissance." She beat her chest with pride. "And I'm responsible!"

Grendel rose, yawned, stretched, and laughed her hideous laugh.

"It feels so good to laugh for joy after a job well done!"

She laughed for eighteen years.

Then she sighed: "I'm tired after all this work. I need a break."

She lay down in the Grand Canyon for a long nap.

When she woke, Papa Abraham Cyclops stood before her.

"Time to come home," he said.

Grendel yawned and stretched. "Okay, Pop," she said. "I'm ready. Anything you say."

She jumped into the Atlantic, swam to Israel, and hiked to her favorite marsh near the Dead Sea. Near the Qumran Caves, she saw Bi Cyclops riding a two-wheeled mechanism he'd invented.

Later she found Multi Cyclops lying on a pile of sand sunning himself and reading the Dead Sea Scrolls through an eye in his leg.

Leaping to his feet, he shouted: "Grendel! You're finally home!" He gave his brother a huge slobbering kiss. "How about a welcome drink and some fruit?" he asked, offering the Jordan River and an orange tree to eat. Then he examined her more closely. "You have bags under all your eyes, my dear."

"I'm tired, Cousin Multi."

"Of course, it's been a long trip. Why don't you lie down? Dinner is at six. I'll set the alarm."

Grendel sat down in the sand. She pulled back a blanket of Dead Sea marshland, and tucked herself beneath it for a well-deserved, seven hundred-and-seventy-seven year rest.

Poems

The War God

The people of the country
Tremble at the name
Of the fire-breathing monster
Spitting balls of flame,
Thunder in the sky.
People shout and run.
Red flames rise—
The monster has come.

Its greenish black belly through the brown earth bores,
Pushing its ashen head through the city floors.
Its roar of open hatred makes every person cower
As it overturns the buildings, the factories and towers.

This fire-breathing madman next to the ocean turns
And, with his lashing legs, kicks out the waves he churns.
The people hide in holes when they see his insane eye,
Bloodshot, as the monster tears a star out of the sky.

His laughter cracks the heavens and opens vaults of land;
His crushing hulk treads on the rocks, turning them to sand;
He howls defiance out at all beauty and splendor,
Roaring out a terrible denial of the tender.

Equally he destroys the weak, the strong, the lame;

Turning them to ashes, he makes them all the same.
He pounds the helpless mountains, kills elephants and flies.
His face reveals no mercy as, around him, people die.
Death and destruction in his mangled brain do sit.
Upon the strong and weak he casts his lethal spit.
He breathes his fire into everything he sees,
Forcing all of Nature down upon her knees.

The people of the country tremble at the name;
The people of the country rupture into flame.
He points his finger at them, and he sends another stroke;
Mothers, fathers, children, all go up in smoke.

Now the monster understands that his desires are fed,
He rolls his eyes insanely backward to his head.
No man remains alive the burning earth to see,
Or hear the fire monster's ghastly laugh of victory.

House of Fear

I saw the giant house
With portals made of stone,
The roof of fashioned iron,
And walls of polished bone.
Trees lay dead and dying;
They leaned as if to speak
To that cold and ancient house
Surrounded by the creek.

There I met a man.
I felt his freezing breath.
"My name is Mr. Fear," he said.
To me he looked like Death.
"I'll guide you through my house
And make it all quite clear
Why many people like to live
Inside my House of Fear."

I saw the fear to think,
I saw the fear to know,
I saw the fear to change your ways
Or change the status quo,
The fear to start a new life
Exciting, fresh, and bold,
The fear to leave the dull routine

And safety of the old.

The fear to strike out on your own
Through your despair and grief,
To find out what on Earth you need
And personal belief'
The fear to face the future,
The hardship and the strife,
To open up your mind
And really love your life.

I said to Mr. Fear
As I took another breath,
"I cannot stay with you—
I want life instead of death."
Mr. Fear grinned back again
And said, "Well, we shall see.
Can you get along without me?
Can you stand being free?

If times get tough, remember—
Come back for my key.
I'll tell you evil stories
As I chain you up to me."
When I left the house,
This question I could hear:
"Will I ever want to live
Inside the House of Fear?"

Peter Pogin Paleolithic Painter

Peter gave his wife
A mesolithic lip-kiss;
Then went out to hunt
The horse called eohippus.
Armed with a gray stone hammer,
Hardy bow and arrow,
He hunted in the woods,
The fields and valleys narrow.

Later in the evening,
He came home to rest
And sat down in his cave
With the woman he loved best,
Took his painting tools to him,
Stood up very tall,
And painted a quick reindeer
On the wet cave wall.

Next day he caught a bison
Or a wooly mammoth, maybe,
And brought it back to eat.
With his paleolithic baby,
Peter and his woman
Ate what he would kill.
Peter would pull

And drag it up the hill

He had to hunt all day.
At night his love did start.
He'd devote himself
To his painting art,
Picking up his brush
Dipping it in color—
Without painting in his cave,
Life would have been much duller

Soon many men and women
From the surrounding caves
Began to ask this Peter
To decorate their graves.
Peter said, "Yes. Gladly,
But when, then, will I hunt?"
The cavemen had a meat exchange,
Which made him smile and grunt.

Years passed by the thousands;
Peter's tools grew dull.
Then an archaeologist
Came on Peter's skull.
He found it in the cave
(Whose walls you well remember)
That held the art of Peter Pogin,
Paleolithic Painter.

Jack McQuinn

There was a man named Jack McQuinn.
One day he began to take off his skin—
Took off his skin, threw it in the mud.
And just stood there in his bones and blood.

The neighbors looked, and their hearts failed.
"Put on your skin, or we'll have you jailed!"
They needed illusion no matter how thin.
They couldn't stand Jack without any skin.

Jack said, "My heart was covered with skin.
I do not know what lies within,
The things I might have done or been—
I wanted to know the real McQuinn."

The neighbors saw the bloody cuts.
"Call a doctor! This man is nuts!
To leave him there would be a sin.
We must hide the real McQuinn."

They tried to hide the real McQuinn
But McQuinn began to live without a skin.
"I'm learning about what lies within—
I'm getting to know the real McQuinn!"

Empire Builder

Now I am old,
In sad state of mind,
Leaving the dream
Of the world behind.

Long have I lived
In this world of sad sighs,
World of illusion,
Violence, lies,

Blood-drenched and battered,
World of all strife—
Memories have vanished
Of quieter life.

Fighting my battles
Helped build my throne;
Wrinkles of age
Turned it to stone,
So long I stood
Before crowds all alone
Like a hermit
Before endless faces unknown.

Now I am old

In a sad state of mind,
Leaving the dream
Of the world behind.

Colby's Halls

Colby's Hall sops up sound
Even when no one's around.
My guitar was quite intense
But my listeners so dense
That every note I plucked or struck
Elicited not one bare cluck.
I said, "This crowd is sure slim pickins—
I'd rather play guitar for chickens."

Sleep, Sleep, Slender Sam

Sleep, sleep, slender Sam,
Snore away like roasting ham,
Dream of darkness velvet black,
Feel your shoulders sinking back.

It's so soothing—now you find
Cares and worries fall behind;
Heavy waters bathe your eyes;
Darkness comes as daylight dies.

Snore away like roasting ham.
Sleep, sleep, slender Sam.

It's So Hard To Start

My friend, I ask you from the heart—
Why so hard, so hard to start?
To start to fight, to start to write,
To turn the darkness into light,
To turn the brain from dismal dust,
To shine the spirit, scour the rust,
To build the bridge, to try, to trust,
To have the urge. I must, I *must!*
So I ask you from my heart,
Why so hard, so hard to start?

I tell you frankly, for my part,
It's hard to open up your heart
And to create! Ah, there's the rub—
When you think your brain's a tub
Of telephone distractions dialed,
They hold you back, they can't get wild
And free, and let your powers loose
To howl like wolf, to roar like moose,
To let your raging savage roam
Across your page to find its home.

Easier to get involved
With troubles that can't be solved,
Let distractions whip your mind ,

Kicking you in your behind.
They help you cry, "Too late, too late,
Too late today. I can't create!
I'll put it off until tomorrow,
When I'll be free from care and sorrow.
Today's distraction is my fetter,
But tomorrow I'll be better.

Though I ache in every bone,
Still I say, "Postpone, postpone!"
I check my mind; I try to borrow
Ideas I want to write tomorrow,
Avoid the struggle and the pain,
Avoid the anguish and the strain,
Avoid the conflict and the strife,
And so avoid creative life.
Writing makes you mad, insane—
Why write at all? What will I gain?

Of course. It could be that today
I just have nothing left to say.
This is, no doubt, the perfect ruse,
The perfect lie, the best excuse—
To say my energy's gone lank
That, today, I'm a total blank.
I'll take a morning walk and fill it.
Tomorrow I'll come back and spill it.
I wish a deli *words* would cater. . . .
But, since it won't, I'll see you later.

The Muse

Look for the Muse—she is gone.
Call the Muse—no answer.
Run to the Muse—she runs away.
Make a demand: She leaps into darkness.
Hoping for return is hopeless.
Best to give up.
One day when she's ready,
She'll appear in splendor
To guide you on the divine trail.

The Nicestrikings

Ah, the Nicestrikings!
Could they be windfalls
Or soft noodles sweeping vast oceans?
Delve deep. Light the heart,
Stoke the embers along the coronary highways
Here it comes . . . a Nicestriking!
The moment where God and man hold hands!
But only a moment, mind you—
God is hot stuff;
You can get scalded, even destroyed.
We don't want good liquid spilled in the streets.
Even so,
A Nicestriking makes the day dance!

The Loudest Sound in the World

Once there was a king
Who ruled with such great poise
The kingdom that he ruled
Was the Kingdom of Noise.
Those in his kingdom
Would rant and rave about.
No one would listen.
Everyone would shout.

"Louder!" said the king.
"You're all too *quiet!*
Louder, louder, louder!
I want a noisy riot!"
People stamped and screamed
Running through the halls,
Pounding on the drums,
Beating on the walls.

The town fool spoke,
And people gathered round.
"The king's birthday is coming.
He'll want the loudest sound!
We'll gather in the palace.
Bring your noisy screams.
We'll give the king a noise

Beyond his wildest dreams."
Running to the palace
To celebrate his birth,
Dashing onward to create
They made the loudest sound on Earth,
Orchestrated by a fool,
Running to a riot.
Then the fool announced,
"Everyone be quiet!"

What a strangest moment!
No one moved around.
What a strangest moment!
No one heard a sound.
The king was flabergasted
At the lack of riot.
Everyone was still;
Everyone was quiet.

The king heard. . .silence.
He said, "What sound is this?"
He closed his eyes, listening
To a sound he'd always missed.
People and the king
Listened on in awe,
Listened to a silence
They'd never heard before.

Better than the riot,
The loudest sound in the world is
. . . quiet.

Universal Hamburger

(How New York City Got Its Trees)

The trees in the forest were hungry.
They wanted food to eat.
They weren't looking for water
But for human meat.
When a man passed by them
To pick a forest flower
The trees lowered their branches
And   him they would devour.

Chorus
Trees would eat
Slurp, slurp, slurp—
Head and feet
Crunch, crunch, glub.

Men soon feared the forest
And none of them came by;
The trees began to starve
And feared that they would die,
So they got together,
Formed a Tree committee,
Said they'd leave the forest

And eat up New York City!

They crossed turnpike and highway
Like fifty thousand drunks,
Staggering from side to side
With fifty thousand trunk.
They walked along upon their roots
And carried signs that read
Trees should not go hungry—
Better fed than dead!

Chorus

Spoken: When people heard the trees
were coming, they didn't know what to do.
"Call out the termites," said Larry.
"Feed them air pollution," said the mayor.
"Feed Republicans to the trees!" said the Democrats.
"Feed our parents to the trees," said the children.

The president called the army out,
Marines and air force, too
"Tanks are rolling," said the generals.
"*We* know what to do."
Soldiers shot their guns,
Hand grenades they threw—
But the trees ate up the soldiers
And the generals, too!

Chorus

Spoken:
The trees kept walking towards the city.
People were desperate. Then a child said,
"Let's feed them hamburgers."
"No tree will eat our cheap, tasteless hamburgers,"
answered the mayor.

"We need a new, juicy, healthy, tasty hamburger."
The people called a meeting.
"*Achtung*, vee must make a powerful hamburger,"
said Herr Flugel.
"Hamburger must be humble and have inner peace,"
said Woo Song.

"You're all nuts," said Mr. O'Bloomer.
"I want my hamburger to be so beautiful that,
when I kiss her, she smells like perfume."
Finally, everyone agreed to put their ideas
into one giant frying pan. They cooked
the Universal Hamburger!

Then they sang Hamburger Hallelujas.

Chorus

Trees staggered down the highway.
The mayor shouted in the street,
"The army and air force failed us!
Let's fight with hamburger meat!
Call the cooks and butchers!

We must save this town!
We'll cook delicious burgers,
And the trees will gulp them down.

Chorus

The trees crept closer, closer.
People trembled in their knees.
They picked up their hamburgers
And gave them to the trees.
The starving trees consumed them
Until they were just *stuffed*—
And they sure felt much better
When they had eat enough.

Chorus

Spoken:
The people had been saved!
They poured out of basements, closets, and attics,
 danced round the trees and under their branches.
The happy trees started dancing "Maple Roll"
and "Oak Tree Rick." A breeze from the Hudson
 River gently rocked their leaves and branches.
Then they planted themselves on every block.

And that's how the city of New York got its trees.

Train With a Brain

There once was a railroad that owned a free train.
This train was different: It had a brain.
From Texas up to Maine, it led all the pack,
But it got pretty tired of riding the same track.

It wanted adventure, it wanted a change!
It wanted some new thing, some thing that was *strange*.
It whistled its whistle: "No slavery for me!
I'm going to have fun; I'm going to be free!"

The cops and the mayor and the governor of Maine
Couldn't quite silence the train with a brain.
People erupted with joy and with glee
When the train went off track and into to sea.

It sank underwater like a submarine,
The speediest submarine you've ever seen!
Pistons turned fast as the old engine roared.
Fish in the ocean were climbing onboard.

It traveled along until it reached France
And sped on to Paris to watch the people dance.
The train didn't stop—through Europe it ran
And then on to China, for that was its plan.

The army and navy both followed the train.
They wanted to catch it and take out its brain,
But moving so fast, round Earth it ran
The train was too smart to be caught by a man.

The whole world ran after—and that's why one day
The train lifted off and had soon flown away
High into the sky, so far did it did race
It sped past the moon and off into space.

It sped among planets, it sped among stars,
A light year from Earth and three light years from Mars.
Astronomers saw a new cosmos appear. . .
But also they saw the smart train disappear!

Days Before Bones and Blood

If you often wondered
How it all began
And where you fit
In this world now ruled by Man,
Think of the days
Before bones and blood
When protozoa crawled
In pre-Cambrian mud
Six hundred million years ago.
All of this took place
And no one ever heard
Of the human race.

Long, long ago,
Before bones and blood
Microscopic protozoa crawled
In pre-Cambrian mud.
They had many offspring
Who grew up quite fast,
And before you knew it
A million years had passed.
Six hundred million years ago
All of this took place
And no one ever heard
Of the human race.

Fish began to swim,
They crawled from sea to sand.
Fins turned to legs,
And they began to stand,
Changed into reptiles,
Grew larger than before,
And grew larger still
To became dinosaurs.
Two hundred million years ago
All of this took place—
And still no one had ever heard
About the human race.

Dinosaurs became extinct.
Up grew the mammals,
With eohippus looking
Quite like a humpless camel.
Mountains still were forming;
Earth did shrink and squeeze,
Pushing up Himalayas
Alps, and the Andes.
Thirty million years ago,
All of this took place,
And no one'd ever heard
Of the human race.

A hungry gorilla
Jumped upon the ground,
Started running wildly,
Looking all around.

Friends began to follow him
And they also found
It's easier to hunt
When you walk upon the ground.
Two million years ago
All of this took place,
And no one ever, ever heard
Of the human race.

Gorillas and their kin
Joined to hunt for grub;
There wasn't much to eat,
Just a nut or shrub.
They made themselves a tool of stone
And slowly they began
To stand up straight, to walk erect
And look just like a man.
Two million years ago
All of this took place,
And, yep, no one had ever heard
About the human race.

Men banded together,
Joining for the hunt.
They developed tools—
Some sharp, but mostly blunt.
They started out to live in caves,
Drew pictures on the walls.
Their grunts turned into language;
They practiced how to call

And then they learned the way to plant,
Found culture and and found grace. . .
And that was the beginning
Of the human race.

So if you often wonder
How it all began,
Where you fit
Into this world now ruled by Man,
Think of the days
Before bones and blood
When microscopic protozoa
Crawled in pre-Cambrian mud,
Andabout the million things
That must have taken place
Before we could exist
As a human race.

Listen to Statue Phil

I like to sit
In the park stone still
Under the tree
On top of the hill,
Listening to wind
And cold rain, too.
Come on over
I'll listen to you.
Listen, listen, listen, listen. . . .

Here's how you listen:
Sit stone still,
Listen to flowers
On the window sill,
Listen to wind
And rain on the hill,
Don't move a muscle,
Sit stone still.

A wristwatch ticking,
Then being wound,
The sound of a verb
Looking for a noun—
Don't move a muscle,
Don't make a sound,

Listen to the ants
Crawl on the ground.
Listen, listen, listen, listen. . . .

Who Is God?

Out of the fire
From under the dead
I heard the voice
Of God, who said,
"You have crossed
The flaming river
To meet me
The Supreme Giver.

"Come to me—
I am the Way,
I live in night,
I live in day.
I belong
To all the races.
And I shine
In all the places.

I live forever
And everywhere;
Though you cannot see me
I am always there.
I live in you,
I live in others—
I am the one

Who makes men brothers."

I listened,
And my eyes grew bright,
My pains vanished;
I felt light.
I was no longer
Weak and small;
Now I
Encompassed all.
My small vision
Had so grown,
I saw all people
As my own.
Then I knew
I was no elf
But something greater
Than myself.

The Wind

I hear the sound
Of the wind in the trees—
Whispering wind
Washing the leaves,

Moving unseen,
Moving with ease,
Touching the rocks,
Pushing the bees,
Washing the mountains,
Washing the trees,
And rolling out
To the worshiping seas.

No one knows
What the wind sends,
No one knows
Where the wind ends,
Touching our feet,
Bathing our brain,
Soothing and cooling
And freeing from pain.

Gentle reminder
Of infinite force

Blowing one way
Then changing its course,
Touching the rivers
And lofty treetops
The wind always moves,
The wind never stops.

Invisible power
Subtle and fine,
Invisible power
Bends the great pine,
Blowing through forests,
Churning the air,
Blowing through fields
When no one is there.

I hear the sound
Of the wind in the trees,
Whispering wind
Washing the leaves.

Songs for
Open Ears

Listen to Your Children

Listen to your children!
Do you dare to hear them?
Listen to your children!
Or do you really fear them?
Often they have honesty
In their eyes that glisten.
Oftentimes they tell truth
If you dare to listen.

Do you dare to hear
Their unanswered cries?
Do they have a wisdom,
Despite their age and size?
Often their approaches
Are different from our own.
Do they have an openness
We have long outgrown?

Do they dare to see
What we would see no more?
Do they let the stranger in
While we would shut the door?
Often they will try new things,
Adventurous and bold.
Often they can see a world

Better than the old.

Listen to your children!
Do you dare to hear them?
Listen to your children!
Or do you really fear them?
Often they have honesty
In their eyes that glisten.
Oftentimes they tell truth—
If you dare to listen.

Long Journey

There was a maple tree standing all alone,
Standing in my yard where it had always grown.
When I was a boy, beneath the tree I played,
Its branches and its leaves always gave me shade.
For years and years that tree protected me
But when I came to be eighteen, I wanted to be free,
I wantedmost to see the world and set myself afloat
The tree said, "Cut my branches.
My wood will be your boat."

Chorus
It's such a long journey from birth to stone.
I'm with you. my friend, and you're not alone.
I've seen many coasts, and I've tried to compare
One land to the next as I sailed everywhere—
At loose on the ocean, at loose on the sea.

Sailing on, I forgot my tree.
Then I met my woman, we began to plan
How I'd get myself a job and be a family man.
Returning to my country, I asked, "Where will I live?"
The tree said, "Cut my trunk. My wood to you I'll give."

Chorus

Thirty years passed; our children were full grown.
They got married, and went off on their own.
Their kids called me "Grandpa." *Now* what would I plan?
I went back to the tree, the place where I began.
I stood before the stump that once had given shade.
I stood before the memory of where I once had played.
I said, "What should I do now? I've walked a weary mile."
The tree said, "Friend, it's over.
Sit down and rest awhile."

Chorus

Who Am I?

I know where I'm going, I know where I've been,
I know what I'm doing, I know what I'm in,
I know what I think and I know what I feel,
I know I can love and I know that I'm real.

One day I realized with a single anxious breath
My life had been completely planned, from birth to death,
By those before me who had thought that I'd look good
Living an intended life that I misunderstood.
I searched in books and music notes;
I asked my friends; poems I wrote,
My search unending, sailed the seas—
But where'er I traveled I came back home to me.
I was my lasting problem, I was my only hope—
To be so lost, to be so blind, to stumble and grope,
To find my way so awkwardly,
And know that what I wanted was all just up to me.

Through fog and pain my roads one lovely morning met.
It was a time that I will not so soon forget.
The troubles on my mind all dwindled down to none.
I opened up my eyes and saw all things as One,
The colors all around me blending into white;
The darkness lifted off me, restoring me my sight;
The waters, mountains, people, flowers

Poured into my soul their mighty powers.

Then a harmony filled my mind.
I felt like a god in heaven sublime.
I accepted my best and also my worst.
I became part of the universe.

I know where I'm going, I know where I've been.
I know what I'm doing, I know what I'm in.
I know what I think, and I know what I feel.
I know I can love and I know that I'm real.

Eli The Elephant

Eli the Elephant walks down the street
Swinging his trunk all over his feet.
Clumpety, clumpety, clumpet he goes,
Swinging his nose all over his toes,
Tail like a whale or gargantuan fish—
Swishity, swishity, swishity, swish.
Flowery ears flip-flop as he goes
Swinging his nose all over his toes.

Chorus
Elephant, elephant, elephant nose,
Elephant, elephant, elephant toes,
Elephant, elephant, elephant goes
Swinging his nose all over his toes.

Eli the Elephant wanted romance.
He wanted to dance, so he put on his pants.
I dance like a klutz, I know some folks say;
But I still want to jazz, and to dance rock and roll,
to folk dance, and disco, and even ballet.
He went to a dance school, where they said, "No way!
"Get out of here now! You can't dance ballet!
You roll like a tank, and you smell like the zoo.
Get out of here! We can't do nothing for you."

Chorus

Eli then said, "It's true I'm a klutz,
But I promise I'll try. I know I've got guts."
The teacher paused, listened, and uttered a sigh.
"Okay," he said. "Come on, let's give it a try."
The music began, and the elephant clumped.
He walked the room, and he hopped and he jumped,
At last lost his balance and with it his poise,
And fell to the floor with a thunderous noise.

Chorus

"Try once more," the dance teacher said.
"Straighten your shoulder, hold up your head,
Keep your back straight, stand up with pride,
Tighten your stomach, and lengthen your stride."
Eli danced like a beer without malts,
Fid a two-step, then started to waltz
Rhumba, and polka, and even ballet!
His teacher observed him and shouted, "Hurray!"

Chorus

Dinosaur Rock

Dinah the dinosaur put on her sock.
Dinah the dinosaur wanted to rock.
Dinah the dinosaur, she got soul.
Dinah the dinosaur wanted to roll
Down in the swamp where the dinosaurs go
To rock and roll, rocking and rolling real slow. . . .

Chorus
Dinosaur rock, oo, oo, ooo
Dinosaur rock, oo, oo, ooo
Dinosaur rock, oo, oo, ooo
Dinah, Dinah, dinosaur rock, oo, oo, ooo.

Triceratops started to hop.
Tyrannosaur Rex, he just couldn't stop.
Brontosaur quickly was tapping his feet.
Dinosaurs danced a reptilian beat
Down in the swamp where dinosaurs go,
To rock and roll, rocking and rolling real slow. . . .

Chorus

Tyrannosaur Rex, man, you gotta rock!
Brontosaurs, each of you babies got soul!
Come on, Stegosaurus, let's rock and let's roll

Down in the swamp where dinosaurs go
To rock and roll, rocking and rolling real slow. . . .

Chorus

Clam Chowder

The dog at my side snores like a man.
He likes to sleep in a clam chowder can.
No other dog can bark any louder
He's my best friend, I call him Clam Chowder
When he's by my side, I do not feel fear.
We walk out together, and soon I will hear
The friendliest bark of my own Clam Chowder
Getting louder and louder and louder.

Chorus
Clam Chowder, Clam Chowder,
His bark'sis getting louder—
I've nothing to fear or to hide
With Clam Chowder there by my side.

Clam Chowder came whenever I'd call,
He'd lick my face when I would fall,
And every time that I would fight
He'd start to growl with all his might,
Sticks by me when I break a rule,
Wakes me up to go to school,
With the friendly bark of my Clam Chowder
Getting louder, louder, louder.

Chorus

Rain of fog, sleet or snow,
My dog comes with me wherever I go.
When I'm in my bed at night
I know I'm gonna sleep all right.
I see Clam Chowder across the floor
I hear him snore, then bark some more
The friendly bark of my Clam Chowder
Getting louder, louder, louder.

Chorus

Dear old Clam Chowder, my best friend,
Remained my pal until the end.
Up in heaven, I know I'll see
My dog Clam Chowder wait for me.
I'll never forget the day he died.
I sat for hours, and cried and cried
For the friendly bark of my Clam Chowder
Getting louder, louder, louder.

Chorus

Bubblegum Home

There once was a gum from the town of Tubblebubblegum
Who had a friend named Rubbledoublebubblegum.
Both gums talked because it was troublesome
Finding a home if you are a doublebubblegum.

The first gum said, "You'll be a treat
If you practice being sweet,
You'll find a home that's right for you
If your taste is fresh and true.

"Rubble!" said the bubble named Rubblehubblebubblegum.
"I won't be sweet for a man from Tubblehubbledom!
Being sweet is much too troublesome.
I'd rather be a sour piece of doublebubblegum.
Gums are the same both North and South.
You can find a home in anybody's mouth.
The sweet gum said to Rubble, "Go back to school
Or you'll become a bubblegum fool!"

Then into the store in the town of Tubblehubbledom
Strolled a little kid who was looking for some bubblegum.
He tasted Rubbledouble, and he said, "This is rubbledom!"
And spat it on the sidewalk in the town Tubblehubbledom.

The other gum he found first rate,

Chewed it and announced, "It's great!"
The happiest kid in the town of Tubblehubbledom
Blew a double bubble with his piece of Rubblebubblegum.
That's the end of the gum from Tubblehubbledom
And his friend named Rubbledoublebubblegum.
Both gums talked because it was troublesome
Finding a home if you are a doublebubblegum.

Ballad of Jack Reeves

Jack Reeves was an executive.
He wore the best that he could buy.
He had a suite of thirteen rooms,
Walked through them with his head held high,
A tall man of distinction,
White-haired and quite well groomed,
Every secretary sighed
When he crossed the room.

"That's a real man!" they all said
"If I were him I'd die.
His wife divorced him, business failing
Still he walks with his head high."
"He's really tough," said another.
"Look at the strength in his stride—
He's made of iron, can't be broken.
Like a rock inside."

Jack Reeves passed his secretaries,
Entered the room on the right,
Locked the door behind him,
And shut the windows tight.
Then he pulled the shades down
So that none could see
When he fell down on his knees
Shouting, "Mommy, please!"

Art of Gargling

Do you want your voice to sing?
Then try the art of gargling;
The finest music that I know
Is the *Gargle Concerto*.

Chorus (everyone gargles)
In order to avoid debate,
In order to communicate,
Words are very hard to sing—
But everyone knows gargling.

Chorus

Are you looking for peace of mind?
This I know you'll always find
When you sing with mouth and soul
To the sound of a gargole.

Chorus

Group Guitar

I used to be a struggling creature
An unknown, underpaid guitar teacher.
I searched for pupils of any size
But only found those in my eyes.
Then one day, while eating soup,
I decided to give all my lessons by group.
I wrote on my front door and car
Unite our nation by playing guitar.

Chorus
Guitar students are never bored.
They all strum the old C chord.
When together they did strum,
Down came Yankee Stadium.

People who passed my door and car
Said, "Unite our nation with guitar!"
Thousands of students then did come,
So I rented Yankee Stadium.
I taught the crowd from second base
As seventy thousand guitars filled the place.
I stepped to the mike and happily roared,
"Strum your guitars and play the C chord!"

Chorus

I heard a crash; the roof fell down;
The C chord thundered through New York town.
I listened with fear as the stadium rumbled.
My students all ran as the mezzanine crumbled.
The police came from New York town.
There was a crash. The place fell down!
Seventy thousand guitars
Were the sound that put me behind prison bars.

Chorus

The Backward Clock

Spoken:
Once there lived a grandfather clock
That hung on the wall and went tick tock.
One sad day this old clock got sick—
Instead of tick tock, it went tock tick!

Chorus
Tick tock, tick tock, tick tock, tock tick—
Instead of tick tock, it went tock tick!

In this house there lived Pauline:
Pretty brown eyes and age fourteen.
She heard the sound of the backward clock
And got younger—tock tick tock.
Thirteen, twelve, eleven, ten,
Soon she was a baby again
Three months, two months, one month neared
Tock tick tock—she disappeared!

Chorus

Her father grew younger, a little boy,
Crawled on the floor with his choo-choo toy.
He lay in his crib and sucked his thumb
And said, "Goo-goo, want Mommy come."

The backward clock in a backward whirl
Turned Mother into a baby girl
The baby mother was mad as a viper
When a safety pin stuck in her diaper.

Chorus

The paint on the house crawled into the can.
The boards walked out of the walls and ran—
They turned back to trees! The house disappeared!
Tick tock tick, this is getting weird!
The earth grew hot, and burned and cracked.
The sun went ashen, the sky turned black,
The moon disappeared, the stars cooled to rock—
The only thing left was the backward clock.

Spoken:
You couldn't see a thing,
There was darkness all around.
The clock was utterly confused
By its backward ticking sound.

Its backward tick got worse and worse;
It felt all alone in the universe,
So it started ticking a crazy way:
Tick tock, tock tick, tock tock, tock tick,

Tock tick, tick tick, tick tock, tock, tick. . . .
Tick tock sounded good.
Tick tock sounded right!

The universe began to rock
When that clock went tick tock!

Chorus

The sun and the moon returned to the skies.
All the stars opened their eyes.
The house returned, the paint unpacked,
The mother and the father both came back,
And with them came the girl Pauline,
Pretty brown eyes and age fourteen—
And that's the story of the backward clock
Which one day went tock tick, tick tock.

Chorus

Bonality Breakdown

There lived a musician named Tom Repent
Who didn't play an instrument
But made the very finest tones
By cracking his neck and snapping his bones.
Every day he practiced scales
From his knee bone to his nails.
Oh, he was sure a sight to see
As he cracked his bones so free.

Chorus

On his tibia and fibula and cranium, yes, he did play—
Occipital, parietal, mandibular, and vertebrae,
Maxillary, zygomatic, cervical, coccygeal,
Clavicle and sacral, lumbar and vestigial.
When he cracked his humerus
His radius was well employed,
Ulna and the phalanges
Sounding with the sesamoid.
Sternum hit a minor chord
as often as the clavicle
Ischium and ileum
both rattled rhythms radical.
His tibia and fibula
Played marching songs in genera'l

Patella and all cartilage
Together with the femoral.
Pelvic, lumbar, digital,
They almost turned to gelatin;
He was cracking every bone
In his entire skeleton!

First Tom lay down on a mat
And cracked his neck: He got A flat;
Cracked his hips, he got C sharp,
Shoulders jiggling like strings on a harp;
Cracked his knuckles in a way so free
And called the thing "bonality"
Hip bone, ankle bone, loosen when light.
Shoulder bone. neck bone. left arm. right.

That's the story of Tom Repent
Who didn't play an instrument
But he made the finest tones
By cracking his neck and snapping his bones
Every day he'd practice scales
From his knee bone to his nails.
Oh, he was a sight to see
As he cracked his bones so free.

Chorus

Grendel the Nightmare

Last night when I went to sleep,
In my room I heard a creak—
Grendel riding through the door
Riding her nightmare over my floor.

She was a horrible sight to see
Her legs were skinny like those of a flea.
Her mouth looked like an empty pocket.
She had no eyeballs, only sockets.
Her sunken face was all in wrinkles.
When she walked, her bones all tinkled.
She picked me up with much delight
And dropped me in her bag of night.

Then she cackled in my ear,
"Heh, heh, my little one, do not fear.
  Mount my nightmare ride with me
Into the world of fantasy.
I will bring you endless dreams,
Dreams of witches, snakes, and screams
Dreams to make your skin turn stiff
Dreams where you fall off a cliff."

My dream began. I saw my brother;
Then he changed into my mother.

By a leash a rat she led.
It broke away and toward to my bed.
Right across my chest it raced,
Its hairy belly brushed my face,
My mouth was open, the rat jumped in,
And crawled beneath my skin.

Then I felt an awful pain—
The rat was eating up my brain!
I kicked and shouted, "Oh, no more!"
And woke exhausted on the floor.

Grendel travels in disguise.
She stands right here before your eyes,
So do come closer *if you dare!*
Meet Grendel, the Nightmare!

Swami of Salami

A girl from Mumbai came to 42nd Street
And went into a deli for a bite to eat.
Max the owner said, "I serve each kid and Mommy.
Why don't you try our rye bread and salami?"

Chorus
Swami, swami,
Swami of salami
Swami, swami,
Swami of salami.

The girl said to Max as she was being fed,
"I think you're kind of cute. I like your balding head.
Your face is also handsome. You look just like a swami."
Max said, "Well, I am. The Swami of salami."

Chorus

The girl said, "Glad to heat that you're a swami.
Let's get married while the weather's balmy!
We'll have lots of kids. The first boy we'll call Tommy
I'll be the mom of Tommy, son of Swami of salami."

On their wedding day, the the guest who showed up first
Gave them, as a present, a pound of liverwurst.

Max said, "It's the kind of gift that really fits a swami."
He ate it with his new bride, Mrs. Swami of Salami.

Chorus

Booni Hated to Wash

Booni said, "I hate to wash my face."
His mother said, "Your face is a disgrace!
If you don't get that dirt off from your face,
Get out of here and live in outer space!"

Chorus
puh-tuh-kuh, puh-tuh-kuh, puh-tuh-kuh, puh-tuh-kuh

That night Booni wanted to scream,
But instead he had a dream—
His room became a space ship flying past stars
On its way to Mars.

Chorus

Putting his hand on the space ship throttle,
He landed on Mars, met a Martian in a bottle.
"You're the strangest sight I've ever seen!"
The Martian said, "I live here to keep clean."

Chorus

Booni heard marching music afar.
The President of Mars appeared in a jar.
"Booni," said the President, "I'll show you all of Mars.

Get into this bottle, or one of these jars."

Chorus

"I won't get *there*. I'm afraid that I'll be *squashed*."
"If you don't get in here, then you'll have to be washed.
Martians live in bottles. We live in them from birth.
Get in the bottle, or go back to Earth!"

Chorus

Booni woke from his dream and had milk to drink,
Went to the bathroom, and straight to the sink.
He concluded, "I'll wash up as soon I play
I don't want to live in a bottle all day."

Chorus

If You Want Love to Fill Your Cup

Do you often get violent and shove
When you're secretly in search for love,
And your woman starts to say, "We're through"?
Here's a philosophy—here's what you do.

Chorus
If you want love,
To fill your cup,
When you're wrong, admit it.
When you're right, shut up.

There's no need to argue or fight.
If it's true you're really right,
Your woman will smile at you
Because you speak these words so true.

Chorus

It's hard to say, "I have been wrong."
To come to this, you must be strong
If you're strong, you can say what's true.
Here's a philosophy, here's what you do:

Chorus

Gargoon's Bassoon

I'll tell you the story of Efrum Gargoon,
Who once had a dream he would play the bassoon.
He worked to earn money; at last came the day
He brought a bassoon home and learned how to play!

Chorus
Efrum, Efrum Gargoon—
Children would dance to his magical tune!
Efrum, Efrum Gargoon—
Efrum Gargoon loved to play his bassoon.

When he walked down the street, all the people would stare.
They liked Ef Gargoon and his wild wavy hair.
Gargoon strolled along dressed up in maroon,
Took out his bassoon, and played them a tune.

Chorus

He played his bassoon quite without pain or strain.
He played his bassoon for his girlfriend Elaine.
His playing got wilder, his rhythm ran drastic,
Until Elaine giggled, "Gargoon, you're *fantastic!*"

Chorus

Elaine danced with abandon beneath the full moon
While Efrum Gargoon crooned a tune on bassoon;
He played through the morning and then until noon;
Yes, Efrum Gargoon loved to play his bassoon.

Chorus

His girlfriend Elaine quickly started to swoon—
Swoon to the tune of Efrum Gargoon.
They happily married the third day of June
And he played at their wedding upon his bassoon.

Chorus

For Efrum Gargoon the days ended too soon
Bassooning and crooning from morning to noon,
Bassooning at night beneath the full moon,
Efrum Gargoon loved to play his bassoon.

Chorus

Beedle Dee Bop Song

I was walking down the street
Singing the song,
Singing it and singing it
All night long.
No matter what I did,
No matter what I said,
I couldn't get that melody out of my head—
And it went. . .

Chorus
Beedeldeebop a deedle beedledee bye
Beedeldeebop a deedle beedledee bye
Beedeldeebop a deedle, Beedeldeebop a deedle
Beedeldeebop a deedle bye.

Back at my home, my Papa felt sad,
But hearing this diddy made him feel glad,
And old Dad started singing lilting and slow
In a voice real mellow, and real low.

Chorus (Sing it mellow and low)

Grandma sat on the porch alone.
She had an ache in every bone,
Heard my song, put a smile on her face,

And soon she was dancing all over the place!

Chorus (Sing it in high-pitched "Grandma" voice)

A grocer drinking tea from a cup
Said, "I got a cold. I'm all stuffed up."
I said, "This song can *cure* a sick man—
Come on and try it!" And soon he began:

Chorus (Sing it in stuffed-nose style)

I worked all day, got home at last.
That song was spreading awfully fast.
I lay me down on my soft bed,
But I couldn't drive that song from my head.

Chorus

Next day I went out to eat.
The mayor was dancing in the street.
Kids were jumping up and down,
Everyone singing all over town.

Chorus

My Guitar

When I'm down and can't go on,
When all my fight and drive are gone,
I strum those notes so soft and sweet.
They put me right back on my feet.

Chorus
My guitar I start to play.
Playing at night and playing by day
Bring to me a sweet release
Soothe my mind and bring me peace.

It helps give me a better sight,
Helps me see what's wrong and right.
Music soothes the hawk *and* dove,
Brings me peace and brings me love,

Makes me feel so light and free,
Fills my mind with harmony.
All my worries, all my fears,
For that moment disappear.

Chorus

Good things come, then pass away.
Nothing lasts, the wise men say.

First you fight, and then you cease.
First it's war, then it's peace.

In the future far away.
There will be another day
When my voice and song are gone.
My guitar will carry on.

Chorus

Long Island Yodel

The Long Island railroad broke down on the tracks.
In one of the cars sat a man named Jack Black.
Some folk read papers for news of the day,
But Jack Black sat back and just yodeled away.

Yodeling Chorus

A salesman from Hicksville a that point turned around
In astonishment hearing that yodeling sound.
The riders from Great Neck all did agree
They wanted to hear Jack Black yodel in key.

Yodeling Chorus

Jack Black then declared, "I'll try this old song."
The salesman from Hicksville sang right along.
From Great Neck they yodeled; it made them feel glad.
Soon the whole car was yodeling yodels like mad.

Yodeling Chorus

Now there is a moral to this short refrain:
If ever you ride on a broken-down train,
Take a tip from Jack Black, and you'll be okay
Relax. . . sit back. . . and yodel away.

Yodeling Mad

A man from a band
In Switzerland
Came across the sea.
When he appeared,
He had a long beard.
Sometimes he sang off key.
He said, "My son,
If you want to have fun
When you're feeling sad,
Jump out of bed,
Throw back your head,
And yodel like mad."

Arpeggios would vibrate my nose
Mi mi mi mi mi mi!
I did not fail
To yodel my scale:
Yodeldeodeiii!
I stood up tall
When I could call
To my Ma. I was proud.
"That's great," she said,
"When you throw back your head
And yodel that way out loud."

Later that fall
For Carnegie Hall
A concert I prepared.
I went over and over all the words,
And I was pretty scared.
My girlfriend Joyce
Said, "With your voice,
You'll really make them glad."
The curtain drew.
On stage I flew,
Yodeling like mad.

In the End, You Simply Vanish

You go through life, you rant and rave
To please the bank with cash you save,
You sit in your tub of troubles and soak,
But in the end it's all a joke.

Chorus
It doesn't matter if you're black, white, or Spanish—
In the end you simply vanish.

No matter what you hope to gain
By riding the fame and fortune train,
You sweat and worry to earn your name,
But in the end it's just a game.

Chorus

Why bother thinking of creed or race?
Everyone's heading straight for the same place.
Why worry 'bout looks or the shape of your face?
In the grave we all take up about the same space.

Chorus

The Bee and the Flower

Once upon a time there was
A great big bee whose name was Buzz.
He liked to fly to every flower
And show to them his buzzing power.

Chorus
Buzz, buzz, buzz, buzz.
Buzz was a bee who knew how to buzz.
Buzz was a bee who knew how to buzz.

One day Buzz saw a pretty flower,
Said, "I'll show her my buzzing power,"
But he sounded much too rough.
Soon the flower'd had enough.

The flower then her petals closed.
Buzz flew at them but banged his nose.
His eyes with tears began to brim—
The buzz was knocked right out of him.

Chorus

Buzz realized he had hurt the flower,
And that their friendship had turned sour.
He changed his ways from what he was

And put some love into his buzz.

The flower then heard Buzz's buzz,
And what a lovely buzz it was.
The bee and flower became fast friends—
And that is how this story ends.

Chorus

| 376 |

Red Hot Lover

Come on, baby, you're the gal for me.
I'm gonna love ya and set you free
When ah touch yo finger tips,
With the red hot fire of my lips.

Chorus
Ah'm a red hot lover, baby, and yo drivin' me insane.
I'm a red hot lover—fire's a-comin' from ma brain.
I'm a red hot lover—fire's a-comin' from ma brain.

I met her at the laundromat.
She was wearin' her wide-brimmed hat,
Pair of gloves on her fingertips,
Red hot fire on mah lips.

Chorus
Her hair hung down, her belt was tight.
I kiss her, and she starts to bite.
Come on, honey, gimme the light—
Love me, baby, I'm dynamite!

Chorus

Blow the Clouds Away

Jonny was the kind of kid who never liked to eat.
For breakfast, lunch, and supper, he ate air instead of meat.
He ate so much air, let me say, that, finally, one day,
His breath became so strong, he could blow the clouds away.

Chorus
Blow the clouds away,
Blow the clouds away,
Blow the clouds with a mighty breath
And see the sun today.

One school day a storm came up; the kids all ran to hide.
Jonny took a deep, deep breath, and he went outside.
He blew and quickly sent the clouds off on the run,
The sky turned blue, and out came the sun.

Chorus

Kids ran back into the yard, and everyone agreed
Blowing all the clouds away was a mighty deed.
Jonny got a part-time job at a weather station.
Now he blows the clouds away during school vacation.

Chorus

Song of the Dishwasher

Chorus

All day long I wash each dish.
Every meal, I'm like a fish—
My hands swim speedily, with grace
Through the water that cleans off taste.
At night, when all my work is done,
Into bed I quickly creep.
But when I close my eyes to dream,
I dream of dishes in my sleep.

Busboys bring their trays to me
Piled so high they cannot see
With peels and bones and greasy meats.
Salad leaves. and peas and beets.
I like to sing whene'er I work
A song about another place,
But before my song is through
Plates are piled up to my face.

Chorus

When I see the stars at night
Shining just like bulbs of light,
There's a dipper in the sky
First to wash. and then to dry.

Then each star becomes a dish
Circling round the universe.
When I reach eternity,
Washing stars will be my curse.

Chorus

www.ingramcontent.com/pod-product-compliance
Lightning Source LLC
Chambersburg PA
CBHW020931020726
47495CB00002B/451